Praise for The Minstrel and the Prophet

The plot was phenomenally designed with a slow reveal that teases the reader and drives them to keep reading. ... I eagerly await the next book to find out what happens.

- Ronél Steyn for Readers' Favorite

The Minstrel and the Prophet is Larry Z. Daily's brilliant debut novel. ... The plot teases readers with bewildering intrigue and offers an unforgettable adventure.

– Nino Lobiladze for Readers' Favorite

Daily's plot is well-developed, clearly written, and is an absolute joy to read. This book had me captivated from the start. I highly recommend The Minstrel and the Prophet and applaud the author. I look forward to reading Book Two.

– Teresa Syms for Readers' Favorite

The Ring and the Sword

Book Two of the Chronicles of the Lawbreaker

Larry Z. Daily

The Ring and the Sword / Larry Z. Daily – 1st ed.
ISBN: 979-8-9913879-3-4 (eBook)
ISBN: 979-8-9913879-2-7 (paperback)

To my sons, Benjamin and Jonathan. The world would not have been the world I loved without you.

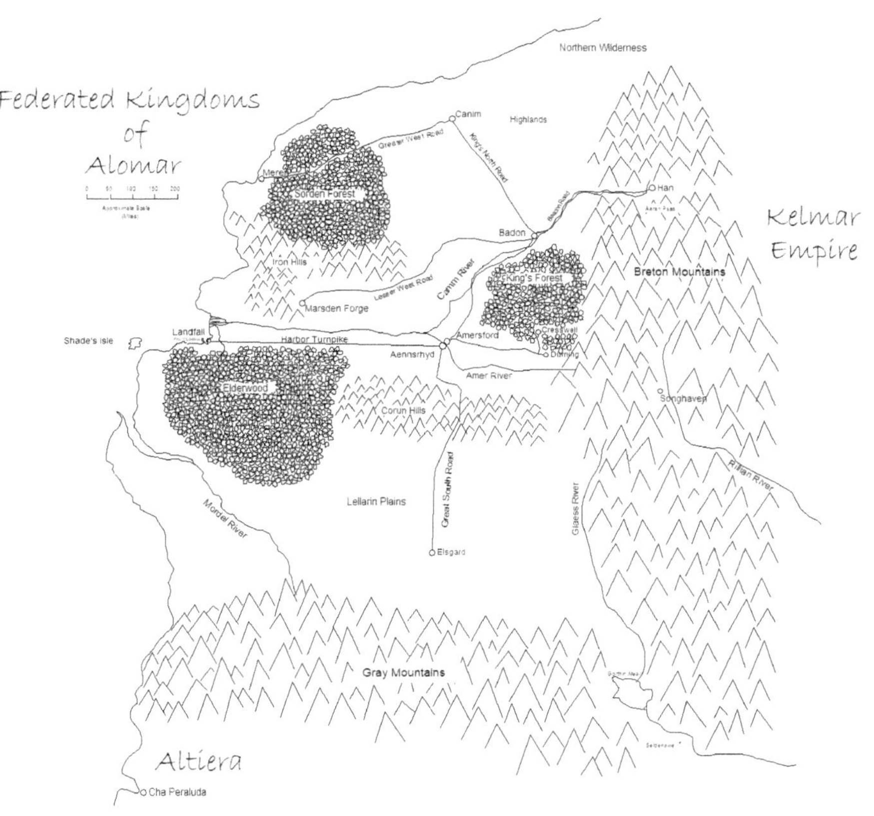

Federated Kingdoms
of
Alomar
Approximate Scale
(Miles)
0 50 100 150 200
Kelmar Empire
Altiera
Northern Wilderness
Canim
Highlands
Greater West Road
King's North Road
Han
Aeron Pass
Meris
Sorden Forest
Badon
Iron Hills
Lesser West Road
Canim River
King's Forest
Breton Mountains
Marsden Forge
Crestwall
Shade's Isle
Landfall
Harbor Turnpike
Amersford
Dunning
Aennsrhyd
Amer River
Songhaven
Elderwood
Corun Hills
Glaess River
Rilan River
Mordel River
Lellarin Plains
Great South Road
Elsgard
Gray Mountains
Selbenhoe
Cha Peraluda

Part Three

Race Among the Ruins

When you wake up to the promise

Of your dream world comin' true

With one less friend to call on

Was it someone that I knew

Away we'll go sailin'

In a race among the ruins

If you plan to face tomorrow

Do it soon

- from Race Among the Ruins

- Gordon Lightfoot

CHAPTER ONE

I paused to take a sip of my wine. It was a white and really should have been chilled–and had been when the server brought it–but mine had been sitting on the table for hours and it had warmed to room temperature. I swallowed it but decided against drinking the rest. It had not been all that good chilled and warming hadn't improved it. I set the goblet down and pushed it away. I looked around the room; there were far fewer people in the inn now than there had been when we started. My companion politely cleared her throat.

"You were there when Ambrose the Prophet died?" she asked.

I nodded and she shook her head, the expression on her face some mix of awe and disbelief. She had her mother's eyes and the accent of her mother's people. That cut to my heart. I fought back tears and nodded.

"But that was…"

"A very, very long time ago," I said softly and slowly.

"And he…" she started, but I cut her off.

"And he called me evil. One of my teachers, one of my mentors, one of my closest friends, a man I had known for many rounds of the seasons, he called me the most evil thing that he knew of and then he died. He died believing that's who I was."

"Tell me," she said.

It was a hot day, the nineteenth day of the first moon of *Tymnacynn*, the season of growth. Ambrose and I were riding out of Badon, accompanied by ten of the High King's Guard, to meet Marc, King of Amersford, and his cavalry. We were passing through a small wood not far from the meeting point when we were set upon by a rogue band of soldiers from Meren. Most of our men were slain in the first few moments of the fight and before Marc's troops reached us, Ambrose was mortally wounded.

With his last strength, he revealed to me that he had the ring of the Lawbreaker. Shortly after the Elven King Lorrestian had forged it, he had passed it on to a minstrel. In secret, it had been handed down from one minstrel to the next until Colin, Ambrose's master, had passed it to him. Now Ambrose was passing it on to me and asked me to swear to keep it secret and to keep it from the Lawbreaker. But when I touched it, the stone set in the ring–which had been dark and unreflective–woke.

"Merciful Mar preserve us," Ambrose said. "It is you. You are the Lawbreaker."

"Master, what are you saying? I can't be..."

But Ambrose was not looking at me, he was looking behind me.

"Marc," he said, his voice weak. "Marc, it is him. Lauren is the Lawbreaker. He must..."

Ambrose's voice trailed off and the light faded from his eyes.

"Master, no," I cried.

Rough hands seized me from behind, dragged me back away from Ambrose's body, and threw me to the ground. Marc stood over me, anger and fear on his face.

"Give me the ring," he demanded.

I was suddenly aware that I was no longer holding the Lawbreaker's ring. I held up my hands in a placating gesture, intending to say that I didn't have it, when I saw that it had somehow ended up on the ring finger of my right hand.

"I can't," I said. "I promised Ambrose that I would keep it safe."

"He called you the Lawbreaker. I must stop you from whatever it is that you're planning."

"Sire, I'm not planning anything. I can't be the Lawbreaker. The Lawbreaker killed the High King. I was with Ambrose when the High King was killed."

Men from Amersford were gathering around us, looking from Marc to me and trying to understand what was happening. I tried again to get through to Marc.

"Sire, the Lawbreaker is supposed to be evil. I'm not evil. I helped save your life. I saved Prince Anders. I..."

"Boy, all I know is what Ambrose said. He has never once told me something that wasn't true. With his dying breath he named you. I know what the Lawbreaker is, and I know my duty. I'll have that ring."

"Marc, I..."

The King gestured to his men. "Four of you hold him. I want that ring off his hand."

Four of the men rushed me and pinned down my arms and legs. I struggled against the restraint, but they had a solid hold and after a moment I gave up. The one holding my right hand began to struggle with the ring, trying to remove it from my finger. It wouldn't budge.

"Relax your hand," he ordered.

"I am," I said.

He spent several more moments trying to remove it, then looked up at Marc.

"It will not come off, Sire."

Marc stood silent for a heartbeat, then said, "Then take the hand. He cannot be allowed to keep that ring."

I felt as if my mind was somehow receding into my head and the edges of my vision went gray. Fear overwhelmed me. I was a minstrel; my hands were everything. I couldn't play without them.

"Marc, no," I cried.

The King simply gestured to his men. The man holding my right arm shifted and another joined him to completely immobilize my arm. I began to struggle again, but I couldn't move my right arm at all. Another man stepped to my right, and I heard a sword slide out of its scabbard.

"No," I wailed.

I caught a brief glimpse of movement to my right, and I felt something deep in my chest uncoil and explode out of me. I heard several large objects hitting the ground and men yelling in surprise and dismay. Suddenly I was free to move. I sat up and lifted my right arm, dreading what I would see. I still had my right hand, though, and the ring still glittered on my finger. I looked up at Marc, who was staring at me, astonishment and fear written on his face. I slowly stood and looked around me. Seven of his men were lying on the ground in a circle around me and I knew that they were the ones who had been holding me. Their bodies were twisted in ways that bodies were not meant to twist, and it was obvious that they were all dead. I looked back at Marc.

"Marc," I started to say, then someone hit me from behind and bore me to the ground. My breath was knocked out of me, and I struggled to breathe as my arms were roughly pulled behind me and bound at the wrists. As my legs were being tied, I tried to speak.

"Marc," I gasped.

"Gag him," was the king's response.

A filthy cloth was jammed into my mouth, and another tied in place to hold it. I was turned onto my back then. I was surrounded by Marc's soldiers, all of them holding unsheathed swords. The king himself stood at my feet glaring down at me.

"I trusted you," he said, his voice harsh. "Were you actually the one behind my poisoning? Is that how you knew what to look for?"

I frantically shook my head, but it had no effect.

"Did you sell out your accomplice to make yourself look good?"

He didn't wait for an answer but turned away from me.

"Throw him over a horse. We'll take him to Badon. We can't get the ring from him, but maybe between the High King, the wizards, and the Repentant someone will know what to do with him." He looked at the seven fallen men. "He has much to answer for."

None of the men moved. The king took several steps before he noticed.

"I said get him on a horse," he snapped. "Now."

Two of the men sheathed their swords and moved toward me. One grabbed my shoulders and the other my ankles. They hoisted me up and carried me to a horse and managed to sling me facedown across the saddle.

"Mount up," the king called. "They're expecting us in Badon."

Within moments, we started to move. I could barely breathe; all my weight was resting on my chest and gut making it difficult to take a breath. The way I was lying, it would have been hard to breathe even without the gag in my mouth. Every step the horse took jostled me, forcing the air out of my body and bouncing my face against the saddle fender. I tried to twist in a way that would relieve the pressure on my body but felt myself begin to slip. After that, I held as still as I could, but to no avail. Within a few minutes, I felt myself go and I tumbled off the horse.

Luckily, I didn't land on my head and the horse didn't step on me. I managed to twist just enough to take the main force of the landing on my back, but the fall knocked the wind out of me again, and my vision blurred as I fought to breathe. I was just beginning to catch my breath when I heard frustrated shouting and footsteps, and I was hauled to my feet by two of Marc's men. A third pulled a hood over my head.

"Don't move unless I move you," one of them ordered.

My hands and legs were untied, and I was led to a horse.

"Mount," the same man ordered.

Clumsily, I climbed onto the horse and immediately felt men tying my feet to the stirrups.

"Put your hands on the saddle horn," the man said.

I did as instructed, and the man tied my hands to the saddle horn.

"Ready," the man called.

"Forward," Marc ordered, and we began to move again.

After that, I lost track of time. The bag over my head was thick and no light got through it. I could see enough out of the bottom to tell that it was still daylight, but that was about all. It was a hot day and the air in the bag grew stifling; sweat was running down my face. Still, I could breathe and that was a small mercy. I could hear quiet conversations from the distant members of Marc's forces, but I couldn't make out what they were saying and the men near me stayed silent. That left me alone with my own thoughts and all I could think of was that Ambrose was dead. Every time that I thought those words, tears welled up in my eyes. Not all the moisture on my face was sweat.

The sound of the horses' hooves changed, and I guessed that we were crossing the bridges over Badon's defensive ditches. That guess was confirmed when I made out the guards at the Southgate challenging Marc. I think we passed through three more gates and the noise of the city receded enough that I could tell that I was now accompanied by only a few men. Then we stopped and I felt someone loosening the bonds on my feet.

"I'm going to free your hands now," said the man who had given me orders before. "Don't try anything."

I felt the blade of a knife as the man severed the bonds holding me to the saddle horn.

"Alright, get down."

I dismounted awkwardly and nearly fell. Someone laughed. Then men grabbed my arms.

"Come with us," I was told.

I had no choice but to comply. The sound of our footsteps changed; we were walking now on a wooden floor instead of the ground. Then the sound changed again and suddenly the air was noticeably cooler. Out of the bottom of the hood, I could see the flickering of torchlight on bare dirt ground. We walked for some time. I couldn't tell whether we made any turns, but then we stopped and someone in front of me said, "In here."

We changed directions and took a few steps. Then the men holding my arms released me and I heard them step away. A door closed, a key grated in a lock, and I heard footsteps receding into the distance.

I stood there in silence for long minutes, wondering what was next. I heard nothing; it seemed that I was alone. Hesitantly, I reached up and removed the hood and the gag.

Before me was nothing but darkness. I turned and could see a small square of faint light at the level of my face. I took a careful step forward with my arms stretched out in front of me. My hands made contact with a heavy wooden door. I ran my hands over it. There was, of course, no knob and the hinges must have been on the outside of the door. At my eye level was a small, barred window that allowed in the faint light from some distance source. At the bottom of the door was a slot, too thin to get my arm through, that I presumed–that I hoped–would be used to pass me food.

I stood and leaned forward with my hands on the door, my head bowed. I stifled a sob.

I was obviously in the High King's dungeon.

I spent some time then exploring my cell, mostly by touch; the window in the door was the only thing I could see, and it was just barely visible. The room was roughly four paces by four paces, and it contained nothing except me, my gag, and my hood. There was no cot, no bench, nothing to sit or lie on except the stone floor. The walls, what I could make out of them, were featureless except for the distinction between the dressed surface of the building stones and the mortar. There was no chamber pot and no hole in the floor, not even any straw; when I needed to relieve myself the only way to do so was on the floor of the cell.

Periodically I was brought food. I'm guessing it was no more often than once a day. The first time, I noticed my little lighted window growing brighter. Soon, it was clear that someone with a torch was standing outside the door. My heart lightened just a little; I wasn't sure how long I'd been alone in the darkness, but I welcomed the possibility of human contact, however minimal. I was just taking a breath to speak when the person outside spoke.

"Don't say anything."

The voice was rough and sounded angry.

"I have food and water. If you say even one word, I'll leave with them. I'm going to slide them under the door. You eat, you drink, you slide the bowl and water skin back under the door. If they're not outside when I get back, you don't get the next meal."

I heard a scraping sound and could barely see a bowl and waterskin in the slot at the bottom of the door. Even as I bent to pick them up, I heard the man outside walking away and the light faded. I sank down with my back against the door, the bowl in one hand and the waterskin in the other. There was no spoon, so I brought the bowl to my lips and took a sip. It was gruel, but of far better quality than I would have expected. At a guess, I'd say it was made with milk and oats. I finished it as quickly as I could and literally licked the bowl clean before I slid it back under the door. I took my time with the water, figuring that if my guard returned, I could gulp the rest down and get the skin back under the door before he arrived. I wasn't sure when I'd get more.

Mostly I was left alone in the dark. After that first time, the guard who brought my food didn't speak to me again. I heard no other sounds, nothing to indicate the presence of other prisoners or even of rats or other vermin. I guess there was nothing to draw them; I ate the only food available as quickly as I got it.

At first, my thoughts were consumed with the fact of Ambrose's death and what he'd said about me. One of the most influential and wisest counselors for the kings of the Alomar was gone. My friend, my mentor, was gone. Worse, he died believing that I was evil, that I was going to destroy the world.

In the dark, I couldn't see the ring, but I could clearly remember how the dark stone woke at my touch. I couldn't deny that. I also couldn't deny that three times in my life, something inside me–some power–had acted to save me from serious harm or death. I couldn't seem to call it up, not even to get out of my cell. I'll admit that I tried. I tried to unlock the door. Thinking of the tree and the men who attacked me, I tried blasting the door. Nothing happened. I wondered what the ring was supposed to do. I tried pointing it at the door and willing a blast of energy to set me free. Nothing happened. I had killed seven men without willing it–something that caused my heart to falter each time I thought of it–but I couldn't open that door. In the end, I was left in the cell, in the dark, and back at the beginning of the cycle of thoughts: Ambrose was dead.

If I thought too long about my own situation, I began to panic. I was alone and people I knew and respected, people I liked, believed that I was evil. I wondered whether they simply planned to keep me locked up forever or if they'd decide to simply stop feeding me. What would I do if they did? I thought a great deal about Peg. I was afraid that I'd never see her again and I was afraid of how she'd react if I ever did. I was locked in a small cell, and when I thought about that, I could feel the walls closing in and the panic grew. Pacing back and forth helped wear me out and I'd fall into a troubled, unsatisfying sleep.

I tried to count the number of meals I was brought, but with no way to mark down the count and grieving over Ambrose's death and my own imprisonment, I lost track. My thoughts kept going in circles until, exhausted, I'd drift into fitful sleep, then I'd wake with a sudden remembrance that Ambrose was dead, and it would all start again.

I was thinking of Peg, longing for her, really, when I noticed my little window slowly brightening and heard approaching footsteps. A bowl of gruel and a waterskin were pushed in under the door and I heard the guard moving off. As the light died away, I hurriedly sat down with my back against the door and began slurping down my food. I was halfway through the bowl when I noticed that there was enough light coming in through the food slot that I could see the waterskin on the floor. In a near panic, I tried to push the bowl back under the door, but then I heard a key in the lock.

"Lauren," an unfamiliar voice called softly.

The sound of another voice confused me, and I couldn't answer. Then the door opened, and I fell back into the hall. I found myself flat on my back, blinking up at a man who appeared to be wearing the sable and gold of the High King's Guard. He held only a single torch, but my eyes were unaccustomed to the light, and I couldn't see clearly.

"*Mirdl*," he swore softly. "What have they done to you?"

He turned and put the torch into a sconce on the wall. Then he crouched by my side.

"Lauren?"

My eyes had adjusted somewhat, and I peered up at him from the floor. I couldn't get my thoughts together enough to form a coherent utterance. Something about him, though, seemed familiar.

"Lauren," he said again, "I'm Steafán, Peg's brother."

That's why he seemed familiar. I'd never met him, but he did resemble Peg. His face was thin where Peg's was round, but his nose and eyes were similar to hers. His hair and his neatly trimmed mustache were the same shade of brown as Peg's hair.

"Thirsty," I managed to get out, my voice raspy from thirst and disuse.

"Sorry, I don't have anything with me."

"Inside," I said. "Skin."

I was lying half in and half out of the cell and Steafán was kneeling beside me, so all he had to do was lean slightly to one side to find the waterskin.

"Got it," he said.

He helped me sit up, wrinkling his nose a bit–I must have smelled terrible–and brought the waterskin to my lips. I drank deeply, nearly emptying the skin.

"My thanks to you," I said in a hoarse whisper. I looked at him, puzzled. He was, indeed, wearing the uniform of the High King's Guard. I seemed to recall that Peg had once said that one of her brothers was in the Guard. "Why?" I asked.

He looked at me, puzzlement fading into a slight smile as he understood what I was asking.

"For what you are to my sister," he answered. "She loves you. She loves you very much. And Peg might not be a great princess—I still don't know why she chose to give it up to be a minstrel—but she's an excellent judge of people. If she gave you her heart, you cannot be what they are saying you are."

I glanced at the ring. It glittered on my hand, somewhat more red than violet in the torchlight. He saw but didn't say anything.

"Why now?" I asked, my voice harsh and grating from disuse.

"Because the guard just brought your food. No one will be back for another day."

"Not what I meant," I said.

"Ah. I understand. Everyone has been arguing over what to do with you. They decided to wait until Prince Anders returned and have him decide. Today, though, a group of Repentant arrived, demanding that you be turned over to the Church. Prince Anders is due back tomorrow, so the Chancellor told them that they could discuss the situation with him. I thought it might be best if you weren't here at the end of that discussion."

"I think I agree," I said. "What now?"

"We need to get you out of here. I have a merchant waiting with a wagon. She's heading out of the city to the villages on the north side of the Camm River. She'll take you as far as Willow Bank. I'll meet you there with your things. We do need to make one stop, though, before we meet Ottilie."

"Where's that?"

"Somewhere you can clean up. They'd be able to find you by your smell alone. What have you been doing in there?"

"The only place to go was the floor."

"Sweet Mar and the Keepers," he said. "What a way to treat a person."

He stood and then helped me to stand.

"Let me close and lock the cell," he said. "If we're lucky, they'll think you used magic to escape. It would be better if you could blow down the door..." He paused and his gaze flicked to the ring on my hand. "Could you do that? Could you blow down the door?"

"Sure," I replied, with as much sarcasm as I could muster. "I'm only still here because the accommodations were so cushy."

He winced and shook his head slightly as he locked the cell door and retrieved his torch.

"Sorry. Wasn't thinking. Follow me."

He led the way down a passageway carved out of the bedrock of Badon Hill.

"This passageway opens into a guard house on the fourth level of the city," he explained. "There shouldn't be anyone there this time of night. I have some clean clothes for you. You'll need to wash up and change quickly. We don't want to miss Ottilie."

"A washing will be nice," I said. I hadn't bathed or shaved since Ambrose, and I rode out of Amersford. "A bath would be better. And I'd love a shave, too. I haven't shaved in... How long was I in there?"

"Almost ten days," Steafán answered.

"Ten days?" I asked, surprised. "That's all? It felt like much longer."

"That's all it was," Steafán replied. "And I wouldn't shave if I were you."

"Why not?"

"You're looking scruffy and that's good. The less that you look like Lauren of the Minstrels, the better. Every soldier and bounty hunter in the Federation is going to be looking for you."

The passageway ended at a wooden wall with a door. Steafán gestured for me to hang back. I stopped and stepped back outside the circle of the torch light. He carefully opened the door and peered into the room on the other side. Then he stepped back, threw the door open and said, "It's empty. Come on."

The guardhouse was about the same size as my cell. There were no windows and only two doors: the one we just came through and one that, presumably, led to the street. Steafán lit a candle from his torch and snuffed the torch out in a bucket of sand. Then he picked up an empty bucket.

"There's a well just outside," he said. "Go ahead and get undressed. I'll fetch some water. I don't have any soap, but you can at least rinse off. There's a sack on the bench. The clean clothes are in there. You can put your old things in there and I'll dispose of them later."

I began to strip as he slipped out the door. I pulled the clean clothes out of the sack and stuffed my old things into it, everything except my sash. I would not be parted from that, even if I couldn't wear it. In just a few moments, Steafán was back with the water. Then it hit me.

"Steafán, if I try to clean up in here, there's a chance that someone will be able to tell that when they discover that I'm missing. Are there people around outside?"

He shook his head and said, "Good thought. There's an alley just across the street. We could go in there and I'll douse you."

I nodded and picked up the bag and my fresh clothes.

"That'll work."

We opened the door and checked the street. No one was about. I dashed across the street into the alley with Steafán following more slowly with the water. I found a window ledge and placed my clothing there. I stood with my arms and legs akimbo.

"Go ahead," I said.

Steafán dumped the bucket over my head. The water was chilly. I began using my hands to wipe off as much grime as I could.

"Would you get another bucketful?" I asked.

He nodded. I continued scrubbing as best I could with just my hands until he returned. I had him dump that bucket over me and then tried to shake like a dog to dry off. Then I used the outside of the sack as a towel. I was still damp when I went to put on the clothes, but I no longer smelled like a midden on a hot summer day. The clothes that Steafán had brought were plain—a tunic and trousers of simple homespun fabric, with a piece of rope for a belt—the kind of clothes that would be worn by a farmer from a village like Cresswell. If someone were looking for a minstrel, they wouldn't give me a second look.

"One more thing," Steafán said. "Here."

He held out a plain chain of silver. I just looked at him, puzzled.

"You can't go around wearing that ring," he said. "I thought you could carry it around your neck with this."

"That's," I started, but a sudden rush of emotion cut off the rest. I swallowed hard to clear the knot in my throat. "That's how Ambrose carried it all those rounds."

A single tear rolled down my cheek as I took the chain, slipped it through the ring, and fastened it around my neck. As I was tucking it into my tunic, Steafán turned to go and said, "Come. We have to hurry."

I stopped and picked up my bright blue minstrel's sash.

"What are you doing with that?" he asked.

"I can't leave it," I said. "I worked too hard to earn it. Give me a second."

I lifted the bottom of my tunic and tied my sash around my waist. The dangling ends I stuffed down my trousers. When I pulled my tunic down, the sash couldn't be seen.

"That'll work," Steafán said.

Together, we left the alley.

"Where are we going?" I asked.

"Ottilie is a traveling merchant," Steafán replied. "She occasionally delivers supplies to the wizard's college. She made a delivery tonight and is waiting near the college. You'll hide in the back of her wagon, and she'll get you out of the city and to Willow Bank."

We walked in silence a moment. As we walked, I glanced at Steafán in his sable and gold uniform.

"Steafán," I said. "I very much appreciate what you've done for me, but aren't things going to go badly for you if they find out?"

"If they find out, yes. But how will they? No one will even know that you're gone until this time tomorrow. Long before then, I'll have the key back and the bag with your clothes will be gone. So far, we haven't been seen and there's nothing unusual about my being out; I'm off shift now."

I nodded.

"I'd just hate to bring trouble down on you," I said.

We turned a corner and Steafán pointed.

"There's Ottilie's wagon."

As we got closer, I examined the wagon. It was smaller than the other wagon I had ridden in, back when the merchant Kendal had given my father and me a ride back to Cresswell from Amersford. Kendal's wagon had pretty much been a box on wheels, but this one was constructed differently. The wagon bed had sides that were, perhaps, three feet tall. Above that was a canvas cover supported by some kind of internal structure. We were approaching the wagon from the front and a woman stepped from behind it as we drew near.

"Ottilie," Steafán said quietly.

She nodded in acknowledgement. Ottilie looked to be about the same age as Steafán, a few rounds older than me. She was about my height, her brown hair tied back in a long ponytail. Her clothing was relatively plain but made from fine cloth.

"I was beginning to wonder if you would come," she said.

"We needed to stop and douse my friend in a couple of buckets of water," Steafán replied. "He was a bit too noticeable."

She smiled slightly and turned to me.

"I'm Ottilie," she said.

"I'm…" I started, but Steafán cut me off.

"This is Arlow," he said.

Ottilie looked at us for a moment, then nodded and said, "Well enough for me. Arlow it is." She turned her full attention to me. "You'll ride in the back. I've piled a bunch of furs in there. Bury yourself under them and don't come out until I tell you to. We'll stop down in the first level to get the rest of my team and then we'll leave the city. When we're a good distance away, I'll call a halt, and you can come out."

"I understand," I said.

"If by chance," she continued, "we get stopped and searched, I don't know that you're in there. You're a stowaway."

"Fair enough," I said. "I'll confirm that if questioned."

"OK, then, let's go."

I turned to Steafán and offered my hand. He took it.

"My thanks to you," I said.

"Good luck," he replied. "Wait for me in Willow Bank. I'll bring you some supplies and as many of your things as I can manage."

With that, I climbed into the wagon and burrowed under the furs. A moment later, I felt the wagon rock as Ottilie boarded and then we began to move. I was nervous, fearing that at any minute we were going to be stopped and the wagon searched, but at the same time, I was comfortable for the first time in over a quarter moon. The summer night was warm, and it was getting a bit hot under the furs, but I was fighting sleep as we passed through the city. Then we stopped and I snapped awake. I heard Ottilie speaking to several other people, but their voices were muffled by the furs, and I couldn't make out what was being said. Then we were moving again. Presently, there was another brief pause and then the wagon tilted, and I knew we were heading down the slope of Badon Hill. I smiled and surrendered myself to sleep.

My first thought on waking was that the wagon wasn't moving. I listened intently for a while and heard nothing but vague sounds that might have been quiet conversation, so I dug my way out from under the furs. I heard only the sounds you'd expect from a camp and people quietly speaking, so I climbed out of the back of the wagon.

The sky was the color of steel with just a faint blush of pink to the east. A gentle breeze was blowing from the west and the air smelled of rain. The wagons were parked alongside the road. I could hear the faint rushing sound from a small creek that flowed under the road in a culvert. I walked around to the side of Ottilie's wagon and found the others of the party gathered around a fire. A large pot of something bubbled over the fire. One of the men noticed me, nudged Ottilie, and then pointed at me. Ottilie looked at me and gestured for me to join them.

In addition to Ottilie, the group consisted of two men and a woman.

"Good morning, Arlow," Ottilie said, with just a slight emphasis on the name. I realized that she knew that Arlow was not my true name. "I came to wake you after we were away from the city last night, but it was clear that you needed the sleep, so I left you to it. I trust that you're fine with that."

"I am. My thanks to you for your consideration," I replied.

"Would you like some oatmeal?" Ottilie asked.

"Yes, please."

One of the men selected a metal bowl from a stack, ladled a generous helping into it, and passed it to me. As I began to eat, Ottilie addressed the group.

"Arlow will be riding with us to Willow Bank," she said. "My understanding is that he would prefer to avoid chatting with any of the High King's men and I've agreed make sure that doesn't happen until we get him to Willow Bank. We shouldn't run across any of the king's troops before then, but should that happen, I wanted you all to know what the deal is. Are there any questions?"

No one spoke, though a couple shook their heads.

We finished eating in silence. I stood and began gathering the empty bowls.

"What are you doing?" Ottilie asked me.

"I'm going to clean the dishes," I answered.

"There's no need for that."

"I very much appreciate your help," I explained. "I don't want to be a dead weight, and I don't believe that I can assist with whatever your business is. The dishes need to be cleaned, though, and I can clean them. I know that it's not much, but it is something."

Ottilie stared at me for a moment and then nodded, so I finished gathering the bowls and spoons and headed for the creek. A few moments later, one of the men joined me carrying the now empty pot. We worked in silence, but as I finished and prepared to return with the clean dishes, he nodded.

We were underway not long after. The growing light of day revealed that the sky was full of clouds. Shortly after we set out, it began to rain, a gentle rain, but our clothes were soon wet clear through to our skins. The group was obviously familiar with the route; we stopped for our midday meal at a spot that made it easy to get the horses down to the river for a drink. The rain finally let up in midafternoon and the hot summer sun burned off the last of the clouds. The air was humid and, instead of drying out, our clothes stayed wet, this time with sweat.

When we stopped for the evening, I helped to unharness and care for the horses. As I was examining the hooves of one of them, the man who had washed the pot that morning came and stood watching me. After a moment, he spoke.

"We been talkin' about ya," he said without any preamble.

I just glanced his way and then went back to caring for the horse.

"Ya obviously know how to work and you're not afraid of it," he continued. "So, we figure ya ain't no lord or any such thing. Your hands are soft, though. Kinda makes us think maybe you're some lord's house servant."

I let go of the last hoof and began wiping the horse down. My companion joined me.

"Question is, why ya runnin' away? Men don't run from cushy jobs. Ya know what I think?"

He didn't wait for an answer from me.

"I think ya done some noble lady and got caught at it."

I glanced his way, but still didn't say anything.

"That's it, ain't it?" He grinned, but the grin quickly turned to puzzlement. "If that's it, though, why's it the High King who's lookin' for ya?"

A look of surprise washed across his face, and I cocked my head in question.

"Mar's left tit," he swore, his eyes wide. "His sister. Ya did the High King's sister, didn't ya?"

I allowed the ghost of a smile to play across my face as I finished wiping down the horse and added the cloth I'd been using to a growing pile of dirty cloths.

"Would you mind hobbling this guy for me? I'd like to go wash up a bit before we eat."

"Damn," he said as I headed for the river.

It was still hot and humid when we bedded down for the night. Unlike the others, I had nothing to change into, so I was trying to sleep in damp, sticky clothes. I felt like I laid awake most of the night and, when I did sleep, I was troubled by dreams of a spreading darkness, huge and powerful, that hid something that was frantically searching for me. When there was enough light to see by, I went down to the river, stripped off my clothes, and waded in. The water was cool, and my clothes had finally dried by the time I finished rinsing the worst of the dirt off; I had no soap. When I returned to camp, everyone else was up. We broke our fast with bread, cheese, and fruit and then I helped harness the horses. By the time it was fully light, we were underway.

As I had the previous day, I rode with Ottilie. We rode in companionable silence for a while, sipping from mugs of tea.

"They're talking about you, you know," she said.

I nodded. "I know."

"Mitch says that you claim to have slept with the High King's sister."

I smiled.

"He came up with the idea that I'd slept with the wrong person all on his own. I just asked him to hobble the horse I'd been caring for."

"You didn't deny it, though."

"I didn't. If anyone asks them about me, I'd rather they tell the story of a servant fleeing a romantic indiscretion than the story of a mystery man who was avoiding authorities."

She nodded.

"Makes sense," she said. "Care to tell me what the real story is?"

"It would probably be better if I didn't."

She simply nodded once in acknowledgement and didn't bring it up again.

We reached Willow Bank just after midday the next day. Willow Bank contained a dozen or so cruck houses with wattle and daub walls and thatched roofs. Each had a small vegetable patch and most had odds and ends related to fishing leaning against the walls or hanging from the eaves. The land between the houses and the river was lined with willows, no doubt the source of the village name. There were several small boats drawn up on shore under the trees; several more were visible out on the river.

As we rolled into the village, people looked up from their garden patches or came to the door of their house. When the people recognized Ottilie, they left what they were doing and met us in the middle of the village. We climbed down from the wagon and people gathered around Ottilie, smiling and all talking at once. A few glanced my way, took in my plain clothing and dismissed me as unimportant, and then turned their attention back to the wagoner. Ottilie spent a few moments greeting the villagers, then broke away to move toward the back of the wagon.

"The wizards were pleased with the herbs you sent, and the vegetables sold well in the marketplace," she announced. "I was able to get everything you requested and there are a few crowns left over."

She and her colleagues began unloading things from the wagons: many bolts of cloth, mostly wool, but I did see one bolt of linen, new pots and pans, and several small containers of spices, mostly salt. The new supplies were quickly whisked away.

"Have you had your midday meal?" one of the women asked.

"No, we haven't," Ottilie responded.

We were served a meal of bread and cheese and some kind of smoked fish. After we'd eaten, Ottilie asked me to join her and one of the women from the village.

"Arlow, this is Rhona," she said. "And Rhona, this young man is called Arlow. He's stumbled into a bit of hard luck and had to leave Badon with nothing but what he's wearing. He has a friend–someone I know and trust–who will be along in a few days with his belongings. Since he's been riding with us, I've found him willing and able to work to earn his keep. Would you be willing to give him a place to lay his head and a bit of food until his friend arrives?"

The woman–Rhona–looked me up and down, her look cautious and colored with a bit of suspicion.

"I am willing to help with any work that needs to be done," I confirmed.

Just then a little girl rounding up some of the used dishes screamed, dropped the plate she was carrying, and began running and flailing around. Several of us ran to investigate and found that she was being attacked by a yellowjacket that had been attracted to the food on the plate. Mitch managed to kill the offending insect, which had already stung the girl twice. She was crying and not even her mother seemed able to comfort her. I squatted down in front of her.

"Hello," I said as calmly as I could. "That really hurts, doesn't it?"

Suddenly faced with a stranger, the girl stopped screaming and inched back toward her mother, but she nodded.

"I might be able to help. May I look at it?"

Tears were still running down her face and she shook her head.

"I won't touch. I'll just look. I promise."

Hesitantly, the girl held out her arm. Two large splotches of red marked her forearm where the yellowjacket had stung her.

"You know what might feel good?" I asked her.

She shook her head again.

"I'll bet the water in the river is cool. If you dipped your arm into the water, I'll bet that would feel really good."

She looked up at her mother who nodded her assent. Together, we walked down to the riverbank. Aided by her mother, the girl laid down and dipped her arm into the water. Her face calmed and the tears stopped. After a moment I asked, "How's that feel?"

"Better."

"That's good. My name is Arlow. What's yours?"

"Emilie."

"That's a very pretty name. Emilie, do you think you could let me help you now?"

She glanced at her mother again, got another nod, and said, "Yes."

I turned to the others who had followed us to the river.

"Would someone go and fetch some soap, some clean cloths, and some apple cider vinegar?"

One of the village women left to retrieve the items I'd requested.

"Has anyone got a knife?" I asked. "If so, could you peel off three or four small strips of bark from one of the younger branches of one of these willows?"

One of the men in the group did as I asked and brought the strips to me.

"Emilie, could you chew these for me? Just chew them and swallow the juice. Don't swallow the strips. Can you do that?"

She nodded and I helped her sit up. Before I handed them to her, I said, "They aren't going to taste very good, but the juice will help you feel better."

She took the strips and put them in her mouth.

"Remember, chew, but don't swallow the strips, just the juice."

She made a face as she began to chew. Just then, the woman returned with the items I had requested. I took them and turned to the girl.

"Emilie," I said, I need to wash your arm. I'll be very careful."

She held her arm up for me; apparently, I'd won some degree of trust from her. I wet one of the cloths, added a bit of soap, and carefully wiped down her arm. I rinsed away the soap using the cloth to dribble water over her arm. Then I wet another of the cloths with vinegar and laid that over the bites.

"You can spit out the bark now," I told her.

She spit and then said, "That tasted real bad."

"I know," I said. "I'm very proud of you for not spitting them out. How are you feeling?"

"Better. My thanks to you."

"Glad to help," I said. I turned to her mother. "You can put a cloth soaked in vinegar over the bites to control the pain and itching whenever she needs it. The worst pain should be over in a few hours, but the swelling and redness can last a couple of days."

"My thanks to you," she said. "You were so good with her. Are you a father?"

"No," I replied. "But someday…"

She smiled and then helped Emilie stand. Together, they headed back toward the houses.

Rhona walked up to me then.

"You have some experience as a Healer," she said, her tone making it a question.

"I know a little," I replied.

"Well, with luck we will not need to call on your healing skills again, but you are welcome to stay until your friend arrives."

I spent that night on a blanket spread out on the floor of Rhona's house. Her husband, Fergus, had been wary of me when he came in from the river, but Rhona pulled him aside for a whispered conversation and he agreed to allow me to stay. He snored, a deep rumbling that sounded for all the world like there was a bear in the house, so I didn't get much rest. The next day, I worked with the villagers, tending to their gardens, and repairing the roof of one of the houses. I kept one eye on the road from the east, but there was no sign of Steafán. By nightfall, I was so exhausted that I slept despite Fergus' snoring.

When Steafán rode in the next evening, I wasn't in the village. I was down on the riverbank helping patch one of the small rowboats the villagers used to fish the river. Fergus brought the news. He simply walked up and said, "Yer fren's here." Then he gently pushed me aside and took over assisting the boat owner.

I found Steafán in the center of the village speaking with Rhona and a few of the other villagers. He was holding the reins of a chestnut gelding and a fully laden donkey. When he saw me, he smiled widely.

"Well, here's my friend Arlow," he said as I joined the group. "I will let you return to your supper preparations, and we'll tend to the animals. Do you have a stable?"

Rhona nodded and pointed to the largest structure in the village.

"That's our shared barn. You may keep your animals there overnight."

Steafán handed me the lead for the donkey, a medium sized one with a brown coat and sad-looking brown eyes that somehow conveyed the idea that he simply couldn't believe what he had been asked to endure. We headed for the small communal barn and, once inside, I led the donkey into an empty stall while Steafán did the same with his horse. Steafán then made a quick check to see that we were alone and joined me to help unload the donkey.

"This is everything I could get," he said quietly. "I didn't bring any of your clothes; they'd be far too fine for the wandering vagabond you're posing as and would attract too much attention. I did get you an extra tunic and trousers, though. I also found a small pouch in your room that had a few irons and a couple of copper crowns in it. I assume that's yours."

"Yes, it is."

"I also got you some typical traveling supplies: some travel bread, cheese, and dried meat and fruits. A tent would be out of character, but I did get you a blanket and a tarp for shelter. And a bit of rope."

There was one wooden box atop all the other things.

"What's in the box?" I asked.

"Your guitar. My sister is a minstrel; I know how important your instruments are to you. I thought the box would disguise what it is, though it might attract attention."

"Less than an obvious guitar would," I noted.

"I did get one other thing. I hope it's alright."

"What?"

"I got Ambrose's pouch of medications and the like. I thought maybe you'd want it."

I felt tears welling up in my eyes.

"Steafán, my thanks to you. That means a great deal to me."

He simply nodded and turned to the donkey.

"This guy is yours as well. Perhaps not the kind of mount you're used to, and I wouldn't try riding him anyway. He's very good at carrying things, though. His name is Budge."

That struck me as an odd name for any animal, much less a donkey.

"Budge?" I asked, frowning.

Steafán shook his head, smiling.

"I didn't name him."

Once the donkey was unloaded, I brushed him down. Steafán did the same for his horse. Then we joined the villagers for the evening meal. It was fish. Again. Steafán was delighted, but after three days of eating fish with almost every meal, I was growing tired of it. Neither of us spoke much–just what was required for politeness' sake–and the villagers didn't push us, but instead spoke about the events of the day, the work that was done and that which still needed doing, and the number of fish caught.

There were still a couple of hours of light left when the meal was ended. We helped clean up the dishes and then Steafán turned to me and said, "Can we walk a bit?"

I nodded and led the way down to the riverbank. Here, so near the village, the bank was kept clear, and the villagers' boats were drawn up out of the water. In places, the branches of the willows hung out over the water, and we walked under green archways.

"Has anyone been out this far looking for you?" Steafán asked quietly.

"I haven't seen anyone," I responded.

"It took them two days to realize that you were gone," Steafán informed me. "By that time, I'd been able to get into your room to get your belongings. I was able to get the stuff down to a safe place on the first level before they began looking for you. They think that somehow you managed to magic your way out and up to the palace to get your things. By the time I left, no one was even suggesting that you had help."

"What was the reaction when they discovered that I was gone?"

"Shock. Fear. Some were angry. Messengers have been sent to all the federated cities, with drawings of you. A reward has been offered: ten silver shields for information leading to your capture. People everywhere are going to be looking for you."

"What about you, Steafán? If they figure out that you helped me, they'll kill you."

"If they haven't figured it out by now, I don't think that they ever will. There were no witnesses; if there had been we'd know by now. Ottilie won't talk, if they even think to track her down. She was just one of a score of traders to go in and out of the city between the last time they know that you were in your cell and the time you were found to be missing."

He paused for a few steps and then said, "I won't be going back to Badon anyway."

"What?" I looked at him in surprise.

"Laur..." he started, then caught himself. "I'm worried. Something strange is happening in the Aeran Pass. I'm sure you remember that Han was under attack."

"Yes. Prince Anders rode out to bring what aid he could. Has there been word?"

"There has. By the time the prince and his men arrived, the battle was over. The Kelmar mounted a half-hearted assault on the outer wall for the better part of two days, and then just stopped. When Anders arrived, the Kelmar army was camped well out of bowshot, but they filled the pass east of the city. Watchers say that they see men coming and going from the Kelmar camp, more coming than leaving. But there's a huge army camped right outside Han, doing nothing."

I just looked at him in surprise.

"My father and brothers need me. I'm heading home to Han to provide whatever assistance I can to them. I've resigned my commission in the High King's Guard. As third in line for the throne, I was just sent there to give me something to do. I'm really more of an honorary member. I won't be missed."

I finally found my voice.

"The Kelmar are just sitting there?"

"Yes. They haven't attacked since that first assault. They haven't sent anyone out to negotiate. They did fire some arrows at a group that my father sent out under a parley flag, but it was clear that the shots deliberately missed and were meant to signal the Kelmar unwillingness to talk."

"That is strange," I agreed. "I cannot recall from any of my history lessons a single time that the Kelmar ever behaved that way."

"Just before I left, a messenger came in from the prince. He was returning to Badon to rally additional troops to send to Han. He left your father in command at Han. I feel like something is coming, something big, but I have no idea what it might be."

It was nearly dark by then, so we returned to the village. Steafán slept in the home of Emilie's family, and I again spent the night with Rhona and Fergus. Steafán and I were both up with the sun and, with a few others from the village, broke our fast with fresh baked biscuits slathered with butter and jam, and the ubiquitous fish. Then we made our way to the barn to pack up.

I went to the stall where the donkey was tied up. My things lay undisturbed in the corner. With the exception of the box that housed my guitar, it was clear to anyone thinking of robbing me that nothing in the pile was of much worth.

I began loading my things onto Budge and Steafán turned to saddle his horse. He finished before I did and joined me in loading the donkey. I tied the last bundle into place and turned to my friend.

"Steafán, my thanks to you for all you've done. If it weren't for you, I'd still be in that cell."

"I was glad to help. I will admit that I was a little concerned about getting you out of there; the things people were saying about you were bad. But my sister loves you and given my experience of you in the last few days–plus what the people here are saying about you–I'm glad that I did."

"Safe travels, Steafán. Be safe if the Kelmar attack again."

"You, too, Lauren" he replied, very quietly.

We led our animals out of the barn then to find that most of the villagers had turned out to see us off. Rhona stepped forward.

"Rhona," I said, with a slight bow. "My thanks to you and to Fergus for your hospitality."

"Arlow, you have been a great help in the few days that you've been here. You'd be welcome to stay if you'd like."

I smiled but shook my head.

"As much as I might want to, I think it best that I move on," I said.

"Then let me offer this," she replied and held out a couple of irons. "You did far more work that would be required for a place on our floor and some food. This amount doesn't even cover the aid you gave to Emilie."

"What kind of person would refuse aid to a child in need?" I countered. "Rhona, please use your money for your family and your village. If you truly wish to compensate me, there is something I would request."

"And that would be?"

"The High King's men may come here looking for a man. It would be better for me if they did not hear stories about the stranger who came through Willow Bank."

She stared at me for long moments, obviously weighing what she knew of me and what she could see in my face. Then she nodded.

"It shall be as you ask."

Steafán spoke up then.

"Rhona, you have my thanks as well for your hospitality."

In reply, she simply said, "Safe travels, wayward travelers. May Garth guide your footsteps and put you on the path back to Mar."

It would have been best for me to reply with the ritual response, but some obscure impulse moved me and instead I replied, "May your fields be fertile and the river kind."

Rhona cocked her head at that, looking puzzled, but then smiled. Steafán mounted and rode out of the village to the east. I, with Budge following behind me on his lead, headed west.

CHAPTER TWO

I followed the road west out of Willow Bank. It was unpaved, but for about a mile out of the village it showed signs of fairly regular use. After that, it was simply a pair of parallel dirt ruts in a sea of knee-high grass. The land this near the river was mostly flat, but there were some gentle rises and dips, and occasional stands of trees dotted the landscape. On either side of the road, the grass often reached waist high, leading me to believe that enough traffic came this way to keep the grass on the road shorter. Scattered patches of wildflowers–Black-eyed Susans, purple coneflowers, cardinal flowers, and others I did not know–formed islands of color in the sea of green.

The sun was almost directly overhead when the ground sloped gently down to where the road crossed a shallow creek. The soft sounds of the water on the stones made me aware that I was thirsty and with that awareness came the realization that not only was I thirsty, I was also filthy and tired and in no real hurry to get anywhere in particular. When Budge and I climbed out of the creek's little hollow, I spied a small wood in the distance. I thought it might provide a decent place to camp.

When we reached the trees, I found that the wood was bigger than I had first thought, and the road ran through the middle of it. To my left, the trees were all pines, and the wood looked as if it reached all the way down to the river, which was well over a hundred feet away. To the right, the pines mixed with deciduous trees, and extended as far as I could see. Since I really wanted to wash up, I decided to get off the road and head for the river. While I'd been considering our options, Budge had found some sweet grass to chew on and wasn't happy when I tugged on the lead. I got a little more forceful with my tug and he followed, looking for all the world as if he were disappointed in me.

As we neared the riverbank, I saw a small trail that led into the thick underbrush. A short distance in, the trees and underbrush opened onto a broad grassy sward that was surrounded on three sides by the pine wood. On the fourth side, the ground sloped gently down to the river. It was the perfect place to camp. A quick search revealed no signs of recent occupation, so I unloaded Budge, hobbled him, and left him to munch on the sweet grass or whatever else struck his fancy. Then I spread out my things to take stock.

Steafán had given me a pretty accurate accounting of what I had. Several of the bags held foodstuffs. Even if I couldn't find other food, I had enough for a little over a week if I was careful. I had Ambrose's stock of medicines. There were no remedies for headaches–he'd obviously exhausted his supply in the days leading up to his final prophecy–but I had treatments for a wide variety of common ailments. If there were more willows ahead of me, I could make a replacement for the headache remedies. With what I had, I could possibly earn food and lodging as a self-taught healer. Another bag held my second set of clothes, poor stuff that was similar to what I was wearing. There was a surprise at the bottom of that bag, however: a small cake of soap.

Smiling, I took the cake of soap and headed for the river. It was obvious that someone worked to keep the riverbank clear at this spot; the brush and reeds that grew elsewhere nearby had been cut back here. I wasn't going to be able to stay in the clearing for long; I couldn't be sure when whoever it was that maintained this place would come back. After taking off my shoes, I waded into the water without undressing. The river here was slow moving and the water was cool, a welcome relief from the summer heat. I stripped off my tunic, washed it and tossed it onto the bank. My sash and trousers followed. Then I spent a good amount of time scrubbing myself. I hadn't felt clean since I'd first been locked into my cell.

I hung my wet clothes over some bushes to dry. When I was dry myself, I dressed. I started to tie on my minstrel's sash, then stopped. I couldn't wear it openly; Steafán was right that everyone was going to be looking for me. A person could live quite well for a long time on the reward of 10 silver shields that was being offered for me. Even wearing it under my tunic as I had been was a risk. I turned to the box holding my guitar.

It was constructed of a hodgepodge of boards that appeared to be leftovers from other projects. The top was held on by a pair of ropes tied around the box. It took me a few minutes to worry the knots loose and then I lifted the top. The box seemed to be filled with old worn-out clothing. I picked up one piece, a pair of trousers with both knees out and the crotch seam split wide open. Digging deeper, I found my guitar, still in its leather case. I had to hand it to Steafán: the deception would not fool a determined thief, but someone looking for a quick score would most likely pass the box by even if they opened it, and my guitar was reasonably well protected.

I glanced around, weighing the risk of playing. I hadn't seen anyone since I left Willow Bank, and I was hidden from view of the road if anyone chanced to come this way. I decided that as long as I didn't play loudly or sing, I could practice a bit. I gently took my guitar out of its bed of rags, set the top back on the box, and used it to sit on. I started by practicing scales and bass runs, but my mind began to wander, and I ended up simply playing soft chords as I thought.

At first, I simply weighed carefully where I should go. I desperately wanted to see Peg; I felt that if I could just get to her, everything would go back to the way it had been before I left Songhaven. I wanted to speak with Ryan, too, because I was sure that he'd know more about what was happening to me than anyone else. He'd know what I should do. The last time I saw him, he'd been heading for Songhaven. Peg was at Songhaven, too. But Songhaven was one of the first places anyone would think to look for me.

That thought led me to my immediate situation and why it was that people were looking for me. Ambrose had named me the Lawbreaker. The ring he gave me, the ring that he said was the Lawbreaker's, seemed to confirm that. In contact with me, the stone set in it glittered, but was dark and unreflective otherwise. The idea that I might be the Lawbreaker sent a chill along my bones that broke my concentration, and I stopped the gentle fingerpicking pattern I'd been mindlessly playing. I suddenly felt as if everything I had ever done had been a lie and that I didn't even know who I was anymore. The Lawbreaker's ring answered to my touch. Whether I willed it or not, I'd killed seven men. I held my guitar up and looked it over. It was beautiful, but somehow no longer felt like mine. I carefully placed it back its case and then into the box with my sash folded neatly beside it. I covered them both with the rags and tied the top back on.

I just sat with my back against the box watching the river. Occasionally I saw concentric rings spreading out from what I thought was a fish breaking the surface of the water, probably to snap up an insect. I saw dragonflies darting about over the water and some kind of bird–it looked like a swallow–skimming low over the surface. Thoughts were crowding my consciousness, but I pushed them away, trying not to think. I felt empty, but fear was seeping in at the edges of that emptiness. Nothing in my training, nothing in my life, had prepared me for this, for being on the run. I needed to be Arlow, at least for a while, but I wasn't sure who he was. I longed to be Lauren again, but I didn't know if that was even possible, or whether the Lauren that I believed that I had been had ever truly existed. My mind shied away from considering my other possible identity, but I slowly became aware that my fingers were twisted in the front of my tunic, holding the ring. I'd seen Ambrose do that but hadn't realized what it was that he was doing. I forced myself to l et go.

I felt as if I came back to myself then, almost as if I was waking from a nap. I looked around the clearing. Budge was drowsing to one side. The shadows told me that it was well past the usual evening mealtime and, as I realized that, my stomach rumbled. I stood and stretched and decided to look for something to supplement the food Steafán had provided. There was thick underbrush under the trees all around the clearing. I picked a direction at random and waded in. Five or six feet in, the growth thinned out, cut off from the sunlight by the trees. After a few moments, I found red mulberries and then some blueberries. Faced with how to carry a good number back to camp, I resolved to buy some kind of pot the first chance I got. I settled on removing my tunic, laying the berries on it, and then bundling it up as an impromptu bag. I got a bit scratched up pushing back through the underbrush, but I had fresh berries to go with my hard travel bread and dried beef.

As the light began to fade, I removed Budge's hobble and tied him to a tree. Then I spread out my blanket. Crickets and frogs were singing all around. I laid on my back and watched the sky fade from blue, to indigo, to black, more and more stars becoming visible as it got darker. They seemed somehow more cold and remote than they ever had before. I thought I saw two of the Seven Sisters but faded into sleep before the others rose above the trees across the river.

I started awake the next morning to some sudden sound. I sat up quickly and scanned the clearing, but–other than Budge–I was alone. The morning was beautiful, a bit cool for high summer, but very comfortable. Thin wisps of mist hung over the river and somewhere beyond the woods an early rising field sparrow sang his plaintive song, the soft notes speeding up into a trill at the end. Then Budge brayed, breaking the spell. That must have been what woke me. I climbed to my feet, walked over to the donkey, and put my hand on his shoulder.

"What's the matter, boy?"

I don't know whether he truly understood, but he looked at the river.

"Ah. Well then, let's get you a drink."

I untied him and led him down to the water. He spent several minutes drinking, then I hobbled him and left him to his own devices to find a morning meal. I packed away my blanket and checked on the clothes that I had washed the day before. They were now dry, so I packed them up as well. I broke my fast with more of the travel bread and some dried fruit and then loaded Budge and headed back to the road.

The morning passed pleasantly enough. The wood wasn't particularly large, and we passed through quickly. Soon we were back in the sunlit rolling meadows. In several places the road crossed shallow streams on rickety wooden bridges. At each one I led Budge down to the water and let him drink. It was nearing midday when I spotted what looked like a village in the distance.

As we got closer, however, I could see that it wasn't any kind of village I'd ever seen. On the south side of the road between the road and the river were a pair of long, two story buildings. The long side of each building was parallel to the road, with a door in the center of the wall at ground level and many windows at both levels. The facing walls each had a chimney. On the north side of the road were two huge buildings that were obviously barns or stables and behind those were large, fenced in pastures full of horses. The buildings were all painted white and were clearly well maintained. A group of men stood in the large open door of one of the stables. As Budge and I drew nearer, one of the men left the group and met us at the edge of the compound.

"Good day, wayward traveler," he said, his tone guarded. He was several inches shorter than me and a good deal older. He was thin and wiry, his skin browned from long rounds in the sun. His close-cropped hair was blonde, as was the stubble on his face, but so sun lightened as to be almost white.

"Good day," I responded. "What is this place?"

His eyes narrowed slightly at that, but he answered civilly enough.

"This is Keffnael Ranch. We breed horses for the High King." He watched me intently for a moment, then added, "We don't get many people coming through here."

"My name is Arlow," I said in response. "I have some training as a healer and I'm looking for places to ply my trade. I was heading south out of Badon and saw a side road off the King's Road and thought I'd explore. I spent a few days in Willow Bank but felt that it was time to move on."

"Arlow, I'm Jess. We got our own Healer stationed here. No real need for another." He paused. "Word come from Badon a bit ago," he started, and my blood ran cold. "The

Kelmar attacked Han. The army needs us to get forty horses to Badon as soon as possible. That means we're busy. You can stay the night, but no one has time to entertain you."

"Fair enough," I said, relaxing when it became clear that they hadn't heard about me yet. "I don't need to be entertained and I'm willing to work for my keep, even if that means mucking out the stables."

He grinned.

"Well then, young man, I think we can find a pitchfork for you," he said, and turned toward the open stables. He led me into the shadowed interior and pointed out an empty stall. "You can put your donkey there. In a bit I'll send someone to show you where you can put your things and bed down for the night. For now, here you go."

He handed me a pitchfork.

"Start wherever you like."

After Jess left me, I unloaded Budge, checked his hooves, and wiped him down. Then I grabbed my pitchfork and went to work. I'd finished two stalls when a boy came to show me where I could put my things. He carried my bags while I carried the box with my guitar in it.

"What's in that box?" he asked as we headed toward one of the bunkhouses.

"Rags," I answered. "Old worn out clothes. I have a woman in Amersford who makes quilts. She pays me to bring her scraps from all over the Federation."

"You been to lots of places?"

"A fair number. Amersford. Badon. Durning."

"Durning? Where's that?"

"Out east in the foothills of the Bretons. It's a fairly small town."

"I never been anywhere but here," he said. "I was born here. My mom's one of the cooks. I wish I could see some of those places."

I smiled at him. "I'm sure that you will someday."

"Here you go," he said, pointing to a simple bed near one end of the bunkhouse. "You can put your stuff here now and sleep here tonight."

I set the box down between the bed and the end wall of the building and laid my bags on top of it.

"My thanks to you," I said to the boy. "I should get back to the stables now."

"Maybe I'll see you at evening meal," he said.

Once outside, he scampered off toward the pastures and I returned to the stable. I worked the rest of the afternoon, only stopping when Jess came to call me to the evening meal. He looked at all I'd accomplished and nodded, an approving look on his weathered face.

"You've certainly earned your keep," he said. "Come, let's clean up and go eat."

There was a screw pump between the two bunkhouses that drew water from the river to feed a large washbasin. I turned the screw for Jess, and he washed the worst of the day's grime off himself and then he did the same for me. He then led me to the second bunkhouse, the ground floor of which was the ranch's refectory. The end of the building closest to the other bunkhouse was a massive open kitchen where pots hung boiling over open fires and meat—it smelled like beef—was sizzling on huge grills. The meal turned out to be thick steaks with boiled potatoes and broccoli. It was the best meal that I'd had in some time; everything was grown there on the ranch and so was amazingly fresh.

Jess invited me to sit with him and we chatted between mouthfuls. The conversation was strained, though, and after a time, I noticed that I was attracting notice from others in the room, suspicion and distrust written plain on their faces. By the end of the meal, it was growing dark, and the ranchers were beginning to settle into bed for the night. I returned to my assigned bed and found that someone had been into my things. I couldn't tell whether they'd found my guitar, but my bags and pouches had been moved around. I had no doubt that they'd been searched.

I wanted nothing more than to leave but packing up and leaving then would simply have confirmed whatever suspicions these people had about me. The ranch belonged to the High King and the ranchers worked for the Crown. Was it possible that word of the search for me had somehow already reached here? Were the ranchers just typically suspicious of anyone wandering this far off the main roads or were they hoping to capture me and earn the reward?

I didn't sleep well at all. Every small sound snapped me awake, listening intently for the approach of a captor. When the first hint of dawn light appeared, I rose and gathered my things. It was awkward carrying the box with my assorted bags and pouches piled on top of it, but I managed to get out of the bunkhouse and into the stables without rousing anyone else. As quickly as I could, I loaded Budge and led him out. Jess was crossing the road from the bunkhouse to the stables as I did. A trace of a frown flitted across his grizzled face.

"Heading out?" he asked.

"I am."

"Probably for the best."

"Can you give me any idea what's ahead?"

"Not much for a long way. Road gets a lot worse. About a day's walk out there's a small group of people that live all by themselves. Never come this way. Don't bother us and we don't bother them. Beyond that, I'm not sure until you reach Cammford. Heading anyplace in particular?"

"Amersford, eventually," I lied. I didn't realize that it was a lie until I said it, but as the words left my mouth, I realized that during the night I'd reached a decision about where to go and it wasn't Amersford. Jess might not believe me–his look was skeptical–but if they sent someone after me, my lie–plus what I'd told the boy the day before–just might send any pursuit in the wrong direction.

"Well, then," he said and turned away without another word.

Jess had been truthful with me; the road deteriorated rapidly past Keffnael. Within a short time, it was nothing more than a couple of barely visible rutted lines of dirt in the sea of mostly waist-high grass. The day was beautiful, warm but not too hot, the cloudless sky like a cerulean bowl placed upside down over the landscape. A little past midday, I led Budge off the trail–I couldn't think of it as a road anymore–and doubled back the way we'd come. An hour later we were setting up camp in the shelter of a stand of trees I'd noticed earlier, close enough to see the trail, but far enough back and overgrown enough to hide us from anyone who might be following. I unloaded Budge and tied him to a tree near some delicious looking greenery, grabbed a bit of dried beef and fruit from my food supply and settled in to watch for signs of pursuit.

To my relief, night fell with no indication that anyone was following us. I fell asleep quickly and woke the next morning feeling refreshed and somewhat more at ease. After a quick meal, I loaded Budge and led him back to the trail. I could see no signs that anyone had been through during the night, so we set out away from Keffnael. A short time later we came to a shallow stream crossing our path. It was barely deep enough for Budge to drink from, but he managed. While he was drinking, I stepped upstream a little and took a long drink myself.

On the west side of the King's Road, the Camm River–and the road that paralleled it–ran roughly southwest. From Willow Bank to Keffnael, the direction was more west than south, but just past the ranch the river and the road–the trail–bent to run more south than west. More and more the grasslands were broken up by stands of trees and small woods. We crossed several small streams that morning, stopping to drink at each one. As the sun rose higher, the temperature rose and by midmorning, sweat was stinging my eyes and gluing my tunic to my body. We were walking through a fairly large wood. Up in the trees, cicadas sang all around us, an eerie, pulsating sound that seemed far too loud for simple insects to make. That's when I heard the music.

At first, it seemed to be part of the cicada song, but as we neared the edge of the wood, I could discern that someone was playing some sort of flute. It was a haunting, plaintive melody that nearly brought me to tears but was also the most beautiful song I'd ever heard. Excited, I rushed forward, dragging poor Budge behind me. As I cleared the trees, I could see the player. He looked to be about my age and build. His long brown hair was pulled back in a ponytail, and he had a neatly trimmed beard and mustache. He wore a tunic and trousers of drab, undyed wool and–in spite of the heat–a sleeveless vest of wool dyed dark brown. He was playing a small wooden flute as he watched over a small herd of perhaps fifteen or so sheep. At that moment Budge, his patience exhausted by my insistent tugging on the lead, brayed his frustration. The music ceased and the player turned toward us, obviously surprised. He stepped forward to stand protectively between me and the sheep.

"That was the most beautiful thing I ever heard," I said.

The shepherd looked even more surprised.

"And you would be?" he asked, his voice deep and resonant.

I realized then that I was acting like an overexcited unmannerly child.

"My apologies," I said. "My name is Arlow. I was walking along the trail and heard your music. I didn't mean to startle you."

"Arlow, I am Tadgh," he replied and then added, "We don't get many visitors out this way."

"I've been wandering," I answered. "I have some training as a healer, though I never took the Green. I've been looking for new places to ply my trade. Is there a village nearby?"

"Not so much a village," Tadgh said guardedly. "Just a few families living together in a small community. We value our privacy."

"I won't stay long then," I said. "Or I can just pass on through. May I ask you about your music, though? What is that song? Did you write it?"

Before answering, he looked over his little flock. They were contentedly munching the grass in the clearing. Then he turned his attention back to me.

"Nay, I did not write it. I learned it from my father and he from his as far back as anyone can remember. It's called the *Arimë Daelyr.*"

"I've never heard anything like it."

One of the sheep chose that moment to wander away from the others. Tadgh went after it, shouting as he went. As he returned, he said, "My apologies. Our herd is small, and I can't afford to lose even a single one."

"I understand. That song, though, what did you call it?"

"The *Arimë Daelyr.*"

"The *Arimë Daelyr.* Can you tell me anything more about it? What does *Arimë Daelyr* mean?"

"I really can't tell you much," Tadgh answered. "I once travelled all the way to Amersford, and I asked several minstrels there whether they knew of the song or what the title means. None of them had ever heard it. They also said the title isn't Altieran or Kelmar. Because I played it on a flute, though, they didn't seem interested. At least, not as interested as you."

"I'd like to learn it," I said. "Would you be willing to teach me?"

He just looked at me for a moment, trying to gauge my sincerity.

"I'll consider it," he said finally. "Noweth is where I live, and it is just a bit further down the road. If the others agree that you can stay, perhaps I'll teach you."

"My thanks to you," I said. "Will I see you there this evening?"

"I'll be back for the evening meal."

"See you then."

With that, I tugged Budge into motion, and we passed by Tadgh and his sheep and reentered the woods on the far side of the clearing. A short time later we reached the hamlet of Noweth.

It wasn't much, really. Noweth was located in a large clearing surrounded by pine trees and a faint smell of pine permeated the place. There were six small houses on the west side of the trail. They were arranged to form a broad half circle with the opening facing the trail. As in Willow Bank, each house had a small garden plot next to it. Behind the three houses to the north were a barn and pens for livestock, one empty, one containing pigs, and the other a few black and white spotted cows. A man was in the pen with the cows, inspecting each one. Noises coming from inside the barn suggested that some of the other residents were in there. A creek flowed behind the two southernmost houses. Beyond the creek, something was nestled up under the edge of the trees, but I couldn't make out what it was from where I stood.

In the space in front of the houses a series of some two dozen logs had been set on end in a rough circle. They were obviously to be used to sit on, probably for group gatherings. On the east side of the trail, the ground was mostly cleared of trees and sloped gently down to the river. There was a single small boat pulled up on the bank there. I didn't know whether that was the only boat these people owned or if there were others out on the water fishing. I hoped that it was the only boat; I'd had my fill of fish in Willow Bank.

"Ho, visitor," a man's voice called. I turned and saw that the man who had been inspecting the cows was fastening the gate to the pen behind himself. He turned and waved to me. At the same time, people appeared in the doorway of some of the homes and in the wide door of the barn.

"Good day," I called back. In just a few short moments I was surrounded by a dozen or so people. "Good day," I repeated. "My name is Arlow. I've been exploring, looking for places to ply my trade, and my wandering has brought me here."

"And what is that trade?" asked the cow inspector, a slim man of about my height who appeared to have completed thirty or so rounds of the seasons.

"I have some training as a healer, though I never took the Green."

The residents looked at one another, considering what I had said. I looked them over. In the little group there were nine adults of various ages, five men and four women. There were also five children, four of them girls. One woman stood out; the fair skin on her face was marred with the red blotches of rosacea. She was watching me eagerly but was obviously nervous about speaking up.

"I don't know," the cow inspector said, shaking his head slightly. He seemed to be something of an informal leader.

"I'd be interested in talking with him, Nevyn," the woman with rosacea said. "I'm sure there are others who might want that, too."

Several others nodded but didn't say anything. They all looked expectantly at Nevyn.

"Very well," he said and turned to me. "You may stable your donkey in the barn. While you're meeting with whomever wishes to speak with you, we'll decide where you can sleep for the night."

With that, he turned and went to the northernmost house, grabbed a hoe that was leaning against the wall, and went to work in the garden. I led Budge into the barn and found an empty stall. I unloaded my things and piled them neatly against a wall outside the stall. After caring for Budge, I grabbed my bag of medicines and returned to the center of the little hamlet.

The woman with rosacea was waiting for me. Like Nevyn, she appeared to be in her thirties. Her ash blond hair was long and bound back in a ponytail that reached halfway down her back. She smiled shyly as I approached.

"I'm Shailey," she said. "I think you can see why I wish to see you."

"Shailey, I'm Arlow. I'm assuming that you're concerned about the redness and bumps on your face."

"Yes, I am. It just started a month ago and it doesn't seem to get better."

"Do you know what it is?"

"No. But, Arlow, I'm afraid that Nevyn–he's my husband–I'm afraid that he won't want to be with me anymore. I'm hideous."

I shook my head.

"Shailey, you're not hideous. And I don't really know Nevyn, but in the brief encounter that I just had, he doesn't strike me as the kind of man who would set you aside over this."

"What is it?" she asked, running her fingers lightly over her face. "Do you know?"

"It's a fairly common skin condition. It's called rosacea. It often occurs for the first time in women about your age."

"Can you make it go away?"

I tried to convey as much sympathy as I could as I answered.

"Not permanently, no. But there are some things you can do to control the outward signs of the condition somewhat. Have you any honey?"

She nodded the affirmative.

"Then do this. Twice a day–morning and evening would work–wash your face gently. Pat it dry–don't rub. Then apply pure honey over the affected areas. Leave it on for half an hour, then gently wash your face again. That should help control the outward signs."

She looked cautiously hopeful, but asked, "But it will come back?"

"Probably. There are some things that you can do to reduce the chances of that, though. Exposure to bright sunlight can bring it on. For some people, eating certain foods can. Make sure to wear a hat that shades your face when you must work outdoors and keep track of what you eat. If the condition flares up consistently after eating a certain food, try to avoid that food."

She nodded and then smiled shyly.

"My thanks to you. I will do as you suggest."

As she went to join Nevyn in their garden, I sat on one of the log seats and waited for another patient. I didn't have long to wait. I spent the afternoon tending to small hurts and illnesses and by the evening meal had seen nearly everyone in the place. My last patient of the day–a man named Login–had a knife cut on the palm of his hand that wasn't healing and looked like it might go bad. I cleaned it and applied a salve made with burdock and then wrapped a clean bandage around his hand.

"My thanks to you, Arlow," he said as he stood. "I need to go help my husband finish our contribution to tonight's meal." He smiled. "You should have just enough time to clean up and then everyone will be bringing food out here. We don't often get guests, so this will be a big celebration for us."

As he left, I stood and stretched. Movement toward the north end of the settlement caught my eye; Tadgh was coming in with the little herd of sheep. I watched as he headed for the empty pen and then I turned and walked down to the river to wash. By the time I returned, the sheep were safely in their pen and Tadgh was speaking with Nevyn and Shailey. As they spoke, a woman called Karstyn joined them. They huddled together, obviously speaking quite earnestly. Occasionally one of them would glance my way, and I realized that they were deciding whether I could stay. I sat on one of the logs and, as I tried to tamp down the sudden concern that I felt, I realized that I really wanted to stay here for at least a few days.

The group split up and Tadgh came to join me while the others disappeared into Nevyn and Shailey's house.

"I hear that you had a busy afternoon," he said as he settled onto one of the logs.

I nodded as I said, "I did. I grew up in a place like this. Not quite as small, but every bit as isolated. It reminds me of home."

Tadgh just studied me for a moment, then said, "Karstyn says that you are quite knowledgeable when it comes to healing."

I looked at him, a puzzled frown on my face.

"She doesn't wear the sash here, but she's a Healer," he explained. "We couldn't get by out here without a Healer."

I smiled.

"You were testing me."

He nodded.

"As I told you, people rarely come out this far and we value our privacy. We wanted to see if you were what you said you were."

"I could still be the kind of person that you don't want here," I noted.

"True enough. But you didn't just treat the people who came to see you. You talked to them, got to know them, and you treated them with compassion. That's telling."

People began to join us then, each family carrying some food dish. Nevyn and Shailey and their daughter Imogen brought several types of cooked vegetables. Login and Sloan brought a dish consisting of noodles, chunks of beef, vegetables, and cheese all mixed together and topped with toasted chunks of bread; I'd never seen anything like it before. Others brought baked potatoes or fruit or–I had to groan–fish.

The food was all excellent and the people of Noweth were open and friendly now that they had accepted me. As we ate, I noticed that a couple of the children slipped away quietly, each with some small bit of food. They crossed the little creek to the place I had noticed earlier and then returned without the food, all done as unobtrusively as possible. I tried to hide the fact that I'd noticed; it was clear that what they were doing wasn't meant to be shared with me.

Long after everyone had eaten their fill we sat and talked. I was surprised to find that all the adults were well-educated and well-read and that they were taking pains to ensure that their children were as well. All of them had settled there after growing up in other places; it was unclear to me how they had come to know about Noweth. I had certainly never heard of it before I found my way there. It was growing dark by the time people began to gather their things and return to their homes. Tadgh stood and turned to me.

"Arlow, I have to no spare bed for you, but if you don't mind sleeping on the floor, you're welcome to sleep in my home tonight."

"My thanks to you for your hospitality, Tadgh. Let me fetch my things from the barn."

Tadgh went with me and helped me carry my things to his house. He asked what I had in the box, and I simply said that it contained old rags. For some reason, I was loathe to lie to him. As we approached his house–the southernmost one in the hamlet, I tried to get a better look at the place the children had gone earlier. All I could make out was that it appeared to be a collection of fairly large stones.

"Before we settle in," I said, "I'd like to go see what that is across the creek."

Tadgh shot me a sharp look.

"I don't think that would be a good idea," he replied, and his tone told me to drop it.

Tadgh's house was all one room, rough built, but homey. A fireplace dominated one end wall, but in the late summer heat there was no fire lit. The furnishings were few, just a bed, some shelves that were serving as a pantry, a small round table with a couple of chairs, and a bookshelf that was mostly full.

"Just spread out wherever you think you'll be most comfortable," Tadgh said.

I laid my blanket along the wall near the door.

"Sleep well," I said.

"You, too," Tadgh replied. "If you're willing to help tend the sheep tomorrow, I'll begin to teach you to play the flute."

"I'd be happy to help."

I was standing alone in the center of the circle of log seats. Thin scraps of mist drifted amongst the trees, but overhead I could see the stars blazing in all their remote glory. Almost I thought I could hear the faint chiming of their melody. Then I became aware of a light at ground level, a soft glow coming from the place where I had seen the children take the food. Though I was aware that Tadgh told me not to go there, I went, moving forward without actually walking, almost as if the will that moved me was not my own. As I approached, I saw a figure there, a woman clothed only in her long golden hair. She smiled as I drew near and I recognized her: *Aenn*, the earth mother.

"*Vorath, Endollin,*" she said, her voice faint, as if from far away, and I knew that I had heard that phrase before. I tried to speak, but no sound came out of my mouth. I tried again, desperate to say something to her...

Straining to speak woke me to the first faint fading of the night in Tadgh's house. I knew now what the place across the creek was. It was a shrine to *Aenn*. And I now knew why these people were so leery of outsiders: they followed the old ways and gave reverence to the Old Ones.

I laid there until I heard Tadgh stir. I sat up to see him rubbing the sleep from his eyes.

Tadgh had a small metal washbasin on a stand outside the door to his house. We took turns washing our faces and hands and then Tadgh shouldered a small pack, and we joined several others in the center of the hamlet. The smell of fresh baked bread hung in the air. My stomach rumbled.

"Karstyn bakes bread most mornings," Tadgh told me. "There's also usually sausage or bacon to make sandwiches. I'll pack some for us to eat and then we'll get the sheep out to graze."

I knew that I was taking a risk, but I did it anyway. I broke off a small piece of bread and headed toward the shrine with it.

"Arlow, what are you doing?" Tadgh asked in alarm and warning.

"It is customary to share a bit of food with her, is it not?" I asked. "To thank her for sharing the earth's bounty."

Tadgh and everyone else just stared at me, some with looks of surprise, others with sudden misgiving.

"That is a shrine to *Aenn*, isn't it? I know that she is one of the greatest of the Old Ones. All the earth and all the things that live on it are hers."

They all now had shocked looks on their faces.

"How could you know about the shrine?" Tadgh asked, some strange mix of emotions coloring his voice. "I'd swear that you didn't leave the house. I sleep lightly; I would know if you had gotten up."

"*Aenn* showed me," I answered. "She came to me in a dream last night."

No one answered that. They simply stared at me, shock and surprise turned to awe. I turned to go to the shrine and Tadgh fell into step beside me, carrying a piece of bread of his own. The creek was perhaps a foot deep as it passed the hamlet, so the villagers had created a rough bridge from downed trees, two were laid parallel to one another across the water with logs sawn in half laid across them to form a walkway. As we neared the tree line, I got my first good look at the shrine. Small stones–they reminded me of the standing stones of the Lost settlements–formed a half circle facing the stream. At the apogee of the semicircle stood a much larger stone–a waist-high boulder really–the face of which had been sheared off flat. A niche had been carved into the face of the stone, giving the impression of an arch, and in that niche stood a statue of *Aenn*. The sculptor had captured her exactly, the long, flowing hair accenting rather than hiding the curves of her body, the gentle smile on her lips. Twice I had seen her; the likeness was so accurate that this now felt like a third. I knelt and gently placed my piece of bread at her feet.

"My thanks for your bounty," I whispered.

Tadgh followed suit. We knelt in silence for a moment and then–without looking my way–he asked, "Who are you, Arlow?"

"Just a man," I replied quietly. "Trying to make my own way in the world." After a slight pause, I asked, "May I ask you something?"

"Of course."

"Have you ever heard the word *endollin* before?"

"No. Why?"

"*Aenn* said that in my dream. I don't know what it means."

Tadgh was looking at me with surprise written in his features again.

"What?" I asked.

"She spoke to you?"

I nodded.

"I've never heard of such a thing," Tadgh told me. "I've heard of *Aenn* or one of the other Old Ones appearing to the rare few in their dreams, but I have never heard of anyone that they ever spoke to."

We knelt there in quiet contemplation for a few moments, then Tadgh stood and brushed the dirt from his knees.

"We should go," he said as I stood. "We need to get the sheep out to graze."

I followed him back to the others. We took some bread and bacon and stored them in the pack he carried. Then he asked me to wait a moment while he went into his house to fetch something. He returned quickly and we went to the sheep pen and together herded the little flock out and to the west of the hamlet. We passed through a small apple orchard, through a relatively untouched part of the pine woods, and into a broad grassy meadow. After a few moments making sure that the sheep were munching away contentedly, we pulled out our food and ate in companionable silence. When we finished, Tadgh reached into the pack again and pulled out two wooden flutes.

"My father carved these," he told me, holding one of them out to me. "This one he made for me."

I took the flute and examined it. The workmanship was amazing. The flute was made of cedar, lovingly sanded and polished so that the red brown wood almost seemed to glow. Near the mouthpiece, Tadgh's father had inlaid an ornate letter "T" using some lighter wood. I handed the flute back to Tadgh.

"It's beautiful," I said. "And from what I heard yesterday, it sounds even more beautiful than it looks. Your father was an excellent craftsman."

"My thanks to you for saying that," he replied. He then handed me the second flute. "He made this one for my brother Lorcan. I'd like you to have it."

The flute was the twin of Tadgh's, except that it had an ornate "L" inlaid near the mouthpiece. It struck me as an odd coincidence that the letter carved into it matched my own true name. I looked at Tadgh, feeling tears welling in my eyes.

"Tadgh, this is a kingly gift, but I can't accept it. Will your brother not miss it?"

Tadgh didn't answer for a moment but stood with his head bowed. Then he looked up at me, tears in his own eyes.

"Lorcan died many rounds of the seasons ago. He had no wife nor any children. As his only living relative, his flute came to me. Mine will go to my child when the time comes. Given what's happened here since yesterday, something tells me that you should have this one."

"My thanks to you, Tadgh, and to Lorcan, for sharing this gift with me. I promise you that I will always treat it with the care and respect that it deserves."

We stood watching the sheep for some time, neither of us speaking, allowing the deep emotions we'd been feeling to settle somewhat. Then Tadgh said, "Part of that respect is playing it properly. Let's begin. Hold it like this..."

The flute proved to be a deceptively simple instrument. Within moments I was able to play a simple melody, but by the time we returned to the hamlet for the evening meal, I had not learned enough about breathing and fingering techniques to even attempt the *Arimë Daelyr*. The next day, I was much more comfortable with my flute and as the sun reached the zenith, Tadgh said, "Let us try the *Arimë Daelyr*."

I first watched him play the song, without trying to play myself, but trying to mimic his fingerings. The second time through, I tried to play along, but I fumbled the fingerings several times. All afternoon we worked on the song, but I couldn't seem to quite get it right. After one particularly screechy attempt where I couldn't seem to get my fingers in precisely the right place, Tadgh said, "Let's give it a rest, eh? One of the sheep is drifting away, let me go get her and then we can try again."

As he turned and walked away, I let my hands drop to my sides and closed my eyes, trying to let my frustration drain away. I took a deep breath, held it, and then slowly let it out. Then another, and another. I could feel the afternoon sun warming my forehead and the bridge of my nose and the tops of my shoulders. I heard a gentle breeze shushing through the pine trees edging the meadow we were in, felt it cooling my cheeks and my arms. I could hear the sheep quietly munching. Something in me seemed to shift and I lifted the flute to my lips and played.

The *Arimë Daelyr* seemed to flow out of someplace deep inside me, as if I had always known it. As I played, I felt a deep sense of loss, of a sorrow that went down to the roots of my being, of a pain that was always there just below my awareness. And all of those feelings flowed out through my flute and then the song was done. I opened my eyes, feeling somehow drained but at peace.

Tadgh was standing directly in front of me, his mouth open in an "O" of surprise and his eyes overflowing with tears. Behind him, the entire herd of sheep was facing me, staring at me, not one of them moving, not even so much as to chew their cud. I suddenly felt extremely self-conscious.

"Tadgh?" I asked hesitantly.

"Arlow, who are you? What are you? I have known the *Arimë Daelyr* all my life, I've played it since I had ten rounds, but I have never heard it–never felt it–like that before. My heart still weeps with the beauty and the sorrow. There was more than music there."

"Tadgh, as I said this morning, I'm just a man."

"A man the Old Ones speak to. A man who–after a little more than a day–laid bare the heart of the *Arimë Daelyr* with no previous musical training."

I shook my head slightly.

"I never said that I had no musical training."

Tadgh started to speak, but I cut him off.

"Tadgh, except for my name, everything I've told you about myself is true, but I haven't told you everything. I can't. It wouldn't be safe for you to know it all."

He started to say something but stopped. He turned to check on the sheep, who had gone back to grazing.

"I won't push," he said hesitantly. "I trust you. But if I'm honest, I'm not sure why I trust you."

We spent the rest of the afternoon tending the sheep, speaking no more than was necessary to accomplish that task. As we had the day before, we returned to Noweth just in time for the evening meal and, again, I spent the night in Tadgh's house.

I was outside on one of the tiers in Songhaven, in a part of the city that I had somehow never seen. I had come to do... something. I couldn't remember what it was. I suddenly realized that I was supposed to be in a lesson with Ambrose and alarm ran cold through me, chilling my fingers and toes. I turned to go back the way I had come, but retracing my steps brought me to a dead end. I turned to go in the direction I had originally been going, but that brought me to a dead end as well. Then, within a brief heartbeat, the light faded from the sky. Black clouds rolled up and over the city from the east. Some power, huge and angry, was searching for me. Exposed, standing there in the open, I knew that it would find me in seconds, but I could not move. Then I sensed something more. Behind the desperation, behind the anger, there was fear...

I awoke in the darkness in Tadgh's house. A cricket was chirping somewhere nearby. I couldn't tell whether it was in the house or just outside. A whippoorwill called and the final note seemed to echo slightly. Down by the river, frogs croaked. I was completely awake and alert, and I knew that I wasn't going to be able to get back to sleep. As quietly as I could, I rose and stepped outside.

It was clearly the small hours of the morning. There was no hint of dawn in the sky and from the sounds I could hear, the nocturnal creatures were still up and about the business of living. One of the cows quietly lowed and a sheep bleated an answer. I wandered to the center of the hamlet and sat on one of the seats there. I was comfortable in Noweth, and I very much liked the people. But my dream was telling me that whatever it was that was searching for me was still out there, was still looking. The King's men were no doubt still looking for me as well. It would not go well for the people of Noweth if I were found there and I didn't want to risk bringing trouble to them.

The big question was where to go. Any of the Federated cities were out; in ordinary circumstances it would be easy to lose myself in the crowds in a place such as Amersford but too many people would be looking for me, tempted by the reward that was being offered for my capture. I desperately wanted to go home to Songhaven but that wasn't an option either. I'd already realized that people would be looking for me there. However, the thought I'd had in Keffnael still seemed reasonable: I could continue down the north bank and cross the Camm at Cammford. Then I could head west into the Breton Mountains and camp near the trail leading to Songhaven. I could keep watch on who was coming and going and, if one of my friends passed by, I could make contact. If I was lucky, Ryan might come by. Or, possibly, Peg...

With a start, I realized that everything had gone silent. Birds, insects, animals—nothing made a sound. Something was moving in the world, something huge and malevolent, and I felt a chill that brought to mind the standing stone in *Aennsrhyd*. Overhead, the stars seemed dimmed, as if I was looking at them through a thin layer of smoke. I felt odd, as if something deep inside of me had gone still.

And then it passed. The stars were clear again, and the night creatures resumed their calling. I wasn't sure why, but I felt like a rabbit who had just watched a hunting fox pass by. For the rest of the night, I sat and tried to understand what had happened.

After a time, I could tell that dawn was approaching. It was not so much that the sky lightened as it was that the quality of the dark changed. One by one the nighttime birds and insects fell silent, but the morning birds had not yet begun to stir. I sensed movement to my left and turned to find Nevyn easing himself onto the seat next to mine.

"Trouble sleeping?" he asked quietly.

"Yes," I answered.

"Care to talk?"

I thought for a moment before answering. I wasn't sure how much to say.

"I have to leave," I said. "Today. This morning."

"Not on our account," Nevyn replied. "We've talked it over. You'd be welcome to stay. You could stay with Tadgh until we could build you a house of your own."

"That's generous, Nevyn, and you have my thanks. But I have to go. Something is searching for me."

The sky was light enough now to show me the puzzled look on his face."

"Some... thing?" he asked. "Not someone?"

"Yes. I don't know what it is, but I've sensed it several times. I thought at one point that I knew what it was, but I turned out to be wrong. All I know for sure is that I don't want to be here when it finds me. I will not put you all in harm's way."

"My thanks for your concern, Arlow, but what will you do if it finds you all alone?"

I shook my head.

"I can't say. It's hard to even consider possibilities when I don't know what it is that pursues me."

Noweth was waking. The sheep began to bleat, and several cows lowed. The smell of baking bread drifted out of Karstyn's house. Nevyn went to tend the cows and others tended their gardens or prepared food for the morning meal. Tadgh stepped out of his house, his pack over his shoulder. He waved when he saw me, then stopped to wash his face in the basin outside his door. I walked over as he was finishing.

"Arlow," he said. "Good morning. You mentioned yesterday that you needed to seek out some plants to replenish your supplies. I thought we could let the sheep graze in their pen today and..."

Something in my face stopped him.

"What is it?"

"Tadgh, I must leave. Something is seeking me. I think, perhaps, it got close last night. You–all of you–have been kind to me. I will not stay here and expose you to whatever happens when it finds me."

"We could help you."

"I don't know that you could. I don't know what it is that is hunting me. You all are not warriors, and I don't want you to be. I appreciate your hospitality, and I am more grateful than I can say that you taught me the *Arimë Daelyr*. I will not repay your kindness by getting you killed."

He helped me pack then. It didn't take long to have my things loaded on Budge. By the time we finished, everyone in the hamlet was gathered around me.

Tadgh embraced me.

"Safe travels, Arlow. May the Old Ones watch over you and keep you safe."

"And you as well, Tadgh."

I turned to the others.

"Be well," I said and as they called out their farewells, Budge and I headed south.

CHAPTER THREE

South of Noweth, my way followed what was now just a single narrow track through the woods and meadows. The sun was barely up and already the day was warm and humid, without even the hint of a cooling breeze. Though I set a leisurely pace, my clothes were soon soaked through with sweat. Overhead, the sky was clear, but through gaps in the trees I was sure I could see clouds on the western horizon.

Late in the morning the ground sank down toward the level of the river and the track led into a broad marshland. An egret was foraging at the edge of the water to my right, its white plumage in stark relief against the verdant green foliage behind it. Just off the path to my left a turtle slid beneath the surface as Budge and I approached. The murky water closed in on either side of the path and the cattails and other plants grew so tall in places that I couldn't see more than a few feet ahead. We came to a fork in the trail, and, after a moment's consideration, I chose to take the righthand path as it led away from the river, reasoning that higher, dryer ground lay that way. A quarter of an hour later, though, the path sank into the muddy water and disappeared, and we had to backtrack.

The lefthand fork took us closer to the river. In places, the path sank into the water, but I could see where it emerged on the other side. Budge balked at getting his feet wet the first time we had to wade into the water, but gradually became accustomed to the idea. We came across a red-winged blackbird clinging to the cattails, and he showed off his scarlet and gold epaulets, obviously trying to exert his dominance over us. When we continued to advance, he shifted to calling "chip" followed by a pause and then another "chip", alerting others of our aggressive manner. As we got even closer, he gave it up, took wing, and disappeared.

By early afternoon we'd found our way back onto firmer ground. I was coated in mud to my knees and the hair on Budge's belly was dripping muddy water. A breeze had sprung up as we navigated the marsh, driving the clouds I had seen earlier before it and they now covered the sky. It was obvious that a storm was coming, and I hoped that I'd find someplace where we could weather it indoors.

As we walked, it became clear to me that we were nearing some kind of settlement; the land on either side of the path had been cultivated. To my dismay, however, the crops were all blighted, the corn and wheat lying black and rotting on the ground. We passed an apple orchard and found the trees blighted as well, barren of leaves and limbs cracked and falling. Leaves turned black and brown covered the ground and rotting fruit was everywhere. The loss was grievous; it would take generations to regrow the trees. Then we came across a fenced pasture. I walked over to the fence, scarcely believing what I saw. Most of the cattle inside were dead, their bodies bloated and covered in oozing sores. The few that were not dead were clearly dying, lying on their sides, and struggling to breathe. I'd been hearing reports of such things for many rounds of the seasons but had never before encountered them myself. Budge was yanking hard on the lead; he clearly wanted to move on. I agreed; I didn't want to linger there either. A feeling was growing in me, the same feeling I'd had the night before when the stars dimmed, and the night fell silent. I felt sure that the two events were connected, but I couldn't believe such devastation could occur in a single n ight.

Not long after coming across the dead cattle, we reached the edge of a village about the same size as Willow Bank. The center of the village was full of people; nearly every person living there must have been present. People were shouting. I couldn't make out what was being said, but the tone was angry and fearful.

Just then a man stepped out of the nearest building, a small barn. He was holding a pitchfork aimed at me like a weapon, and he was scowling.

"Who in Mar's stinky arse are you?" he demanded.

I raised my arms in front of me, my hands open and palms out.

"Easy, friend," I said quietly. "My name is Arlow. I've been following the river down from Willow Bank, doing a bit of healing here and there."

"Healing won't do us any good," the man said. "Ain't no one sick." He paused and then added, "Yet."

I let my hands drop.

"What happened here?"

"Don't know," he replied. "Happened overnight. Yesterday, everything was fine. This morning, everything is gone. All the crops, the animals, everything. Even our stored food went bad."

He shifted his gaze from me to Budge.

"What's in the box? You got food?"

He took a step toward me, and I saw his grip on the pitchfork tighten.

"No, I don't have food. I was hoping to buy some here."

"We got nothing to sell, and we don't need another mouth we can't feed."

I turned toward the river.

"I'll be leaving, then," I said and tugged Budge along with me.

"Did you do this?" the man yelled at me. I turned back to him. "Did you bring Mar's wrath down on us? You one of them crazies from up the river? You bring their dark ways down here?"

"I'm just a traveler," I said as calmly as I could. "I didn't bring anything here but what's on my donkey. I'm sorry to see what's happened here, but I had nothing to do with bringing it about."

As I slowly backed away from the man with the pitchfork, I hoped what I'd said was true. I'd sensed the thing that hunted me. Had it sensed me and lashed out in my general direction? Was I responsible for this? I was supposed to be the Lawbreaker, the great evil, but I had never done anything like this. What was it that hunted me, that would treat innocent people so badly?

"But you killed seven men," a quiet voice said inside my head. Shame and guilt blossomed in my chest. I hadn't meant to kill those men, but I had. Could it be that I had done this?

The man from the village finally lowered the tines of his pitchfork to the ground and leaned on it like a staff. He was breathing heavily and still glaring in my direction. I turned and continued on toward the riverbank, nervously checking behind me every few steps to see if the man was following. Soon we were out of sight of most of the village. I kept us near the riverbank until we were well past the ill-starred village—I hadn't even learned its name—and then returned to the trail, which had widened again into a rough road.

The clouds overhead had gone dark and gray, and thunder rumbled in the distance. I could taste rain in the ever-stiffening breeze and so kept an eye open for some place to camp that would provide at least some semblance of shelter. As the first few heavy drops fell, I saw a dense stand of pine trees off to my right. I led Budge off the road and under the trees to a spot where their intertwined branches kept out the worst of what was developing into a downpour. I was already wet, and the ground was soaked, so it made no sense to string up my tarp.

It was a miserable night. Images of the blighted town and the seven soldiers pushed their way into my consciousness, insisted that I was the Lawbreaker, that I was evil. Even though the trees provided some shelter, eventually the rain worked its way through the branches, and I was soon soaked through. Fire was, of course, impossible. I ate some of my dwindling supply of dried food and tried to sleep sitting up against a tree. All I managed to do was to doze occasionally, and when I did drift off either my dreams of death and ruin or my soggy discomfort soon roused me again.

Sometime after midnight the rain finally stopped. Though it was no longer raining, water still dripped from the branches overhead so there was little difference from my perspective. As soon as light started creeping in amongst the trees, I rose and headed back to the road. I thought about breaking my fast, but I felt too tired to eat and just wanted to put more distance between me and the village behind me.

The clouds lightened and I judged that the sun had risen. Budge and I topped a small rise and at the bottom of the hill I saw a small two-wheeled cart heading in the same direction as us. I guessed that they must have come from the village. A small donkey was hitched to the cart, which was laden with what looked like everything a small family might own, but it wasn't moving. Four people–a man, a woman, a boy, and a girl–stood beside the cart. The adults looked to be just shy of thirty rounds in age. The boy had, I thought had maybe thirteen or fourteen rounds and the girl maybe eleven or twelve. The adults were talking with each other; the children looked frightened. As I drew near, I could make out the problem. One wheel was axle deep in a puddle of mud.

The man noticed me then. He stepped toward me, putting himself between me and the others.

"Well met, wayward traveler," he said cautiously.

"Well met," I said in reply. "I didn't look to find anyone on the road this morning."

"Nor did we," he answered. "We were hoping to be in Cammford by midmorning, but last night's rain pooled here, and I didn't realize how deep it was until it was too late."

"Cammford is that close?" I asked.

"Aye," he said and then looked closely at me. "You're not from around here, are you?"

"No. Are you?"

"Yes. From Cammlin."

"Cammlin?"

"The village behind us."

I nodded.

"I left Badon almost half a moon ago looking for new places to ply my trade," I said. "I saw a side road off the King's Road and took it. It brought me down through Willow Bank and Keffnael. I reached Cammlin yesterday, but a man with a pitchfork made it clear that I wasn't welcome, so I skirted the village and spent the night in the woods. My name is Arlow."

"Arlow, I'm Brody. We left Cammlin yesterday. The blight hit overnight, and it seemed to drive everyone mad. Rather than consider how to recover or how to get food, they argued over who to blame. Everyone was so afraid and angry. It seemed clear to me that sooner or later they were going to get violent, and I wanted to get my family out of there. We loaded up everything we could and set out for Cammford."

"Brody, I'm sorry that you had to leave your home. There's nothing I can do about that, but perhaps Budge and I can help you get going again. Give me a moment to unload my things and we'll see about hitching him to your cart."

"My thanks to you," Brody said. "I'll help unload if you don't mind." As we began unloading my things from Budge, he called to his son, "Shea, find some rope and work up another harness."

It didn't take long for the two of us to unload Budge and we soon had him hitched to the family's cart. Then, with Glynis–Brody's wife–guiding the donkeys and me, Brody, and the children pushing, we freed their cart from the mud. Glynis led the donkeys a safe distance from the mud and then stopped and unhitched Budge from the cart. I took his lead from her.

"Arlow," Brody said, "our thanks to you for your help. I don't think we could have done it on our own."

"I was glad to help."

"Are you heading to Cammford?" Glynis asked.

"I am," I replied.

"We need to take a few moments to break our fast," she said. "Would you like to join us? Then perhaps we could travel to Cammford together."

"My thanks to you, Glynis," I said. "I would be pleased to join you."

"We don't have much," she replied. "All of our food went bad, just like everyone else's. All we have is some berries the children gathered last night."

That touched me. These people had lost almost everything but were still willing to share the little they had with a stranger.

"I have some dried fruit and meats that I can share," I said in reply. "Let's pool what we have."

By the time we finished eating, we had no food left at all. I found myself fervently hoping that I could purchase more in Cammford. With the overloaded little cart to pull, Brody's donkey set the pace, slower than I would have liked, but an hour or so after we got under way, the road became a real road, paved with crushed stone, and the pace improved. As a result, we reached the outskirts of the town by late morning. I experienced a moment of anxiety when we caught sight of the first field; I feared that it would be blighted like the fields of Cammlin. I was relieved when we got closer and it was clear that the crops were fine, the corn growing tall and strong. Still, the closer we got to the town, the more something felt wrong, as if some subtle miasma hung in the air. I wasn't sure whether I was the only one who felt it until Fianait, Brody's daughter, said, "Papa, something feels wrong here."

"Aye, child, it does. Arlow, do you feel it as well?"

I nodded.

"Any idea what it is?" Brody asked.

"No. I can barely sense it, but it's there."

Cammford was a fairly large town, built where the river Camm widened but became shallower, allowing people and animals to cross without the necessity of building a bridge. The town was surrounded by small farming communities such as Cammlin, and the farmers brought their produce to Cammford's markets for sale to buyers from Marsden Forge, Amersford, and Badon. The first buildings we came to were houses, some with two or three stories, but as we neared the center of town, there were taverns, inns, and shops of all kinds. There were few people on the streets and many of the businesses seemed to be closed. I noticed Brody looking around, an uneasy expression on his face.

"Brody, what is it?" I asked as he gestured to the others to stop.

"This time of day at this season, this place should be full of people," he answered. "But there's hardly anyone out and most of the shops are closed."

At that moment, a young boy carrying a pair of buckets came up from behind us.

"Child," Brody said. "What is going on here? Where is everyone."

The boy stopped.

"You not from here?" he asked.

"No," Brody replied. "We just came in from Cammlin."

"You might want to go back," the boy said. "There's a sickness here. Lots of people have it. Me and my mother are helping the Healers take care of some. They sent me to bring water."

"Child," I said. "My name is Arlow, and I have some skill in healing. Will you take me there?"

He nodded.

"I just need to fill these buckets and then you can follow me back."

I turned to Brody and his family.

"Our ways part here, it seems," I said. "What will you do?"

"We can't go back to Cammlin," Brody replied.

"My sister lives here," Glynis said. "Our plan was to go to her. I think we still should."

Brody nodded his agreement and said, "Safe travels, wayward traveler."

"Safe travels," I answered, and Brody tugged their donkey into motion. They were out of sight before the boy got back with his pails of water. He'd filled them almost to the rim and was struggling with the weight.

"Let me take one of those for you," I offered.

He gave me a grateful look and held out one of the pails on a shaky arm. I took it and he shifted that arm to the other pail.

"My thanks to you," he said. "Follow me."

I followed him down the street to a large wooden building. The walls had once been painted white, though paint was now just a memory on the weathered gray of the wood. The streetside wall had a platform at the typical height of a wagon bed and a huge door–which stood open now–allowed entry into the structure. I tied Budge's lead to a ring set into the platform for that purpose and then followed the boy up the stairs to the platform.

As we climbed the stairs, an Altieran woman stepped out of the door, pulling a brightly colored scarf from around her head. Her hair, freed from the confines of the scarf, spread out in a dark nimbus around her head. There were faint touches of gray in her hair, and I guessed that she had completed somewhat more than 40 rounds of the seasons. She was one of the tallest women I'd ever seen, and thin, with long, delicate-looking hands. Her eyes were deep set on either side of a broad, flat nose. She wore a blouse and trousers of plain, undyed cloth and she had a green Healer's sash belted around her waist. It was clear from her posture and her expression that she was exhausted. As we approached, she used her scarf to mop sweat from the dark ebony skin of her forehead and then she leaned against the front wall of the building. Only then did she notice us.

"Kyle," she said wearily. "You took your time."

"But look, Valeria," he replied. "I've brought someone to help."

Her gaze shifted to me, taking in the poor state of my clothes and my disheveled appearance, and weighing how much use I might be. Her eyes lighted on the pail in my hand.

"We don't need anyone else to carry water."

I smiled.

"My name is Arlow. I have some knowledge of healing. The child says that there is an illness here."

"There is, indeed," she replied. "Two days ago, everything was fine. Then we woke up yesterday and people were sick, suffering from fatigue, weakness, fever, coughing, and difficulty breathing. It didn't take long to realize that there was someone with the sickness in nearly every home and inn in town. As near as we can tell, nearly one third of the people in town are ill and many have died. More fall ill every hour. All over town we've cleared out warehouses like this one to provide central locations where people can bring the sick so that we can treat them."

Her speech was slow and measured, as if each word had been carefully considered before she uttered it. Her intonation was different, peaking in unexpected places and colored with overtones that made me think of music. The way she trilled the "r" sound reminded me of Tavis.

"Do you know what's causing it?" I asked.

She shook her head.

"We haven't been able to make sense out of what's happening. The people who are ill seem to have no connection to one another. They live or were staying in different parts of town. They don't appear to have eaten the same foods or drunk from the same wells. We've been so busy treating them that we really haven't had time to track down the cause. We already have our hands full, and more people are falling ill all the time."

"Are there treatments that help?"

She opened her lips to respond, paused for the briefest of instants, and then said, "We've had some success with burdock for the fever and thistle for the cough."

I didn't hesitate in my reply.

"Then perhaps you do need someone else to carry water."

She looked at me quizzically.

"Why?" she asked.

"To clean up all the vomit caused by ingesting thistle. And since burdock is usually applied in a salve, you might want to wash that off as well since it will do nothing for fever."

She let out a short, sharp laugh and smiled at me.

"What did you say your name was?"

"Arlow."

"Arlow, what would you do for cough and fever?"

"For cough, a tea of maidenhair or maybe sarsaparilla or houndsbane. For the fever, willow or birch tea."

She nodded and began tying the scarf around her head again, binding as much of her hair under it as she could.

"Is that your donkey?"

"Yes. I just arrived in town. I don't have a place to stay."

She turned to the boy.

"Kyle, get that water inside where it's needed. Then come back and unload Arlow's things. Pile them inside and then get his donkey to a stable. Care for it and then get back here."

"I will, Valeria," he said and scrambled off to obey.

"Arlow, you come with me."

She led me into the warehouse. Crates and boards had been used to create makeshift beds, row after row of them, nearly all occupied. To one side, a small group of men and women were preparing teas and other remedies under the direction of a man wearing a Healer's sash. Other men and women moved amongst the beds, wiping people down with cool cloths or helping patients who could still walk to go out the back door, presumably to relieve themselves.

Valeria explained that she and the man were the only two Healers working in this warehouse. The other people were all townspeople who were not ill and who had volunteered to help care for those who were. Another skilled pair of hands would be most appreciated.

"We work until we absolutely cannot work anymore," she said. "Then we snatch a few hours of sleep out back and get back to work. We eat in between caring for people. Are you still willing to help?"

I nodded and said, "I am. Let me wash my hands and I'll get to work."

I lost track of time soon after. I moved from person to person, assessing the severity of their illness, administering whichever treatment seemed appropriate for that individual, and then moving on to the next. I was trying to keep track of the people I saw so that I could greet them when I came back to them, but it seemed that I'd see a particular person once or twice and then they'd be gone. When I thought about that, I became afraid that they were dying and that's why I never saw them again. But each time that occurred to me, my thoughts invariably went next to the one time I had played the *Arimë Daelyr* and how I felt during that playing. Deep inside, I felt that way now.

I was no longer sure how long I'd been working. I was well past exhausted, and I felt as if my head was filled with fog. I looked up from the woman I was treating and noticed that the warehouse seemed quieter than it had been. I finished what I was doing and stepped out onto the loading platform. I was leaning against the front wall of the building with my eyes closed, desperately wishing for sleep when I heard someone step out beside me. I opened my eyes. It was Valeria. As she had the first time I saw her, she pulled off her head scarf and leaned against the wall beside me.

"Arlow," she said, "what have you been doing?"

I glanced her way.

"Just taking a break."

"That's not what I mean."

Her tone of voice said that something was bothering her. I stood up straight, swaying slightly, and faced her.

"What is it, Valeria?"

"When you arrived here three days ago, most of the people brought to this clinic died, despite everything that Quin and I did for them. Then you arrived. You're using the same medicines we are, but somehow the people you treat don't die. After you see them once or twice, they are well enough to leave. Every single one that you have treated has recovered and is now well. What are you doing that Quin and I are not?"

I was so exhausted, so brain fogged, that I missed the import of most of what she said.

"I've been here three days?" I asked incredulously.

"Yes," she replied, a bit of frustration creeping onto her voice. "That's not the point. How is a minstrel a more effective physician than two trained Healers?"

That got through. I felt my face blanch.

"What?" I said, fear and exhaustion making my head spin.

"Arlow, you and I have worked very closely on quite a few people. I noticed the callouses on the fingertips of your left hand. And you've been humming the most beautiful tune while you worked."

"Valeria, I..."

"Look, I don't know why you're hiding," she said. "And I don't really care. After what you've done, you have nothing to fear from me. You have nothing to fear from anyone in Cammford."

I just looked at her blankly.

"You don't know?" she asked.

I just shook my head. I had no idea what she was talking about.

"After we noticed that the people you treated started getting better, Quin and I shifted to simply trying to keep them as comfortable as possible until you got to them. When the people here started going home healthy, the word spread quickly and all the people from the other clinics were brought here. This is the last clinic that is still open, and the people inside right now are the last of the ill."

All I could do was to stare at her in disbelief.

"Arlow, you've saved a large part of the population of Cammford. How did you do it?"

I shook my head. I couldn't understand what she was saying.

"I don't know. I..."

I started backing away from her.

"I need to go treat the people inside."

She just watched me as I backed away, turned, and went back inside. It took three hours or so to finish up with the last of the people in the clinic. Valeria was by my side when I finished with the last one. She took me by the arm and softly said, "Come with me."

She led me to a small office at the back of the warehouse. A cot had been set up there. She guided me onto it, pulled off my shoes, and spread a light blanket over me. I was asleep before she made it out of the room.

The warehouse was empty of people when I woke. The makeshift beds were all empty, the bedding in various states of disarray. I had no idea how long I'd slept, but my mind was clear, and I felt rested though a sense of weariness was still lodged deep in my bones. My things were neatly piled just inside the office door. Across the main storage room, bright sunlight was streaming in the big streetside freight door, which was standing wide open. I rose and stretched. Then, still barefoot, I crossed the empty room to the door and was just about to step into the sunlight when I caught sight of a group of men in green and gold uniforms standing in the middle of the street.

Soldiers of the High King.

I shrank back into the shadowed interior of the warehouse and moved to one side to peer out. There were six of them, all on foot, but two of them were holding the reins of their six mounts. Then my blood ran cold as I noticed that the person they were speaking to was Valeria. One of them was handing her a sheet of paper, no doubt a drawing of me. My vision dimmed and my breath caught as I panicked, then I turned and hurried toward the office as quietly as I could.

They'd be on me in moments. I had very little time to grab what I could and slip out the back door. I pulled on my shoes and knelt beside the box holding my guitar. I couldn't–I wouldn't–leave it behind. I had just succeeded in undoing the knots when I heard footsteps. I looked up to see Valeria standing in the office doorway.

"Lauren, what are you doing?" she asked quietly.

I noticed her use of my real name. My heart was pounding in my chest. I didn't answer, but simply stared at her, unsure what to do. Her gaze flicked to the untied knots.

"You can't go out yet. You need to give them time to get out of town."

She must have noticed my expression then.

"Wait, were you planning to run? Do you think I told them you were here?"

I didn't mean to, but I nodded slightly. She knelt down beside me, her eyes never leaving my face.

"Lauren," she said gently and cupped my face with her hands. "I told you. You have nothing to fear from me or from anyone else in Cammford. The soldiers said that they were looking for a minstrel named Lauren. They said that he was dangerous and must be caught or killed, because he'd bring down irrevocable harm on the Federated Kingdoms." She paused, watching me. When I said nothing, she continued. "All who spoke to them said that we had seen no such man."

"Ten shields is a lot of money," I observed.

"But not worth even one of the lives you saved," she countered. "No one in Cammford will turn you over to them. We owe you too much. The last I saw of them, the soldiers were riding for the ford. I heard them say that they were going to Amersford next."

"They're gone?" I asked.

"Yes. Come, I live not far from here. I can offer you a real meal and a real bed, at least for tonight. Tomorrow, when we're sure they're gone and not returning, you can decide what to do."

I wasn't sure I could trust her. No, that wasn't true. My gut said that I could trust her, but as I had noted, a lot was being offered for me. I couldn't believe that no one in town would be tempted by that much money. Still, I retied the ropes around the box and hoisted it to my shoulder. Valeria picked up my bags and pouches. As we passed through the town, I tried to keep watch on everything around me. I felt naked and exposed and half expected that at any moment the soldiers would reappear. They didn't, though, and all the people we passed smiled and waved. My rational mind was saying that I should continue to be wary, but I could feel myself relaxing.

It didn't take long to reach Valeria's home, which was located on a large plot of land just past the western edge of the town. It was built in the Altieran fashion, in the shape of a large square surrounding a central courtyard. The exterior walls were constructed of adobe, thick and solid and freshly whitewashed. A wide veranda ran around all four sides of the house, its roof supported by carved wooden columns that reminded me of twisted rope. Inside, the rooms were open and airy and decorated with Altieran artwork: sandstone sculpture, red clay pottery, and brightly colored tapestries. The house was oriented to take advantage of the prevailing summer breezes which wafted gently through the large open windows.

Once my things were stored in one of the guest rooms, Valeria and I settled into chairs on the veranda facing away from town. We sat in companionable silence, sipping water flavored with lemons, and enjoying the chance to simply sit. Finally, I turned to her and said, "Valeria, my thanks to you for welcoming me into your home. Outside of the palaces I've visited, it is the most beautiful home I've ever seen."

She smiled and answered, "That's very kind of you to say."

"May I ask you something?"

She cocked her head and nodded her permission.

"How did an Altieran physician end up in Cammford? Why not Amersford or one of the other large cities?"

She paused a moment before answering.

"I was raised in the arid lands south of the Fire Vale. My father came from a family of jewelers, my mother from a family that owned a turquoise mine. Their marriage brought the raw materials and the skills to make the jewelry under one roof. They intended me to enter the family business, but I was always more interested in healing than in profit making. I was raised to believe that I didn't have a choice, however, and I trained to make and sell jewelry. Then they convinced me to visit Marsden Forge to learn what I could from the smiths there."

She paused, a distant look in her eyes.

"I came here from an arid land," she continued. "I was used to wide vistas of browns and greys and muted greens. When I reached the Federation, I could not believe the amount of green. It was everywhere. It was spring and mixed in with the green were flowers of every color of the rainbow. I had never seen anything more beautiful. I fell in love with this land, and I couldn't imagine living anywhere else. I did go to Marsden Forge, and I did send a report home, but I chose not to go back. I drifted for a time but ended up studying for the Green in Amersford. About the time I finished my training, I heard that a Healer in Cammford was retiring, so I came here and took over. I've been here ever since."

She paused for a long time. A cricket chirped once or twice and fell silent.

"As the oldest of my parents' children, I inherited the business when they died. I didn't want it. My brother arranged to buy me out. I got enough to build this house with a good amount left over. My brother has turned out to be far better at business than I ever would have been, and he sends me a share of the profits every summer. I've got enough that I do not need to charge the people I treat. Oh, they pay me what they can–small trinkets, vegetables or fruit, or the occasional chicken–but I would treat them for free. I'm able to give them a level of care they otherwise wouldn't be able to get and that means more to me than pay."

It was pleasant sitting there on the veranda. When neither of us was speaking, it was nearly silent. If there were other people in the house, they were being amazingly quiet. There was a breeze blowing, but so gently that it barely stirred the grass and made no sound. Occasionally, I could hear a bird call in the distance, but that simply emphasized how quiet it was near the house.

Valeria broke the silence.

"And how about you, Lauren of the Minstrels? How did you come to be in hiding with the High King's men searching for you and offering a king's ransom for your capture?"

I didn't look at her as I answered.

"I'm not sure that it would be safe for me to tell you. Even the fact that you know who I am and did not tell them could get you killed."

"I don't believe they will ever find out. I doubt that they'll come back here. They seemed to believe that you were heading for Amersford."

I had to smile at that. Apparently, they'd been to Keffnael before coming to Cammford.

I turned my chair so that I could face her.

"Are you sure that you want to know?"

She nodded.

"This is knowledge possessed by only the Kings and the wizards," I told her. "The Kings and the wizards and one minstrel in each generation. There is an ancient Elven prophecy. It predicts the coming of a man, an evil man who will battle Mar and the Keepers and who will destroy the world." I paused and swallowed. Then I forced the words out. "They believe that I am that man."

She frowned.

"Why would they believe that?"

I'm not sure why, but I took the ring on its chain out from under my tunic and pulled it off over my head. I undid the clasp and let the ring drop into her hand. She held it up and examined it with a jeweler's eye.

"It's beautiful," she said. "The stone is odd, though." She shook her head. "It seems as if it is translucent, but it does something strange to the light. It should be sparkling, but it's not."

"The last Elven King crafted that ring," I answered. "For anyone else, the stone remains dark as it is now. For the man foretold in the prophecy, it wakes. It was meant to be a sign."

I held out my right hand and she slipped the ring onto my extended ring finger. As she did so, the stone lit from within, glittering violet, with hints of red and blue.

Valeria's reaction caught me completely off guard. She half rose from her chair, a look of surprise and awe on her face and then she dropped to her knees at my feet.

"*Sendolen*," she said quietly and bowed her head.

That word echoed in my memory. "What?" I whispered.

She didn't answer. We stayed like that, her bowed to me like a supplicant before a king, for several heartbeats. My discomfort finally found words.

"Valeria," I said quietly. "Please get off your knees. Please don't bow to me."

She rose and stood looking expectantly at me.

"Please sit. I'm still just me, just Lauren. What was it that you called me?"

She sat carefully on the edge of her seat, eagerness and excitement etched in every line of her face, her eyes never leaving me.

"*Sendolen*," she answered me.

"What is that?"

"It is the oldest of our tales," she said, and then it came back to me. Master Ryan and I were on our way to Songhaven, back when we first met. He was teaching me about the constellations as we camped on the western slopes of the Breton Mountains. When he pointed out the North Star, he told me the Altieran story of *Sendolen*.

"*Sendolen* was our greatest leader," Valeria continued, and I nodded. "We were wanderers, drifting from place to place. We were prosperous, but different, and so we were driven from place to place, always homeless. *Sendolen* led us to our home, gave us peace and prosperity and stability. When he died, he took up a place in the heavens. He became the North Star to remind us to live in peace."

"I remember now," I told her. "My Master Ryan told me that story long ago. But why do you call me *Sendolen*?"

"The tale ends with the promise that another great leader, another *Sendolen*, will come and he will bear the star on his hand."

I held my hand up to regard the ring. It glittered very like the sparkling of a star and the color was a near perfect match for the North Star.

"Now I understand," Valeria said.

"Understand what?" I asked, dropping my hand to my lap.

"How you did what you did in town. It is said that *Sendolen* will bring peace and healing."

"That word–*Sendolen*–what does it mean?"

She looked at me, a puzzled look on her face.

"I do not know that it means anything," she answered. "It was the leader's name. Why do you ask?"

"Several times in my life, I've dreamed of..." I paused. I wasn't sure how she'd feel about the Old Ones. "I've dreamed of people who said the word *endollin* to me. I don't think the similarity of that word to *Sendolen* is just a coincidence. Perhaps they weren't just saying *endollin* to me. Perhaps they were calling me *endollin*."

"What does that mean?"

"I don't know," I replied. "I'm beginning to think that it's important that I find out. I don't even know who I can ask, though. For a moment, I was hoping that the meaning of *Sendolen* would help."

Neither of us spoke for some time. I was confused and not sure how I felt. I had just for the first time spoken as if I accepted that I was the Lawbreaker. That was accompanied by a weary sense of resignation, but also a cold stab of fear straight into my heart. Everything I'd ever heard, everything I'd ever read about the Lawbreaker said that he was evil. I didn't want to believe that I was evil. Still, the evidence of the ring seemed irrefutable. On the other hand, Valeria used that same evidence to identify me as *Sendolen*, a man of peace and healing, a man who seemed good.

I guess my conflicting emotions showed on my face because Valeria asked, "Lauren, what troubles you?"

"This ring identifies me as the Lawbreaker," I said. "Everything I've been taught about the Lawbreaker says that he is evil, the greatest evil the world has known. If I am the Lawbreaker, that's me. I'm evil."

Valeria opened her mouth as if to speak but stopped. She had been leaning forward toward me; now she settled back in her chair and crossed her legs, her mouth scrunched up as she considered what to say.

"Lauren," she said. "People are not born evil. People are not born good. People are just born. As they live, they make choices. Some of those choices will be to help others, to serve others. Those choices make the world a better place. Some of a person's choices will be to help only themselves, even to the detriment of others. Those choices diminish the world, make it less than it could be. It is our choices that make us good or evil, not some chance of birth. You are what you choose to be."

Her words echoed something that Ryan had said to me during my training, that only humans could be evil because only humans could choose their note in the Song of the Seasons.

"I haven't known you very long, but I've known of you for some time now," Valeria told me. "We heard here what you did for King Marc in Amersford. When even the King's closest friends and supporters were afraid to speak up, you stood up and helped unmask the man who was poisoning him. And I've spoken to both Brody and Kyle about when you first came here. You heard that there was sickness in the town and your reaction was not to run away. You immediately chose to help, to care for people you didn't even know. Those are not the actions of an evil man."

Valeria's words and the reminder of Ryan gave me comfort.

"My thanks to you, Valeria," I said and realized that I was smiling. "You are very wise."

She smiled back. "Perhaps I am," she said. "But I am hungry for sure. Let me start the evening meal."

"Let me know what I can do to help," I answered.

"Sing for me."

And so I did. For the first time in weeks, I took my guitar out of its case and then settled into a chair in Valeria's kitchen. I spent a few moments tuning as Valeria began cutting up onions and beef and browning them in a large skillet. The first song that came to mind was a simple tune that Denys had written about how important his guitar was to him, so I sang that.

"That's pretty," Valeria said when I finished. "Did you write it?"

"No," I answered as she dumped the beef and onions into a large pot with tomatoes, beans, and a great variety of spices. "A friend of mine wrote it."

"Have you written anything?"

"I've written several songs, but only two of them are good enough be sung to other people."

"Play one of them for me."

As a minstrel, I had come to regard Songhaven and the Breton Mountains as my home. I loved it there and I had written a song about that love. It wasn't a flashy song. There were no particularly clever turns of phrase, no amazing guitar riffs. It was a simple piece that nonetheless captured my feelings exactly. I played that one for Valeria.

When I finished, I looked up to see her watching me intently as she slowly stirred the contents of the pot.

"That's where you're going, isn't it?" she asked.

I nodded.

"I think so. But I can't go to Songhaven. They'll be watching for me there. I figure I can hide out in the mountains near Songhaven, though, and no one will be able to find me. If I keep watch on the trail, I might even be able to make contact with Master Ryan. I'm sure he'll have some idea of what I should do."

She didn't answer but dipped a spoon into the pot and tasted the contents. She added a pinch of salt, stirred, and tasted it again. Then she looked at me.

"Is hiding truly the best thing for you to do?"

"I'm not sure what else I could do. Maybe no one from Cammford will turn me in, but plenty of other people in the Federation will be happy to. I was in the High King's dungeon, and I couldn't even get out of there without help. I don't know why the ring recognizes me, but I'm no powerful being. I'm just a minstrel."

Valeria didn't answer and she didn't look at me. She just stirred the contents of the pot, her expression unreadable.

"Well," she said at last. "I do not believe that you are just a minstrel, but dinner is ready. Shall we eat?"

"It smells delicious. What is it?"

"It is called *cassaca* after the main spice. The spice is named after the type of pepper it is made from. It is one of my favorite dishes. Shall we eat outside?"

I agreed and she used a ladle to fill two bowls with *cassaca*. Then she sprinkled finely cut cheese over the tops. We carried our bowls out to the veranda and ate as we watched the sun sink toward the distant trees. I'd never had anything as spicy as *cassaca* before, but it instantly became a favorite of mine and both Valeria and I had a second bowl. By the time we'd had our fill, it was dark.

"How long will you stay?" Valeria asked.

"I've probably already stayed too long. I should leave tomorrow morning."

"Lauren, I told you, I don't think the soldiers will be back."

"Something other than the soldiers is also hunting me."

"What do you mean?"

I told her about the feeling that I'd had that some dark power was hunting me and about the dimming of the stars in Noweth and the ruin of Cammlin. When I finished, she was silent a moment and then said, "Perhaps hiding is the best thing for you to do."

I started to speak, but then she continued, "For now."

She stood.

"It has been days since I have bathed. When I had the house built, I had them build in a large bathing pool and we set up a system to fill it with heated water. Would you care to join me? It might help you sleep tonight."

I couldn't remember the last time I'd bathed.

"It would be nice to be clean," I said.

The bathing pool was sunken into the floor of the room and was large enough to accommodate five or six people. We quickly shed our clothes and spent some time scrubbing away the sweat and grime of days spent caring for the ill. Then we settled back against the sides of the pool to soak. The water was indeed warm, and I felt days of stress and over exertion drifting away as Valeria and I chatted. I was in the middle of telling her about the first time that Peg and I had sung together when a yawn forced its way out in the middle of a word.

Valeria smiled.

"Well," she said. "You obviously need to turn in."

We both climbed out of the water and dried off with the largest towels I had ever seen. Valeria handed me a robe to wear in place of my soiled clothes.

"I have someone who can clean those for you," she said.

"My thanks," I answered, fighting back another yawn.

"Sleep well, Lauren."

"You as well."

I padded down the hall to my room in bare feet. A gentle breeze stirred the curtains, and I slipped off the robe and lay down. The bed was comfortable, and I slept well past sunrise. After a quick meal of fried eggs and ham, we carried my things back into town. I tried to purchase food to carry with me, but the merchants all insisted that I take what I wanted for no charge. Budge was looking quite sleek and well cared for and he brayed his annoyance as I began loading him, but soon settled down.

Valeria walked with me to the ford. At the riverbank we stopped, and I turned to face her.

"Valeria, my thanks to you for your hospitality and for your wisdom. I hope that my having been here doesn't bring evil down on you or the others here."

"I've been thinking about the things you told me last night," she replied. "I think that evil struck here already. I believe the illness was the result of whatever it is that is searching for you. You drove it out."

She reached out and took my hands in hers.

"Safe travels, *Sendolen*," she said, her voice choked with emotion. "Know that my trust and my faith travel with you."

Then she hugged me, and I found myself fighting back tears. When we separated, she took my hands again and I could see that her deep brown eyes were welling with tears.

"I will always try to be worthy of your faith and trust," I promised. "Be well, my friend."

She squeezed my hands tighter for a moment, then let go and nodded. I picked up Budge's lead and turned toward the ford. When I reached the other side, I turned back.

Valeria was still standing on the far bank. We waved, then I turned away. Two hours later, I entered the King's Forest.

CHAPTER FOUR

The King's Forest was one of the last remnants of a vast forest that had once covered almost all the lands now occupied by the Alomar. Presumably, the first to clear forest land for settlements were the Lost. Later came the Elves and still later, humans. Now, other than King's Forest, the only remnants of that primeval forest were Sorden Forest to the north and the Elderwood to the west. Helm Sorren, the twenty ninth High King of the Alomar, had taken the eastern remnant of the once great forest under his protection and declared that only he and his designees–which included the residents of Cresswell–could hunt there. As a boy in Cresswell, I had explored the parts of the King's Forest around the village. Part of me felt as if I'd come home.

At the edge of the forest, the underbrush was dense and full of brambles. Budge and I forced our way through; Budge's coat seemed to protect him from the thorns, but I was covered in shallow scratches and cuts by the time we got through. Once we were well under the trees, though, the canopy blocked out most of the light, so the underbrush faded away and our going was eased. The trees were huge, so large that if I wrapped my arms around one of the trunks, my fingers would not touch. The canopy was far overhead and tinted whatever sunlight got through green. The ground was covered in centuries of dead leaves and littered with fallen trees and branches. Here and there a moss-covered rock protruded above the detritus. For the most part, it was silent, the only sound the crunching of dead leaves as Budge and I walked. Occasionally, I could hear birds calling, but I never saw them. I saw no animals.

All that first day we headed a bit south of east. I only had two waterskins, so I kept an eye out for water as we walked. By the time I set up camp that night, I had seen no sign of either a spring or a stream. I gave half of one of the skins to Budge and then hobbled him and allowed him to forage for whatever he could find to eat. Given the amount of flammable material on the forest floor, I didn't dare start a fire, so I sat down with my food stores to see what I could find that would go down well cold.

What I found brought tears to my eyes. The people of Cammford had refused to let me pay for food, but they had quietly done more. In each bag of food, I found coins, a few irons in one, a copper crown in another. All told, I had the equivalent of a silver shield in addition to what I'd had when I had arrived in Cammford. I bowed my head in silent thanks.

For almost two days more Budge and I continued southeast, following game trails when we could and wading through ankle deep layers of fallen leaves when we couldn't. Then we turned to the south because I judged that we were coming within the outer range of Cresswell's hunting parties. I hadn't left my childhood home under the best of circumstances, and I wasn't eager to meet a group of the village's hunters alone in the forest, especially with a price on my head. Over the next couple of days, we crossed several shallow streams, and I was able to refill the water skins. On the morning of the sixth day after leaving Cammford, we left the King's Forest and joined the road from Amersford to Durning. Two days later, as the sun was nearing its zenith, we reached Durning.

Durning was situated atop a broad-topped low hill that stood alongside Tolan Creek, which at that point was close to a small river in size. Sturdy walls of stone crowned the hill and kept the town safe from Kelmar raiders. The road split and circled around the hill about halfway up, but there were gates in the eastern and western walls. The town had grown in the rounds since I had last been there. On that previous occasion, only two structures had stood outside the walls: the blacksmith's shop and a mill. Both sat on the banks of Tolan Creek. Now, there were something like a dozen buildings that I could see, nestled up against the outside of the walls. I found myself thinking that my father would be horrified; raiders wouldn't need to bring ladders to scale the walls, they'd just have to reach the roofs of those buildings, and they'd have access to the top of the wall. I was shaking my head at that as I entered the west gate of the town.

I paused just inside the gate to take my bearings. As I stood trying to decide where to go, a Penitent stepped out of a small but ornately decorated building that was obviously the town's church. That was new as well; I didn't remember seeing it on my first trip to Durning. He took up a position near a well while ringing a bell and calling out to the crowd, "Wayward children of Mar, gather round. I would share a tale of Mar's love."

A handful of people gathered around the black-robed Penitent.

"Wayward ones," the Penitent said. "Hear now the extent of Mar's love for us."

He paused to take in the size of his crowd. His eyes met mine and I groaned. I couldn't leave or he'd notice. And that would attract attention that I did not want. The Penitent began to speak:

> *There was once a man who lived in Kerith. This man was known as Lodon. Lodon was not a wealthy man, but neither was he destitute. He owned a home and a plot of land, and a very fine donkey to pull his plough. But Lodon was also a jealous man, who coveted his neighbor's larger home, his herd of cattle, and his beautiful wife. Lodon spent many hours thinking of how he could acquire his neighbor's lands and marry his beautiful wife. One day, while walking along the road, he came across a small man in a brown hooded robe. The man called out to him saying, "Where are you going, Lodon, with your heart so heavy?"*

The crowd around the Penitent was growing as the man continued his tale:

> *Now Lodon wondered how it came to be that the stranger knew his name, but answered back saying, "I am going nowhere, stranger. I am merely walking and wondering how to gain that which I desire." "And what would that be?" the brown stranger asked. "I wish to own my neighbor's land and his beautiful wife," Lodon replied. "Do you not already own land? Could you not find a wife of your own?" the little man inquired. "There is no finer land nor any woman so fair as those of my neighbor," Lodon answered. "And have you prayed to Mar for these things?" asked the little brown man. And*

> *Lodon said that he had, but to no avail. "Well,
> then," said the brown man. "I may be able to
> help. I could arrange it so that your neighbor's
> land and wife were yours for the taking." Lodon
> said how that would be a very fine thing and
> asked what the stranger would want in return.
> "Since you will have your neighbor's wife and
> land, you will have no need of your own. Give
> me the deed to your house and land and I will
> help you," said the stranger.*

The Penitent paused to survey the crowd. The size of the group obviously pleased him, though he just as obviously tried not to show it. Then he resumed the story:

> *And so it was agreed. Lodon gave the deed to his
> house and land to the stranger. At that moment,
> Lodon's neighbor was working in his field. The
> stranger appeared wearing the likeness of Lodon
> and shouted and screamed and frightened the
> neighbor's cattle into stampeding. They broke
> out of their pen and trampled the neighbor to
> death and ruined all the crops in the field. The
> neighbor's wife saw all of this and cried out,
> "Lodon, why have you done this thing? You have
> taken my husband and all that he owned and
> now I am destitute. I shall despise you for all
> time." The stranger then appeared in front of
> Lodon, back in his own form. "And now our
> deal is concluded," he said. "Your neighbor's
> wife and land are yours for the taking." And
> then he laughed.*

The crowd was quiet; the story of Lodon and the Brown Stranger was a well-known one. They all knew what was coming next.

Lodon cried out in despair. He cast his eyes to the heavens and called out, "Is there no one to save me from this calamity?" And even as the words left his mouth, the Destroyer appeared, he who metes out justice as Mar's right hand. His fine black robe was trimmed in warrior's red, and the righteousness of Mar was with him. Without a word, he cast back the stranger's hood to reveal his features. Lodon could now see from his pointed ears that he was an Elf. The Destroyer struck the vile creature down. Lodon's heart was filled with joy for now he could return to his own home and land. But the Destroyer turned to Lodon and said, "Lodon, thou hast turned to Elves for aid and thou hast given thy love and desire to one other than the goddess Mar." And he struck down Lodon as well. The lands that meant so much to Lodon were given over to the church, as were the cattle and the donkey, so that the glory of Mar could be shared with all.

Having finished his tale, the Penitent raised his hands.

"And so, you have seen the love that Mar has for us," he said. "Go now and give thanks."

The crowd began to disperse and a youngish looking man sitting on the porch of an inn stood and approached me.

"Arlow?" he asked when he was close enough that I could hear.

He seemed vaguely familiar, but I couldn't place him. I didn't answer, suspicion narrowing my eyes. He looked at me expectantly for a moment, then decided to continue.

"Arlow," he said again. "I'm from Cammford. You might not remember me, but you healed my sister."

Now I remembered him. His name was Adham, and he was about my age. His younger sister Cori was one of the most seriously ill of the people I treated. I nodded.

"I remember," I said. "How is Cori doing?"

He looked surprised that I remembered her name.

"She's completely recovered," he replied, smiling broadly. "My thanks to you."

"You're a long way from home, Adham" I observed.

"Valeria sent me. I have a message for you from her. Can we find somewhere private to talk?"

"How long have you been here? Is there a cheap inn nearby? I need to find somewhere to stay. I could get a place, and we could talk there."

"I just got here the day before yesterday. I'm staying at the Trader's Rest." He pointed the way, and we started walking. "The innkeep was charging me only 2 crowns a night. I've already been here two nights, though, and I've exhausted the money Valeria gave me. I'll need to leave before nightfall."

"Let me at least buy you the midday meal. We can talk while we eat."

He nodded. "My thanks to you."

It wasn't far to the Trader's Rest. The building appeared to be reasonably well maintained, though the paint was peeling in places. I asked Adham to stay with Budge and my things while I went inside to seek out the innkeeper. The interior appeared to be clean with just a bit of wear showing on the furniture and walls. Overall, the place looked hard used but well-maintained. The innkeeper was a friendly man, also about my age, named Owin. He charged me two crowns for an overnight stay and two more for four meals.

"Before I take your money," he said, "I need to tell you that my stables are outside the wall. Will that be a problem?"

I shook my head.

"I'll need directions to get there."

"I have someone who can take your horse there and bring him back in the morning."

"I have a donkey, but my thanks to you."

By the time I had my things unloaded, Owin's daughter was there to take Budge to the stables. Adham and I stowed my things in my room and settled in at a table at the rear of the inn's common room. We chatted about the weather and how folks were doing in Cammford until Owin brought our meal—a thick stew crammed with beef and vegetables accompanied by bread and a serviceable beer—and left to attend to other patrons.

"So," I said after taking several bites. "You have a message for me."

"I do," Adham replied, glancing around to make sure we were out of earshot of the other patrons. "Valeria wanted you to know that two men showed up looking for you in the afternoon of the day you left. They were strange. They weren't dressed like wizards, but they carried staffs like wizards. And they talked funny, too. Almost like they were from the *Torun Mar*."

"And they were looking for me?"

"Yes. They talked to several people and then they were," Adham paused, looking perplexed. "gone."

"Gone?"

"That's one of the strange things. No one saw them come into town and no one saw them leave."

We ate in silence for a few moments. I was trying to match the description of the men to anyone I'd ever heard of, with no luck.

"They didn't give their names?" I asked.

"No. They just stepped out from between two buildings and stopped people on the street. They said they were looking for a minstrel named Lauren. After they talked to maybe two dozen people, they stepped around a corner and were gone."

"Was Valeria one of the people they talked to?"

"She was. They talked to her longer than to anyone else. They kept asking her if she had seen a minstrel in the town recently and she told them over and over that there hadn't been a minstrel in Cammford since the Summer Day of Passages. It was shortly after that that they disappeared. Valeria thought it was important for you to know, important enough that she paid a merchant heading here to give me a ride. That's how I was able to get here before you."

I used a piece of bread to mop up the last of the stew in my bowl, thinking furiously as I chewed.

"Are you really planning to leave before nightfall?" I asked when I'd finished.

Adham nodded. "I have to. I don't have enough to stay longer, and I need to get back to my family's farm. We're coming up on harvest time and there's a lot of work to do."

"Do you have food for the journey?"

"I have some. And I can forage along the way."

I shook my head.

"You came here to help me out. I'm not going to let you go hungry."

I fished a couple of crowns out of my pouch.

"Here. This should get you plenty of food for the trip."

He took the coins, a look of relief on his face.

"Adham, you'd best be on your way. I don't think those men will have been able to track me here, but if they have, I don't want you nearby when they find me. You have my thanks for coming here. Please give my thanks to Valeria as well. Travel safely."

He smiled and closed his fingers around the coins.

"My thanks to you, Arlow. My trip home will go quicker since I won't have to stop to look for food. May Garth guide your footsteps and put you on the path back to Mar."

I simply nodded at that, and he left. I downed the last of my beer and returned to my room. It was small, barely bigger than the bed, and quite cramped feeling, even with the shutters over the window thrown open. I had been planning to wander the town, maybe try and find a pot that I could use on the trail, but now I wasn't sure that it would be safe to go out. I laid down on the bed and laced my fingers behind my head. I had no idea who the strange men searching for me might be. One thought that occurred was that perhaps they were Kelmar. I had never met a living Kelmar; it seemed reasonable that, given their devotion to Mar, they might speak as the people in the *Torun Mar* spoke. I had no idea, though, why the Kelmar would be searching for me and how they would have tracked me to Cammford.

Then it hit me. The Kelmar were devoted to Mar. If I was the Lawbreaker, I was supposed to do battle with Mar. They would see me as the worst kind of infidel, worse than even someone who was simply an unbeliever. If that was true, not only was most of the Federation going to be hunting me, but the entirety of the Kelmar Empire as well.

My tiny room was suddenly too close, too confining. I had to move. I leapt from the bed, nearly hitting my head on the wall, and stepped out into the hallway. I made sure to lock my door and then set out to explore Durning.

It didn't take long to walk completely around the town. Unlike the cities I'd been to–Badon, Amersford, Songhaven–where the business and residential areas were segregated, Durning was a hodgepodge of homes, shops, and inns all crammed in between the narrow streets cheek-by-jowl. I did have the presence of mind to watch for anyone following me. I found a tinker who had parked his wagon just inside the eastern gate of the town and he sold me a beat-up old pot for just three irons.

I spent the afternoon wandering around the town. My thoughts spun in circles, the men who were looking for me in Cammford, the King's soldiers, the dark power that haunted my dreams. Eventually, I realized that as I had gotten lost in my thoughts, I had been simply circling the town; if anyone was following me, I'd made their job very easy. I looked around me. I was back near the eastern gate. I walked over to the tinker's wagon.

"Back for another pot, eh?" he asked.

"Not exactly," I replied. "I've been past here quite a few times this afternoon."

I laid another iron on the counter but kept my finger on it.

"Aye. Ye have," he said, pointedly not looking at the coin under my finger.

"Anybody following me?"

He smiled and shook his head.

"Not that I've seen."

I took my finger off the coin.

"Thanks, friend. Have an excellent evening."

"You, too, friend."

I cut straight across the center of town to my inn. The evening meal was being served, so I took a table in one of the rear corners. When Owin brought my food, I found it was the same stew that had been served at midday, but the bread was fresh. I declined the beer in favor of a hot mug of tea. I was pleasantly surprised when–halfway through the meal–a minstrel walked into the room and began setting up in one of the front corners of the room.

The minstrel was no one I knew, an older man who played his instrument with an aggressive style, hammering away at the bass strings in a way that I'd never seen before. He had a penchant for tuning the lowest strings down a full step and playing in the key of D, which accented the bass notes on the D chords. He had a marvelous voice and a huge repertoire of songs, and I sat and listened until the room began to empty out. I thought that being one of the last people in the common area would make me stand out a bit too much, so before the minstrel finished, I left and headed to my room.

The interior of my room was pitch dark when I opened the door. Enough light entered from the hall that I could stow my pot in one of my bags, then I closed the door and undressed in the dark. It seemed to take a long time for me to relax but, eventually, I slept.

It was clear even through my closed eyes that it was morning. I very much wanted to sleep longer, but part of me was aware of voices. Angry voices. They were obviously at a distance, and I tried to ignore them, but they were there, just beyond intelligibility and despite my attempt to ignore them, my mind struggled to make out what was being said. Then I crossed some threshold and came fully awake, lying face down on the bed. The angry voices were still there and growing louder. Curious, I got up and dressed and went looking for the argument.

I found it in the common room of the inn. A crowd of people–it looked like most of the guests at the inn–had Owin cornered and every single one of them was shouting at him at the same time. Owin was holding up his hands in a placating gesture, but the crowd was having none of it. I couldn't make out what they were saying, and Owin had no chance to try and speak. Finally, I lowered the pitch of my voice and as loudly as I could I shouted, "Hey!"

The crowd fell silent and turned to face me.

"What's going on?" I asked. As several of the people before me took a deep breath preparing to respond, I added, "One at a time. You," I said, pointing to one large, bearded man. "What's happening here?"

"This little *mirdl* of an innkeeper lost our horses," the man replied, his voice deep and rumbling like summer thunder. I must have looked puzzled because he explained. "His stables are outside the walls. He was supposed to have someone watching them. We trusted him. Now he tells us that someone broke in last night and stole every animal in the stable."

"Every animal?" I asked in disbelief. Budge was gone? How would I carry all my things?

"Every single one," another man replied. "I have a wagon full of goods to take to Kerith and no horses to pull it."

"Me, too," several others chimed in.

I looked over the crowd at the innkeeper.

"Owin?" I asked.

"It's the truth, Arlow," he replied. He was clearly as upset as everyone else. "Someone took every animal in the stable last night. My sister's husband was supposed to be on watch, but he snuck home to be with my sister. When he got back this morning, the stable was wide open, and the animals were gone."

I just stared at him, open mouthed. I needed to leave town that day and I didn't have enough money to buy another animal.

"I'm sorry, everyone," he continued. "I'll refund what you paid me to stay here last night."

"That's not enough to buy me a new horse," the big man complained.

"I know," Owin said. "But I don't know what more I can do. I don't have enough to buy everyone new animals. Even if I sold this place, most of what I got would go to paying off the loan I took when I bought it."

"Take everyone's name," I said. "Give them free rooms each time they come back until you've paid what they're owed."

I saw hope light Owin's face. Several of the crowd turned to look at him.

"I could do that," he said. "Will that suit?"

Most of the crowd nodded. A few grumbled, but in the end they all accepted the deal.

I didn't stay as the others lined up to provide their names and the number of animals lost. I felt the need to get out of town as quickly as possible and I was going to have to do it carrying my own things, including my guitar. I didn't have the time to search for a donkey or a horse to buy and I couldn't afford to buy one even if I found one. Without an animal, I was going to have to give up the rag box; I couldn't lug it around in the wilderness on my back. To maintain my anonymity, though, I needed some way to disguise my guitar as I walked out of town.

It took an hour of searching shops all over the town, but I found a large canvas bag with a drawstring at the top. It was just long enough to hold my guitar. If I stuffed my extra clothes and some of my food around it, the shape of my instrument would be hidden. Some previous owner had sewn shoulder straps on it, so it would be easy to carry. I paid a single iron for it and another for a warm woolen blanket and hurried back to the Trader's Rest.

The common room of the inn was empty when I returned. I hurried up the stairs to my room and began packing my bag. My guitar went in first. Then I carefully stuffed my extra clothes around it and began sorting my foodstuffs to figure out what I could take with me. That's what I was doing when Owin found me.

"I thought I heard someone come in," he said. "Still planning to leave today, I see."

"I have to," I replied.

"I appreciate your helping me out down there," Owin said. "Things were starting to get ugly."

"It was just a spur of the moment thought."

"It worked. I appreciate it."

I went back to packing food into my bag; Owin stood in the doorway watching.

"I'm really sorry about your donkey," he said finally. "If you have a few minutes to give me your information, I'll add you to the list."

"There's no need for that," I said.

"But..."

"Owin, if you really want to repay me, forget that you ever saw me," I snapped. Then I stopped, feeling exasperated, and looked at him. "I'm sorry. I don't mean to be short, but I really need to be going."

I left Durning through the eastern gate and headed into the wilderness. I'd only been that way once before and I'd been following Ryan then, but I'd since learned to read the secret signs that marked the minstrels' trail though the wilds. For two days, the trail sloped gently upwards as I worked my way through the foothills of the Breton Mountains. On the third day out of Durning, the climb began in earnest. I had planned my stopping point that evening well in advance; there was an outcrop of rock that offered a clear view back over the ground I had covered in the last few days. I reached it before the sun set and sat until long after dark watching for movement or a fire or some other sign that I was being followed. I saw nothing.

I sat and watched the stars come out. There was no moon, and the stars seemed brighter and closer than ever. The day had been warm, but the temperature had dropped considerably. I was going to have to wrap myself in my blanket as I slept. I turned my gaze to the north. The North Star–the Keystone, the *Sendolen*–flared in the northern sky, its flickering violet just a little more blue than red that night. There was a faint breeze, just enough to evoke the faintest of whispers from the trees, but the night was otherwise silent. Time passed as I sat watching the star, all the others wheeling around it. Somehow, watching the star, seeing its constancy, gave me comfort, and I found my fear and tension draining away. It was strange, but I found myself feeling as if I was exactly where I was meant to be. It must have been nearing midnight when I finally rose and returned to where I had left my belongings. I dug my blanket out of the bag, wrapped it around me, and laid down. As I did, I felt the ring on its chain slide across my chest.

"The sword is out there somewhere." The thought slipped into my mind, but sleep claimed me before it could disturb me.

Two days later, I left the trail to set up camp out of sight of anyone who might come along. I found a nice spot in the shelter of a very old stand of pine trees. Old needles were thick on the ground and would provide a little cushioning. Just beyond my camp site, the ground sloped down into a hollow and I could hear the faint sounds of a stream down below. Once I'd laid out my blanket and eaten a little of my rapidly diminishing stock of food, I took my nearly empty water skins and scrambled down the steep slope to find the water.

Though it hadn't rained recently, the little stream was full, the water a bit over a handspan deep. It was clear and cool and sweet, and I drank my fill before filling my water skins. As I stood to return to camp, what I saw brought a smile to my lips. Some twenty feet upstream from where I stood was a large, tangled blackberry bush, full of ripe berries. They would supplement my dwindling supply of food quite nicely.

I climbed back to my camp and fetched my pot. I adjusted my downward course to head straight for the bush. The way was steeper, and I was carrying the pot in one hand, so I had to focus to avoid losing my footing. It was that, I think, that kept me from noticing the odd sound that I was hearing. When I finally did notice the deep resonant sound–almost like a purr–I looked ahead at the blackberry bush, now just thirty feet below me. A large black bear was happily feeding on the berries. As I struggled to stop, rustling the underbrush and dislodging some small stones, the bear looked up idly and then returned to the berries.

I'd never seen a bear before, but I knew enough to know that I wasn't going to be having berries. As quietly as I could, I turned and started to climb back up the side of the hollow. I lifted my left foot to step up and the ground under my right foot gave way and I fell. I dropped my pot and grabbed frantically for a sapling, but it gave way as well and I tumbled down the side of the hollow.

I came to rest beside the blackberry bush with the bear just two steps away. For a moment, it looked surprised and made a couple of wuffing sounds. My breath had been knocked out of me and even though I was terrified, I couldn't move. Involuntarily, I let out a loud gasp as I tried to catch my breath. The bear stopped its noise and glared at me, then a low growl started deep in its chest. It took a step toward me and suddenly the growl stopped. My breath was coming in short, shallow pants as I watched the bear, which somehow looked puzzled. It took another slow step forward, its eyes on mine, then it lowered its massive head to my chest and sniffed. Then it nudged me gently and sniffed again. It lifted its head and stepped back slowly, its eyes never leaving me. It stopped and bent its front legs as if kneeling. Then it bowed its head to the ground and held that pose for a moment. It looked as if it was bowing to me. Then it stood, turned away, and lumbered off downstream.

I didn't sleep well that night. The bear's strange behavior disturbed me and even though I had hung my food out of reach over a tree branch, I was afraid it would return. When I wasn't worried about the bear, I found myself thinking about the Lawbreaker's sword. Though the thought hadn't disturbed me that first night in the mountains, I found myself wondering where the sword was and what it might do, what I might do with it. So far, the ring only seemed to sparkle when in contact with me; if it did anything else, I'd seen no sign of it. I'd been hoping that being home in the Breton Mountains would bring me some peace, but my troubles had followed me there and robbed me of rest.

It took me five more days to reach my destination. In the summer of my third round at Songhaven, Ryan and I had been rambling through the forest north of the city. Ryan had been teaching me woodcraft, practicing the skills I'd need to live on my own in the wild. Well off the trail from Songhaven we had stumbled across an old cabin in the woods. It had been built of rough-cut logs with a sturdy stone chimney at one end. The logs on the end opposite the chimney had rotted away, apparently from the bottom up. As each log had crumbled, the next settled down until the whole wall was gone, leaving the gable resting on the ground. The other end of the cabin was relatively intact, that end of the roof still anchored firmly to the chimney. That end provided some shelter from the weather, and I had returned there often during my time at Songhaven. I had told Peg about it and the cabin had been our favorite trysting place when we wanted to be truly alone. It would now be a safe place for me to stay while I tried figure out how to contact Ryan.

The door was halfway between the ends of the building. The opening had been twisted by the partial collapse of the cabin and whatever door had once been there was long gone. I stepped through into the shadowed interior. The wooden floor was covered in a thick layer of dust, dotted with a handful of dried leaves blown in from outside. Long-cold ashes lay in the fireplace, most likely left over from one of my visits. It didn't look like anyone had been there in a very long time.

I spent some time making the place a little more habitable. I cut a pine branch and used it as a makeshift broom to sweep the floor and I gathered a supply of downed wood should I need a fire. There was a small spring nearby, possibly why the builder had chosen this spot. I cleared a fallen branch out of it and let the water flow clear for a time before I drank. Then I searched through the forest for food and returned with a few chicory leaves, some huckleberries, and several handfuls of the fungus known as chicken of the woods. It wasn't much, but it would stretch my food for a few more days.

I spent the next couple of days watching the trail to Songhaven but saw no one. I managed to find only a little more food, mostly berries and nuts, but at least I wasn't starving. On my third night in the cabin, I went to sleep reasonably content.

I woke the next morning to the sound of a woman playing guitar and singing. I was sure that I recognized her voice, but I quietly crossed to the door and peered out to make sure. Then I stepped out, holding up my empty hands to show that I meant no harm.

Rachel saw me immediately. She stopped singing and bit back a scream. She frantically tried to stand, but it's hard to rise from sitting cross legged on the ground while holding a guitar.

"Rachel, it's me," I said. "Lauren."

That didn't stop her from trying to get up and on her second attempt she managed it. To my relief, she didn't run off. She just stood looking at me intently, trying to reconcile the bedraggled, bearded apparition in front of her with the man I'd been just two moons ago when we both took the Blue.

"Rachel, it's Lauren," I repeated.

She frowned. "Lauren?"

"Yes."

She recognized me then and grinned.

"You've looked better," she observed.

"It's been a rough couple of moons."

She nodded. "I've heard. Some of it, anyway. Lauren, why are you here? Everyone in the Federated Kingdoms is looking for you."

Then she ran to me and threw her arms around me.

"It's good to see you, my friend."

I hugged her back.

"It's good to see you, too."

She let me go and sat down. I joined her.

"Lauren, why are you here?" she repeated. "There have been people here looking for you. Soldiers of the High King. Some men who were obviously bounty hunters. Other men hoping to be bounty hunters."

"I figured they would look for me in Songhaven," I replied. "But I didn't think they'd know to look here. I wanted to try and find a way to reach Master Ryan and the last I heard, he was coming to Songhaven. I think he might know something about what's been happening to me."

I looked at her curiously.

"How do you know about this place? I don't remember mentioning it to you."

"Peg told me about it," she replied. "Denys has gone out. I didn't want to go. It's the first time we've been apart since we were children. I come out here when I'm feeling sad and want to be alone."

I nodded.

"Master Ryan isn't in Songhaven," she continued. "He left shortly after news came of Ambrose's death. No one knows where he went."

She looked at me and I saw faint traces of fear in her eyes.

"Lauren, some say that you killed Aerman Sorren. And they say that you were there when Ambrose died. Some even say that you had a hand in his death."

I shook my head.

"I was there when Ambrose died," I said. "We'd been asked by Prince Anders to ride out from Badon to meet Marc of Amersford. We were ambushed by a band of rebels from Meren. One of them killed Ambrose."

I had to fight down my emotions. It still hurt to talk about Ambrose's death.

"What about the High King?" Rachel asked.

"I was with Ambrose when that happened," I answered. "We were riding for Badon because Ambrose had seen that it was going to happen. We didn't get there in time to stop Aerman's death, but I did stop Larsen from killing Anders."

We sat in silence for a moment. She was watching me intently.

"That does sound more like the Lauren I know," she said finally, but there was a tentative note in her voice.

"Rachel, how is Peg?" I asked, finally giving voice to one of my biggest concerns. "How has she reacted to everything you've heard?"

"She's refused to believe any of it. She's afraid for you, though. And she's afraid that she'll never see you again. She loves you."

Something that I hadn't even realized was knotted up inside me relaxed. I smiled.

"And I love her more than I can say."

"Should I let her know that you're here?"

"No. Not yet. If there are people looking for me, they might be watching her. Our relationship wasn't a secret. She might inadvertently lead them here. Worse, it might give them a reason to do something to her."

She nodded.

"That makes sense. Is there anything I can do for you?"

"Could you possibly bring some food? I'm almost out of what I brought from Durning and I'm getting tired of nuts and berries."

She laughed as she stood.

"I'll try to make it back tomorrow," she said. "But I should get back now. I have a class to teach this afternoon."

"You're teaching at the college?" I asked.

"No. I'm teaching some of the children of the city residents. I love working with the little ones."

She paused to put her guitar back into its leather case, then turned to go.

"Lauren, stay safe," she urged.

"You, too," I replied. "Enjoy your lesson."

Rachel did come back the next morning, with food that she snuck out of Songhaven hidden in her guitar case in place of her guitar. We talked for a brief time, and she shared news of our joint friends. Peg had spent a moon tutoring students at the college and then had been asked to begin teaching there. Avery and Tavis had gone out together. The last Rachel had heard, they were in Marsden Forge. Denys was in Amersford but was writing at least once a quarter moon. Rachel said that in his letters he sounded lonely, and she smiled just a bit as she said it. I told her more about what had happened in Amersford and Badon and then she had to go back. I was sad to see her go; for just a short while my life had felt almost normal again.

During the next six days, I settled into a routine. I'd rise with the sun and break my fast. Then I practiced for an hour or so. I'd realized that I was far enough from the trail that I could play as long as I did so quietly. Then I'd creep up to keep watch on the trail, hoping that Master Ryan would come by. I wasn't sure how long I could wait for him; Valeria was correct that I couldn't hide out forever. When the day's light began to fade, I'd head back to the cabin to eat and then sleep.

Rachel returned in the evening of the sixth day. I was just getting ready to head back to the cabin when I saw her striding purposefully up the trail. I stepped out of my hiding place and met her on the trail. She smiled widely when she saw me.

"Lauren, you won't believe it," she said excitedly, a wide smile lighting her face.

"Believe what?" I asked.

"A Keeper is coming to Songhaven."

A vague sense of unease crept in around the edge of my consciousness, and I struggled to think of something to say.

"A Keeper is coming to Songhaven?" was all I could manage.

She nodded.

"Yes. They say it will be Garth, the patron of travelers and minstrels. The Masters say it's a huge honor. The Keepers haven't gifted the Alomar with a visit in several lifetimes. They're planning a concert in his honor for the evening tomorrow."

My field of vision had narrowed to Rachel's face, gray crowding in around the edges.

"Garth is coming here himself?" I asked, my voice strained with unease.

"Yes," she said happily. "Lauren, what is it? You sound... well, not happy. A visit from one of the Keepers is truly an honor."

"Rachel, I don't know. Something about this doesn't feel right, especially so soon after what's been happening."

"Lauren, it will be fine. You'll see. Look, I must get back before it gets dark. Will you come?"

I shrugged my shoulders.

"I don't know. I'm not sure it would be safe for me." I paused, not sure what to say. "Rachel, be careful. I really don't think this is a good thing."

She shook her head slightly and smiled.

"It will be fine. I'll see you soon and tell you all about it."

She turned and headed down the trail to Songhaven and, with a growing sense of fear weighing down my steps, I turned to go back to the cabin.

I didn't sleep well that night. Long after I laid down, my mind was fixated on the thought that Garth was coming to Songhaven. The Keepers had not appeared in the Federation for several generations. Rachel was convinced–apparently because the Masters were–that the visit was an honor. Garth was the patron of the minstrels, so perhaps it was, but why now? Why so soon after the waking of the stone in *Aennsrhyd*, the death of the High King, and the passing of the Lawbreaker's ring to me? Why now, when I was being hunted as the Lawbreaker? I must have drifted off at some point because I woke–drenched in sweat–from some dark formless dream with a single thought in my mind.

Despite what the Repentant claimed, the *Torun Mar* was in no sense a book of Mar's love and compassion. It was a book of the penance owed Mar by the Alomar. For good reason was it known as the Iron Codex.

I rose the next morning before the sun was up. By the time it was light, I was hidden in the thick stand of brambles that provided cover as I watched the trail. All that day I watched, and no one came by on the way to Songhaven and Rachel did not return. Very late in the afternoon, all my senses came alert for no reason that I could discern. A heartbeat later, a single peal of thunder broke the afternoon silence and echoed over the mountains, though there were no clouds in the sky. My anxiety grew. As the day's light was beginning to fail, I heard sounds from the north. It sounded like men on horseback. A lot of men. Soon, the first of them came into sight.

It was a large company of mounted Kelmar soldiers. In the midst of the group rode a lone man wearing a hooded robe of a color very like the bright blue of the minstrels, but there was something about it that seemed off, unsettling. The robe was belted with a black sash and the hem and cuffs and the edges of the hood were all trimmed in black. The man was carrying a long, iron-shod staff of some dark wood. The hood was up and obscured his face, but I had no doubt that I was looking at Garth, one of the Keepers of the Alomar.

I remained still as they passed, daring no more than quiet, shallow breaths. There were nearly fifty mounted men accompanying the Keeper. I found myself wondering why a Keeper on a ceremonial visit would need so many armed men with him. Fear ran cold up my spine.

When the last of the riders was out of sight, I hurried back to the cabin. I suddenly felt the need to be in Songhaven when the concert started. Rationally, I knew that it was a risk; there were likely to be people who would recognize me, even bearded and scruffy as I was. The place was going to be full of Kelmar soldiers and if someone called out my name in greeting...

Still, I had to go. It occurred to me that one more minstrel in a crowd of minstrels might not stand out, might not draw attention. I quickly belted my sash around my waist and slung my guitar in its leather case on my back. Then I returned to the trail and rushed toward Songhaven as fast as I could without risking a fall the dim light.

It was almost completely dark when I exited the forest on the northern edge of the broad field outside the gates of Songhaven. The amphitheater was on the south side of the field and the stage was brightly lit. Torches and lamps flared on top of the city's walls as well. As I crossed the field toward the amphitheater, I could see that the seating was nearly full and that throngs of people were standing behind and to either side of the seats. As I worked my way through the crowd, I kept watch for anyone that I knew. Though I knew it would not be wise, I was hoping to catch sight of Peg. If anyone would recognize me, it would be her.

The Kelmar soldiers were all seated stiffly in the front rows. I stopped on the back edge of the crowd; the ground sloped down from where I stood to the stage, so I could see that all of the Masters present in Songhaven were gathered there. I remembered then that Rachel had said that Peg was teaching at the college, and I searched the people standing on stage for her. I thought I caught a flash of her short brown hair in the back row of the Masters, but I couldn't be sure from where I was standing. As I watched, Master Elissa stepped forward as the others took seats in chairs set on the stage. Again, I thought I caught a glimpse of Peg toward the back, but then Elissa spoke.

"People of Songhaven," she said. "We are gathered tonight..."

She broke off in confusion as Garth rose from his seat, mounted the steps to the stage, and crossed to stand before her.

"Thou art Master over all in this place?"

His voice was cultured and measured, but there was a hint of menace in his tone.

"I am," Elissa replied.

He turned toward the other Masters.

"And ye art also Masters of the College?"

"We are," they answered as one.

I realized at that moment what I was hearing. Garth was speaking like the people in the *Torun Mar*, like the men Adham said had been looking for me in Cammford. It was suddenly hard to breathe; it was the Keepers themselves who were looking for me. And now one of them was in Songhaven, the first place anyone would think to look for me.

"I am Garth," he said. "I have been anointed by Mar as a Keeper of the Alomar. I am sent to render judgement upon thee. Thou hast harbored the Lawbreaker and in so doing hast angered Mar beyond all hope of compassion."

Elissa and the other Masters were looking around in confusion. Garth grasped his staff with both hands and raised it. The lights went out onstage and on the walls of the city. I was sure that all the lights in Songhaven had gone out. Then the stage was lit with an eldritch light, tinged with the same sick parody of minstrel's blue as Garth's robe.

"The gifts granted thee by Mar are rescinded."

He gestured with his staff and the Masters all gasped. Around me, minstrels cried out in alarm. I sensed a tugging deep inside and then it felt as if something in in the very core of my being had gone still.

"Mar is cognizant of thy sins and has declared that thou must be cast out into the outer darkness, forever apart from her."

He paused just for a heartbeat and then, in a voice as cold and as pitiless as the depths of winter, said, "You all shall die."

He pointed his staff at Elissa, and she crumpled to the floor, grasping her chest with both hands, her face swollen and red. The Kelmar soldiers stood, and the sound of their swords being drawn was a cold metallic shriek.

As the soldiers turned and began hacking at the people in the rows behind them, Garth spread his arms and flames sprang up onstage, engulfing the remaining Masters. Their agonized screams tore at my heart and tears began rolling down my face. The crowd around me turned and began to run, some toward the city, some for the cover of the forest. The amphitheater was in chaos, the residents of Songhaven fighting to flee with the Kelmar soldiers close behind them.

The flames had spread across the entire stage, save for a broad circle around Garth, who still stood with his arms spread. Suddenly, the bells of Songhaven began tolling wildly and I knew that the attack had spread to the city.

I heard the laughing, then. It was quiet and it took me a moment to locate the source. Lit by the flames from the stage I made out a figure cloaked in black standing perhaps thirty feet to my right. I couldn't tell whether it was a man or a woman; a hood and cloak covered the being's entire body. But it was clear that it was watching the carnage and laughing. Not sure how, I could sense that the figure in black was feeding power to Garth, enabling the carnage onstage.

Rage flared up in my chest. My entire body was tense, my fists clenched. I unslung my guitar from my back, intending to rush forward and smash it over the black-cloaked being, but suddenly I couldn't move. A thought flitted across my mind, in my voice yet somehow alien, other. It said, "This is not the time."

My teachers were dead in front of me, and my friends were likely dying in the city. The flames onstage burned into my eyes, fueled the rage burning in me. I fought the paralysis, managed to take a single step forward. The figure in black stopped laughing and began to turn toward me. Something from deep inside me reached out and dragged me down, robbing me of my breath and smothering my consciousness. My muscles went slack, and I crumpled to the ground. Just before my awareness completely faded, I felt the great darkness that had been seeking me flash through the spot where I had been. Then whatever it was that held me snuffed my thoughts out like a candle.

Awareness returned slowly. I felt lethargic and warm, as if a blanket covered me from head to foot, protecting me from the cold. Then it felt as if someone suddenly stripped the blanket away and I started awake in fear. I was lying on my back, my guitar clutched to my chest. I looked around me as much as I could without moving anything but my head, but couldn't see anyone, so I carefully sat up. As far as I could see, I was alone. Garth and the Kelmar soldiers were nowhere in sight. The sun was barely up, giving just enough light to make out the broken shapes of bodies scattered over the field. The stage had been reduced to ashes and the ruins were still smoking. The reek of burnt wood and flesh hung in the air. My stomach heaved and I fought down the urge to vomit. I stood, slipped my guitar into its place on my back, and began walking toward the gates of the city.

There were far fewer bodies than I feared, but still so many. Some were residents of the city, people I recognized from my time there. Most, however, were minstrels or students of the college. Minstrels had clearly been a target and, according to Garth, it was because I had studied there. My mind was still, holding my emotions at bay, so I felt numb, empty. I remembered the rage that I had felt the night before, but it was gone, leaving only ashes in its wake.

The gates of the city were intact, untouched, and standing wide open in welcome as always. Inside, the Courtyard of Songs was empty of the living, but a dozen or so bodies lay broken and bloodied where the Kelmar had hacked them down. The stable doors were open, and it was clear that the horses were gone.

I found Rachel sitting in a pool of her own blood, leaning against the stone wall of the well, her delicate hands pressed against the sword wound in her gut. Her eyes were closed, and I couldn't tell whether she was breathing, but my boot scuffed on the paving stones as I knelt, and she opened her eyes. I'd never noticed before how deep a brown they were.

"Lauren," she whispered.

"I'm here, Rachel," I said as I took her hand. It was cold.

"He chased me in here," she said, so quietly that I could barely hear. "Stabbed me with his sword and then left me here bleeding. He said that I wasn't worth the effort it would take to finish me off. It hurt so badly, Lauren."

My heart ached for her.

"The apothecary isn't far," I said. "I'll get something for the pain."

"No need. It doesn't hurt any more, but I'm terribly cold." She looked straight at me. "I'm dying Lauren."

I shook my head and started to deny it, but she continued.

"Lauren, it's too late. Please sing *The Parting Song* for me."

"Rachel," I said. It was barely a whisper.

"Please, Lauren. I tried to sing it while I still had the strength, but the music wouldn't come. I couldn't sing anything. I think maybe Garth did something to us. Please, Lauren, sing for me."

I nodded and tried to swallow the emotions clogging my throat. I took a breath and reached for the words...

They wouldn't come. I knew them as well as any song I knew, felt that they were right on the tip of my tongue, but as I reached for them, they skittered out of reach. I shook my head, trying to clear it, trying to hear the first notes, the first words, but something was pulling them away, keeping them from me. Rachel was watching me, tears welling up in her eyes, her breath going quick and ragged.

"It's you, too," she whispered. "He took our music. Oh, Lauren..."

A tiny flicker of the rage I'd felt the night before rekindled.

"I will sing for you, my friend," I stated with sudden resolve.

I'm not sure why, but I took my guitar off my back and dug my flute out of a pocket in the case. I raised it to my lips, positioned my fingers, and sought for the music. For a moment, nothing came. The wellspring of my minstrelsy had been capped. But then something else inside me stirred and the *Arimë Daelyr* flowed through me and out through the flute. Rachel's look of pain and anguish eased a little as I played. I reached for my knowledge of *The Parting Song* again. I felt as if there was some unseen, barely felt barrier between me and my music. That barrier was inside me and I could somehow sense it inside Rachel as well. My awareness expanded and I could sense the barrier in little pockets elsewhere in the city and all across the Federation. Rachel's eyes were wide with longing, and I pushed against the barrier, and it gave a little, but held. I closed my eyes, gathered my will, and pushed again and it shattered. As the shards of the barrier faded, I caught a brief impression of surprise and fear and then that sense of another mind was gone. I finished the *Arimë Daelyr* and began *The Parting Song* acapella. Rachel smiled faintly and I could see her mouthing the words, though she was past singing. I laid my flute aside and took her hand again as I sang the final lines.

> In this sorrowful dawn
> Are there no farewells, my friend?
> The winding road goes on
> Though you are at your journey's end.

"Farewell," she said, her voice so faint I could barely hear it. Her eyes closed.

"Farewell, Rachel," I replied. I felt tears running down my face. I bowed my head, fighting to keep the pain from overwhelming me. When I looked up, I found her watching me

.

"Lauren," she said. "Peg..."

The light left her eyes then and Rachel was gone.

CHAPTER FIVE

I knelt there beside Rachel for a very long time. I could feel grief and anguish crowding the edges of my consciousness and seeping into my heart, but I kept my mind blank, my feelings quashed, trying not to think or feel. I didn't want to feel and there was a thought that I did not want to think. Could not. Not yet.

Eventually, I stood and settled my guitar on my back. I bowed to Rachel and then checked the others in the Courtyard of Songs. I knew some of them; all of them were gone. The Fountain Courtyard was empty. The entrance to the Rillian Tower was open, the door battered and the frame splintered by the attackers when they forced their way in. I stepped in and called out, but no one answered. I chose not to search the tower.

Holding my thoughts and feelings at bay, I worked my way through the seven levels of Songhaven, visiting the places that Peg and I had frequented. Eventually, I reached the Tier of Time and the door to my room. I reached out to open it and paused. Everything felt unreal, distant, and I felt like an intruder. The person I was in that moment had no right to enter the room of Lauren of the Minstrels. I turned and went to the door of Peg's r oom.

I knocked, but there was no answer. I pushed the door open and stepped inside. It was hushed, still, and a faint scent of lilacs hung in the air. I scanned the room. Everything was neat and clean, as it always was. Peg could have stepped out a moment before I arrived or two months before. A tendril of emotion slipped past my guard, caught my breath in my throat. I fought it down and turned to go. I paused on the doorstep and considered leaving a note but decided against it. I gently closed the door. I had one more place to go.

For a few moments, I stood looking out over the valley. I loved the view from the Tier of Time. Something told me that I might never see it again. Then I turned and followed the path that Peg and I had taken the first night we met. Soon, I reached the clearing in the spruce trees that students called the Grotto.

She wasn't there, of course. She wouldn't be. The Grotto was a place students went. That's when the thought I'd been holding at bay breached my defenses. It burned into my mind, leaving behind it more pain and despair than I had ever known. Peg was no longer a student. She'd been teaching at the College. She was a Master and all of the Masters had been onstage the night before. The world spun, gray pushed in at the edges of my vision, and I found myself on my hands and knees choking back anguished sobs.

I don't remember getting up and was only dimly aware of crossing the little wooden bridge over the Rose River. At one point I realized that I was heading into the wilderness south of Songhaven, heading in the same direction that Ryan did on his mysterious trips. That fact didn't touch me. I needed to move, and one direction was as good as another.

I walked all that day, stopping only to drink when I crossed a small stream. I passed several berry bushes, and it occurred to me that I should eat but I felt no hunger. I didn't feel anything. I refused to feel anything. Walled off from expression, the emotions that I should have been feeling transformed into a kind of nervous energy that movement burned off. So, I walked.

Night came, but a full moon provided enough light to keep going and so I did. Near midnight I stopped, finally too exhausted to continue. I laid down and closed my eyes. Some trick of the mind presented me with swooping, swirling clouds of color, tiny pinpoints of light moving in unison, very faint against a background of black but visible. Yellow faded through orange to red; red through violet to blue; blue through green to yellow. Watching the colors let me keep my thoughts and feelings contained and I laid there mesmerized by the drifting clouds of color.

I must have slept for a few hours, an exhausted, dreamless sleep. I woke suddenly to the quiet sounds of the nocturnal animals. I was shivering; nights in the mountains at the end of *Tymnacynn* could be cold. The moon was far closer to the horizon than it had been. I rose, slung my guitar on my back and began walking again. At dawn, I found a stream and stopped to drink. When I looked up, I was gazing into the eyes of a large wolf that was standing on the other side of the creek. We just stared at one another for a long moment, then the wolf turned and trotted off into the forest.

All that day, I walked. I walked until exhaustion overtook me and then I'd lay down to slip into a restless, haunted sleep. Too soon I'd wake and begin walking again. I continued through the night and the next morning I saw the wolf again. When I woke in the gray light of morning it was sitting an arm's length away, watching me. As soon as my eyes were open, it stood and ran off. All that day, I caught glimpses of wolves shadowing me through the forest. They never came into clear view, but I knew they were there. I guessed that they were stalking me and that sooner or later they'd attack, but I felt detached from that thought, as if I were thinking of a fate that might befall someone else.

When night fell, I stopped and tried to sleep. I laid there on the bare ground, my body aching and my legs and feet throbbing, feeling drained and empty. I was cold, but I didn't have the means to start a fire. Then the night went silent. All the insects abruptly stilled, and a barred owl broke off in mid-call. I sat up, gazing around me with a detached sense of curiosity. The stars overhead dimmed and, as I had several times in the past, I felt that vast darkness hunting me. Somewhere nearby, I heard a wolf growl.

I got up and began walking again. For days, I continued like that. Walking as long as I could and then trying to rest, always shadowed by the wolf pack. And at least once a day, usually at night, I felt that huge, malevolent intelligence searching for me. At last, it all took its toll. Near midday some five or so days after the attack at Songhaven, I couldn't walk anymore. Though the day was warm, I was shivering, and I couldn't seem to hold my thoughts together. I sat down and leaned against a tree. As I laid my guitar across my lap, I noticed that the ring was glittering on the ring finger of my right hand. I couldn't remember taking it out and putting it on. I felt like that should bother me, but it didn't. Then I noticed the wolf—or maybe just a wolf—step out of the forest and sit down facing me. A moment later, another joined it, and then another. I felt like that should bother me, too, but I was past feeling. My vision began to fade to gray at the edges and I felt my consciousness slipping away. My head was slowly drooping to the right, and I willed myself to sit up straighter, but I couldn't control my body anymore. I had a vague sense that I was falling over, but everything went black before I hit the ground.

I became aware that I was adrift in the deep darkness of oblivion. Something was pulling me up toward the surface, toward light and consciousness. It sounded like voices. I couldn't make out what they were saying, though, so I let go and sank back into the depths.

Awareness slowly returned. I felt as if I was floating. But then the ocean of blackness around me began to drain away and as more of the blackness receded, the sensation of floating faded. I realized that I was lying on my left side in a bed, a heavy blanket spread over me, my head cradled by a pillow. I was warm and comfortable but confused; the last thing I remembered was the wolves watching me fall. I hadn't expected to wake.

I opened my eyes. Seated beside the bed was a woman, maybe about my age. Despite her apparent youth, her chin length hair was a pale silver, almost white. Her eyes were dark–blue or maybe green I thought–but the exact color was hard to tell because a large double window behind her was full of sunlight. She wore a pink dress or blouse that left her shoulders bare. There was something about her, some inner light that brought to mind the beauty of the full moon. It was not as bright as the nimbus of sunlight shining around her, but it was there, warm and comforting, a sure guide in the darkness. She was engrossed in the book she was reading and didn't notice me watching her. Something in what she was reading made her smile and she idly reached up with one hand to brush her hair back behind her ear.

Her ear was pointed. She was an Elf.

I must have made some sound then because she looked up. When she saw that I was awake, her whole face lit in a smile. There was such genuine joy in that smile that I couldn't help responding; I smiled back. She set aside her book and said, "*Astolé, Endollin. Selé il manana tul seli navoram.*"

"I," I started, then just shrugged, and shook my head.

She smiled again.

"My apologies," she said. "Rhion told me that you did not know our tongue. What I said was, 'Greetings, *Endollin*. We are honored by your presence.'"

My head was swirling, my thoughts jumbled. She was an Elf, and I had been taught that the Elves had been evil, that they desired dominion over humans. That in consequence, they had all been killed during the Great War, yet she was clearly an Elf. I was still very much alive, but I had thought I was dying. And she had called me *Endollin*. I shifted in the bed to get my weight off my left arm, which was falling asleep, and tried to sit up. As the blanket dropped down, I realized that I was naked. I stopped moving. The Elf was watching me, a puzzled look on her face.

"I," I started again. I had so many questions, all of them begging to be asked first. "I'm Lauren," I said finally.

"My name is Élan," she replied. "How are you feeling?"

"Confused," I admitted. "I thought I was going to die." I looked around the room. "Where am I?"

"You are in *Evendim*, in a guest room of the King's house."

"*Evendim*?" I asked and felt myself frowning. I'd never heard of a place by that name.

"The home of the *Eldar*," she answered.

"*Eldar*?"

"Our name for ourselves. In your tongue it means people of the stars."

"You *are* an Elf?"

She nodded, her face suddenly guarded.

"Élan, I thought all of the Elves died in the Great War."

"Most did," she said quietly. "At the fall of *Elsgard*, Lorrestian and many others stayed to delay the human army. They were slaughtered. They stayed so that some of our people could escape. The ones who did made their way into the wilderness of the southern Breton Mountains and settled here. We have stayed here, hidden, ever since."

I nodded and then asked, "How did I get here?"

"A party of hunters found you lying underneath a tree," she told me. "They said that you were being guarded by a wolf pack. When our hunters approached, the pack left. One of the hunters recognized your ring and so they carried you back here."

"Why?"

"They recognized you as the *Endollin*."

"You called me that. Others have as well. What does it mean?

She looked at me incredulously.

"You don't know?"

"No. Remember, I don't speak the Elven tongue."

"It's not Elven," she said.

"What language is it?" I asked.

She stood. Even in the simple act of rising she displayed an incredible grace. It was a pink blouse she was wearing along with a flowing white skirt. Standing, she appeared to be about my height and slender.

"Let me fetch my father or Rhion. They will be glad to know that you are awake and either of them could explain that better than me."

She went to the door and paused in the act of opening it.

"If you are feeling well enough to rise, there is clothing in the armoire."

Then she was out the door, and I was alone. I looked around the room. It was fairly large and roughly square in shape. The walls were made of some light-colored wood, oak I thought, in its native color but highly polished. To my left was the big double window, open now to admit the light and a gentle breeze. To the right of the window was the door, made of the same oak as the walls, its entire surface carved with an intricate pattern of interlocking elliptical loops and circles. The far wall, beyond my feet, contained a stone fireplace with a raised marble hearth. To my right, the wall contained shelves which were well-stocked with books and a large armoire. To my relief, I could see my guitar in a stand to the right of the fireplace.

I thought I'd get dressed, but when I tried to stand my head spun and my vision began to fade. I decided against trying to get up and laid back against the pillows. I realized then that I was hungry. I couldn't remember the last time I had eaten.

A few moments later, Élan returned carrying a tray of food. With her was a man, taller than her by a head, but by his facial features, clearly her father. His long silver hair was bound back by fine silver chains and upon his head was a silver coronet, set with a thumb-sized piece of the opalescent Elf stone. Behind him came another man, with long dark hair.

"Ryan!" I exclaimed. Then, as the King stepped further into the room, I saw my Master clearly. His hair was bound back for the first time since I had first met him. He had the pointed ears of an Elf.

He smiled at the look of surprise on my face.

"So, now you know," he said.

"Lauren," Élan said. "This is my father Alain, King of the *Eldar*."

I turned my gaze away from Ryan to the Elven King.

"Your Majesty," I said. "It is an honor to meet you. I would do you reverence, but I'm afraid that if I try to stand, I'll fall over."

The King nodded, a faint smile on his lips.

"The *Endollin* needs do me no reverence," he said. "Rather the reverse, I believe."

"About that," I said. "I have been called *endollin* several times now, and not just here. Can you tell me what it means?"

"We shall speak of that," the King replied. "First, though, I would like to know how you came to be in the state in which we found you. What has happened?"

Élan stepped forward then and set the tray on my lap. It contained several slices of toasted bread and a variety of cheeses and fruits. My mouth watered.

"Father, he needs to eat. By the look of him, he hasn't eaten in a week."

Alain smiled at his daughter.

"Very well," he said. "Though perhaps Rhion could do a better job of answering his question than I could."

"Rhion?" I asked.

"My true name," Ryan replied. "Ryan was a close enough human alternative. So, you eat, and I'll talk."

Just then, another man entered carrying two additional chairs. When they had been placed alongside the one Élan had occupied earlier, the three of them sat down.

"So," Ryan began. "The word *endollin* is a curious one. It is a word in the True Speech, the language of Making. The earliest records of its use are in the oldest texts in the library at *Elsgard*. We learned it from the Old Ones. On a few occasions, they used the word *endollin* but would never explain its meaning. What we know has been worked out from the contexts in which it was used."

He paused a moment to watch me eat.

"Slow down, Lauren," he said gently. "I know you've been starving, but if you eat too quickly, you risk vomiting."

In reaction, I put down the piece of toast I was holding and took a sip from the cup on the tray. It was plain water, but never had water tasted so sweet on my tongue.

"*Endollin* appears to be a contranym," Ryan continued. "In some places it seems to mean 'lawbreaker' and in others 'lawmaker.' In still other passages it seems to mean 'lawless' or in others 'the essence of law.'"

"This is interesting," I said. "But why would I be called *endollin*?"

"Lorrestian named the man he saw *Endollin*."

"Why is it translated only as 'lawbreaker' in the *Book of Kings*?"

"I cannot say," King Alain cut in. "It was not so in the *Eldarin* original. The nuance was dropped in the human translations that appeared after my father was killed."

"Your father?" I asked.

"King Lorrestian was my father," Alain replied.

I was about to put a slice of apple in my mouth, but my hand dropped to the tray still holding it.

"You inherited the throne from Lorrestian? You've been King for a thousand rounds?"

Alain chuckled.

"Remember, Elves are immortal unless they are killed," he explained. "So, yes, I did inherit the throne from my father, but we have never allowed one person to serve an unlimited time on the throne. There are five families that rotate the kingship, with a new ruler every two hundred rounds of the seasons. I am only recently returned to the throne."

It was just then that all the implications finally hit me. I looked down at the tray on my lap and then at Élan. I had just been waited on as if I were royalty by the Princess of the Elves. Ryan noticed my look and misunderstood it.

"Have a care, Lauren," he said, teasingly. "You already have a princess."

It felt as if a taloned hand had thrust into my gut and shredded my entrails. Whatever peace I'd been feeling drained away and pain twisted my face. For a moment, I thought Élan looked stricken as well, but I couldn't focus on her. I turned to Ryan. My feelings must have been mirrored in my expression because Ryan's smile melted from his face to be replaced by a look of concern.

"Lauren, what is it? What's happened?"

I focused my gaze on the space between Ryan and the King.

"Master, your Majesty," I said, using formal forms to try and gain control of my emotions. "You asked how I came to be as your hunters found me. Would I be correct in assuming that you know that Ryan was my Master at the Minstrel's College and that I just took the Blue on the Summer Day of Passages?"

The King nodded.

"And I know as well that you and he parted in Amersford," he told me. "There, you and Ambrose prevented Marc's death. After that, our knowledge of events becomes uncertain."

"Ambrose had a vision while we were in Amersford," I told them. "He saw a black-cloaked figure kill High King Aerman Sorren. We rode for Badon to try and forestall the murder but arrived too late. We did, however, prevent the King of Meren from killing Anders Sorren, who then rode out in response to a Kelmar attack on Han. The prince tasked Ambrose and me with greeting Marc when he arrived at Badon. As we rode out to do so, we were attacked by soldiers from Meren. One of them stabbed Ambrose. As he lay dying, he passed this ring," I held up my hand to display it, "on to me. He told me that it had been passed in secret from minstrel to minstrel for generations and that I, too, should keep it secret. But when I touched it, it woke. Just before he died, he named me La wbreaker."

I paused and took a sip of water.

"Marc had soldiers try to take the ring. I..."

My voice faltered. I stared down at my lap, fighting to master my emotions.

"They tried to cut off my hand," I said, barely able to get the words out. "Something in me killed them."

I fell silent. Tears rolled down my face. I looked at Ryan.

"Master, I'm sorry. I violated everything you ever taught me."

"Lauren," he answered, his voice gentler than I'd ever heard it before. "You acted only in self-defense. They tried to maim you. Nothing I ever taught you said that you had to stand by and allow something like that happen."

For a moment, no one said anything. I closed my eyes and took a couple of deep breaths, trying to get my emotions under control. Then I continued my story.

"Marc took me prisoner then and I was locked in a cell beneath Badon. I was released by a friend and made my way back to the area around Songhaven, hoping to contact Ryan. I was staying in that abandoned cabin we found."

That remark was addressed to Ryan, and he nodded acknowledgement.

"My friend Rachel found me there and told me that the Keeper Garth was coming to Songhaven. I followed him and his Kelmar soldiers to the city. The Masters thought his visit was an honor. They had planned a concert to celebrate Garth's visit. Instead, he killed them. All the Masters were onstage with him, and he burned them to death. His soldiers hunted through the crowd for minstrels. They killed as many as they could find."

"Ryan, it wasn't all Garth. I was in the back of the audience. As the crowd fled, I saw a black-cloaked figure laughing at the carnage. It seemed to me that it was somehow feeding power to Garth. I don't know why, but I am sure that that being was the true power behind what happened. I think it was also probably the one who killed Aerman Sorren."

I fell silent. My head was bowed in grief. I was still seeing the room I was in and the people I was with, but I could also see the flames on the stage and smell the smoke...

"Lauren," Ryan said gently. "There's more, isn't there?"

I looked up at him through tear-filled eyes.

"Peg was teaching at the College. She was a Master. She would have been onstage. I think I saw her there."

I felt a warm, gentle touch. Élan had laid her hand over mine. She looked as broken as I felt.

"Lauren," she said. "The sorrow you bear..."

They were all silent for several moments. Then Alain spoke.

"I, too, grieve your loss," he said. "The attack upon Songhaven was unconscionable. As a friend, I hesitate to intrude on your grief, but I am also a King and now I must act as a King. There are things I must ask you."

I took a breath. Élan squeezed my hand and then withdrew hers.

"I understand," I said.

"You spoke of an attack on Han. What can you tell me of that?"

I told him what I could about the attack, and we discussed the odd behavior of the Kelmar. I also told them about the role of King Larsen in the death of the High King and the poisoning of King Marc. We talked for hours about affairs in the Federation. Both King Alain and Élan had a deep knowledge of the history of the Federation and a keen insight into the often-strained political relationships among the Alomar kings. Long after dark, I began yawning almost constantly and they took their leave. As I settled back into the bed, I considered the strangeness of the situation. I'd just spent the evening lying naked in a bed discussing politics with the King and the Princess of a people I would have called a myth even a day before. Just before I drifted off, it occurred to me that, despite the strangeness, I felt perfectly comfortable where I was.

I woke the next morning at sunrise. The windows had been left open, so the room was chilly, but I was warm under the thick down blanket. I hadn't been awake for more than a minute or two when there was a light rapping at the door and a young Elf stuck his head in. Unlike Alain and Élan, his hair was golden.

"*Aduné?*" he said, his tone indicating that it was a question. "*Endollin?*"

"I'm awake," I replied. "But I do not know your tongue."

He stepped in. "I am Truel. If I may be so bold as to instruct you, *aduné* means 'sir' in your tongue."

"Ah, thank you, Truel. And, if I may, please let's dispense with the titles. My name is Lauren."

"As you wish." I could see him biting back the honorific. "Were you ready to rise?"

"I am," I replied. "But before I dress, I'd very much like to bathe and, if possible, shave." He nodded.

"I can take you to the bath house. Just a moment."

He crossed the room to the armoire and retrieved a dark blue robe from inside and brought it to me. Remembering my weakness from the day before, I took care as I stood. I still felt a little weak, but I didn't feel faint as I stood up. While I pulled on the robe, Truel returned to the armoire.

"Shall I bring clothing for you?"

"Yes, my thanks to you. Is my minstrel's sash in there?"

"It is."

"Please bring that as well."

"Very well. There are sandals next to the door for you."

I slipped on the sandals as Truel stepped outside. The morning air was brisk, but the robe was thick and warm. My room opened onto a terrace not unlike the ones at Songhaven. Like Songhaven, the terrace was edged with a low stone wall. I stepped over to see what I could see, but some twenty paces beyond the wall the world disappeared behind a wall of fog.

"It should burn off soon," Truel informed me. "This way."

He led me around the end of the house and a short distance up the slope to a small building constructed of stone. The wooden door was intricately carved in the same style as the door to my room. I was expecting the interior to be dimly lit, somewhat cave-like, but the walls had been faced with the same polished oak as my room. Oil lamps set in golden sconces provided a warm, comfortable light. In the stone floor was a pool large enough for perhaps three or four people, though it was unoccupied just then. Thin tendrils of steam rose from the water. I looked at Truel and he answered my question before I could ask it.

"The pool is fed by a hot spring," he said. "It's very nice at this season and through the winter. At the height of summer, though, it can be quite stuffy in here."

He laid my clothing next to several towels on a small shelf mounted on the wall. On a small stand I saw shaving supplies.

"We thought you might wish to shave, so I brought some things you can use. Is there anything else you need?" Truel asked.

"I don't think so. My thanks to you, Truel."

"Then I have other tasks to attend to. Someone will be here to assist when you are finished. Enjoy your bath, *aduné*."

He was out the door before I could remind him to use my name. As I pulled off the robe and prepared to shave, I realized that he never had called me by name. I smiled slightly and shook my head. Then I picked up the razor, which had the keenest edge I had ever seen, and set to work scaping off over two moons worth of beard. When I was finished, I eased myself into the water. It was almost too hot, but I soon adjusted and could feel myself relaxing.

The clothes fit me perfectly, almost as if they had been made for me. For all I knew, they had been. The trousers were made of some tough fabric dyed a dark forest green and the tunic was dark brown. I pulled on my shoes–which someone had cleaned and polished–and then tied my sash around my waist. I paused as I realized that for the first time since Ambrose and I rode out of Badon to greet Marc, I felt almost normal. Then I thought of Peg and for a moment, I had to fight back tears. When I had myself under control, I stepped out of the bath house.

Élan was there, speaking with another Elven woman.

For some reason, the sight of her helped settle my emotions.

"Princess Élan," I greeted her. I nodded to the other woman.

In response, Élan laughed. Puzzled, I asked, "Why is that funny?"

"You insisted that Truel not use your titles and then the first thing you do is to throw mine at me."

My smile dropped from my face. I didn't know her well enough to read her tone, but I was afraid that I'd offended her. She must have sensed my dismay, because she stepped toward me, smiling.

"Lauren, this is my friend Abria." She turned to the other woman. "*Abria, myl eni Lauren. Sam eni Endollin.*"

Abria's eyes grew wide.

"*Se en manana, aduné,*" she said to me, a slight tremor in her voice. Then she turned to Élan and said, "*Sam eni kalyn.*"

They both laughed quick, mischievous laughs, then Abria bowed to the two of us and left.

"What did you say to her," I asked. "And what did she say back?"

In response, she simply said, "Lauren, would you break your fast with me and my family?"

"I'd like that," I answered.

She led me back toward the main house. Like the bath house, it was built of the native gray stone. The door we entered was also carved with the same loops and whirls as the other doors. It opened into a massive kitchen, where copper pots and pans hung from hooks on the ceiling beams. Two women–one of them was Abria–and one man were baking bread and frying bacon, sausage, and eggs, their movements quick and efficient. They barely looked up as Élan and I passed through and out another door–this one quite plain–into a dining room.

The room was dominated by a table long enough to seat 10 or so people. It, like the walls and floor, was made of the same oak that I'd seen elsewhere in the house. Shelves were built into the upper part of the walls to my left; they contained fine porcelain china decorated with a pale pink floral pattern. Paintings hung on the walls in between the alcoves. The same artist had clearly painted them all and that someone plainly loved the mountains. All the paintings were landscapes that showcased the mountains in all seasons.

"The paintings are beautiful," I said.

Élan smiled.

"My mother painted them," she said. "She also designed the pattern on the dishes."

"She's very apt at creating beauty," I replied.

Élan turned a questioning look on me, a faint smile on her lips. It took a heartbeat, but then I realized what I'd said. I could feel myself blushing and I struggled to find something to say.

Just then, the male cook entered the room. After a brief conversation with Élan in the Elven tongue, he began to set four places at the table.

I decided to change the subject and hope that Élan would forget what I'd said.

"This seems very personal and homey for a King's palace," I observed.

"This isn't a King's palace," Élan replied. "This is my family's home. Remember, Kings do not rule forever. Each of the ruling families has their own home. The palace, such as it is, is down in the valley in the city proper."

At that moment, Alain entered accompanied by a woman who must have been his wife, Élan's mother. She was tall for a woman, of a height with Alain, with long hair that flowed in a silver cascade down her back. Her eyes were gray with just a hint of green that was accented by the deep green robe she wore. Though it was clear that Alain was Élan's father, it was equally clear that Élan's beauty was inherited from this woman.

"Lauren, Élan, *nul sym en elested tul seli navoram*," Alain said. "Our day is brightened by your presence."

"As mine is brightened by yours," I replied, hoping that it was an appropriate response.

Élan's parents smiled and Élan herself nodded approvingly. I felt myself relax a bit.

"Lauren, this is Réalta, my wife and Élan's mother."

I bowed.

"It is a pleasure to meet you, Lady Réalta."

"Please, Réalta will suffice. You are among friends here, not royalty."

The cooks entered, set trays of food on the table, and then returned to the kitchen.

"Ordinarily, our entire household would join us," Alain said. "I have asked for privacy this morning, though, so that we can talk. Please, join us at table Lauren."

Alain took the seat at the head of the table. I took the seat to his left and Réalta and Élan sat next to each other across from me. The others began to serve themselves, so I joined in. The bread was warm and was served with butter and honey. The eggs looked a little different than I was used to; when I took my first bite, I was surprised at how good they tasted.

"The cook adds salt, pepper, and paprika to the hot butter before adding the eggs," Alain said when I remarked on the taste. Then his expression grew serious. "Yesterday you said that others had named you *Endollin*. We were not aware that any of the Alomar were familiar with that word."

"It wasn't a human who called me that."

They were all suddenly looking at me with intense interest.

"Not a human? One of the *Eldar*?"

"No. The first time was when I had nearly completed fourteen rounds. My father was taking me to Amersford for the *magenahr*. We came across a shrine to one of the Old Ones. I heard a voice in my head that said, "*Vorath, Endollin.*""

"That is a phrase in the language of Making," Alain said. "It means 'Welcome, *Endollin.*' Were there other times?"

"As I was falling asleep that night, I heard the same voice saying the same thing again. Much later, as I was entering Songhaven for the first time, I heard a voice say, '*endollin.*' The last time was when I was fleeing Badon after my escape. I had a dream about *Aenn*, and she also said, '*Vorath, Endollin.*'"

Alain looked thoughtful. Élan exchanged glances with Réalta, who spoke up.

"The Old Ones have been silent since before the Great War," she told me. "For many rounds of the seasons they had offered wisdom and advice to us. Then, as tensions with humans rose and we needed their guidance most of all, they fell silent."

"But Grandfather foresaw that, didn't he?" Élan asked. "He wrote that the Old Ones would wake when the *Endollin* appeared."

"That is true," Alain responded. "He could not tell me why they had withdrawn, but he told me to watch for their return when he bade me lead the people away from *Elsgard*."

My right hand was resting on the table, the ring glittering on my ring finger. It marked me as the Lawbreaker, the *Endollin*. I had finally achieved the life I wanted, I had mentors and friends I loved and who valued me, I'd earned the Blue, I had a woman who loved me, and in less than half a round it was all gone. I tried not to make a sound, but a tear slid down my cheek.

"Lauren," Réalta said. "Your grief runs deep. Élan has told me what you've endured. Perhaps we should continue this conversation at another time."

I wiped away the tears and nodded.

"My thanks to you. It is still difficult for me to believe that I am the Lawbreaker, the *Endollin*. I don't want to believe that I am evil, that I will destroy the world."

Alain frowned and said, "The *Endollin* is not necessarily evil. No one is born evil. No one is born good. It is our choices that define us, not our birth."

In my mind, I could see Valeria on the veranda of her house, saying almost those same words to me. A slight smile quirked my lips and Alain looked at me quizzically.

"A very wise woman said that to me not so long ago," I told him. "My thanks to you for the reminder."

He simply nodded and we returned to our food. For a few moments, no one spoke, but then Élan asked, "Lauren, after we eat, would you like to see the city? I'd be happy to show it to you."

"I'd like that," I said.

When we'd finished, she led me through the front room of the house out onto the terrace.

Truel had been right; the fog had burned off and the city was spread out below us.

Evendim had been built in a valley shaped like a bowl, ringed all around by mountains. It was clear from the sun's position that we were south of the city facing north. Below us and on the other mountains nearby, I could make out other houses partially visible through the trees. The valley below was bisected by a river running from west to east. On the far side of the valley, the mountain slopes had been terraced.

Élan must have seen the direction of my gaze.

"The south slopes of the mountains get the most sun," she said. "We terraced them and use them to grow crops. The river is called *Kivin*. That's 'rocky' in your tongue. There are three bridges across the river. The one in the center was built first. It's called *Alten Rhyd*–Old Crossing. The other two are known as Westbridge and Eastbridge."

I nodded.

"Most of the shops and…" she paused, as if struggling for a word. "Shops and *tybith* are between Westbridge and *Alten Rhyd*."

"*Tybith*?" I asked.

"I do not know your word for it," she said. "*Tybith* are places like inns, but they serve food only. No one ever travels here from elsewhere, so we do not need places for outside visitors to sleep."

"I'm not aware of places like that in the Federation. I've only ever seen inns selling food, drink, and a place to sleep."

She nodded and turned back toward the city.

"So, most shops and *tybith* are in Westbridge. There are homes there, as well. Some people prefer living near the water to living on a mountain. Eastbridge is where things are made or stored. There are mills and blacksmiths' shops along with warehouses and grain bins. Few people live in Eastbridge."

"Most people," she continued, "choose to live on the north slopes of the mountains on this side of the river."

"There don't seem to be that many houses, though," I said.

"There are more than there appear to be. Most are built partially into the mountainside or are located well underneath the forest canopy. When we first came here, we were afraid. We felt hunted and we wished to remain hidden. So, we tried to blend the city into its surroundings as much as possible. Eventually, that just became how we do things."

I could see that. There were very few places that I could see that were bare of trees. The city looked almost as if it had grown rather than been built.

"Shall we go down?"

I nodded and she led the way to a staircase that joined a–street really isn't the right word–but I have no better word. Nothing in *Evendim* resembled the straight, paved streets I had known in Amersford and Badon. The streets of *Evendim* were paved, but they twisted this way and that to avoid ancient trees or outcroppings of stone. The buildings were almost universally constructed of stone and were situated to preserve as much green space as possible. Many of them had small trees, bushes, and meadow grasses growing on their roofs. All of them had intricately carved entrance doors.

"It's an ancient custom," Élan explained when I asked. "We brought it with us from wherever we were before we came to these lands. The loops and whirls on the door and the door frame are meant to confuse evil spirits and prevent them from entering."

"These lands? You mean here, *Evendim*?"

"No. The oldest among us tell of arriving in *Ervenschal*, what you call Landfall, in great ships. But that is a long tale, best saved for another time."

"Élan, when you say, 'we came here'..." I started.

Her mouth was frowning, but I could see a trace of laughter in her eyes. I noticed in that moment that they were the same gray with a hint of green as her mother's eyes.

"Are you trying to ask me how old I am?"

I couldn't answer. That's exactly what I was trying to do.

"Are you afraid that I'm old enough to be your mother? Or your grandmother?"

"Élan, I..."

She cut me off.

"Not that it matters," she said sternly, but I thought I could hear a hint of teasing in her tone, "but I'm no older than you. We age like humans until we reach adulthood. Then we just stop."

I still couldn't find words and my face felt flushed. Élan stood glowering at me for a moment more, then burst out laughing.

"I can't keep this up," she said. "You look like a sad little puppy. I'm not really angry, Lauren." She paused and then said, very quietly, "I'm glad that you're interested in me."

We spent hours exploring Westbridge. It was a maze of shops, *tybith*, and homes. I slowly became aware that there was something about the place, some quality that began right on the edge of my awareness. Once I noticed it, however, I saw it in everything: the buildings, the streets, even simple fences or trellises. Everything seemed more real, more present, more right, than had constructed things I'd known before. The Elven people I met all had hair of silver or gold and their eyes were gray, usually with hints of blue or green. Like the place itself, the people we saw were somehow more real, more present, than people I'd known before.

We ate the midday meal in a small *tybith* run by a distant cousin of Élan's. Then she surprised me. She led me down toward the river to one of the few wooden buildings I'd seen in *Evendim*. The exterior was made of wide, unfinished boards that had weathered to an attractive silver-gray color. We entered and I couldn't suppress a small gasp of surprise. It was a luthier's shop.

Large wooden posts supported equally large wooden beams at ceiling height–there was no ceiling, and I could make out massive wooden rafters in the dim light under the roof–and finished guitars hung from the beams. The walls to either side were lined with workbenches, and each held a guitar, all in various stages of completion. The back wall of the shop had a single door that opened out toward the river but was otherwise occupied by racks of the various woods used in the construction of guitars. The smell of fresh-cut wood hung in the air.

The luthier looked up as we entered. He was tall and thin, with a long thin nose and close-set gray-green eyes. His golden hair was cut close to his head. He smiled when he saw Élan.

"*Elnyr* Élan," he said, his baritone voice warm and full of overtones. Then he noticed me and switched tongues. "I had heard that a band of hunters had found a human minstrel. That would be you, I take it?"

"It would," I replied, returning his smile. "I am Lauren, Minstrel of Alomar."

"And I am Gotyr, Master Crafter. I don't believe that I have ever seen a minstrel without his instrument before."

"Mine is up at Alain's home. I was uncertain what the custom was here."

"We treasure minstrels every bit as much as the Alomar," Élan said. "They are welcome anywhere."

"Would you play for me, *aduné*," Gotyr asked. "Any of the hanging instruments will do."

I began to reach for a guitar but paused before I'd even lifted my arm. I wasn't sure that I would be able to play. Garth had silenced the minstrels. I had been able to sing *The Parting Song* for Rachel, but I hadn't tried to play since then. I searched my memory and songs–lyrics and melodies–came easily to mind. I had felt at the time that I had broken whatever barrier Garth had set in place. Then I remembered what Valeria had said when I left Cammford; she felt that I had somehow driven out whatever evil had been visited upon the place. Had I done the same thing with Garth's punishment of the minstrels?

I reached up to take down the nearest instrument, which had a beautiful floral inlay running the length of the fretboard. As I reached, Gotyr caught sight of the ring, and I saw his eyes go wide.

"*Endollin*," he said, his voice tinged with awe. "You honor my shop."

I carefully lifted the guitar down, then turned my gaze to its maker.

"Gotyr," I said. "I do not know what it means to be the *Endollin*. But I am a minstrel, and this is as fine an instrument as I have ever seen."

I took a step and sat on a nearby stool. I lifted the guitar to my lap and tried a few chords. The guitar was in tune with a sweet, balanced tone.

"This is a beautiful instrument. Your skill as a crafter is unequalled."

"It is yours, *Endollin*."

A small spark of anger kindled in my chest. I stood, holding the guitar in my right hand.

"That's not what I meant," I said firmly. "I did not come here to make off with one of your instruments for free. I said that I do not know what it means to be the *Endollin*, but I do know that it doesn't mean taking advantage of people. I wish to be treated the same as you would treat any other guest in your shop. If you can't manage that, I will take my leave."

He looked at me with a mix of awe and confusion, and then turned to Élan, who simply gave a quick nod of agreement. Gotyr visibly tried to relax and gave me a timid half smile.

I sat down again. I strummed a few chords, wondering what to play, and then decided on *The Cylin Witch*, a traditional ballad that tells the story of a Canim soldier who, after receiving a wound that would not heal, follows a series of mystical signs to an unnamed Highlands lake where he is healed by the eponymous Cylin Witch. Halfway through, Gotyr took down another guitar and joined in. When we finished, he smiled at me, a genuine smile this time.

"I've not heard that tune in a very long time," he said. "Could we do it again?"

In reply, I began playing again and Gotyr joined in, but before I completed the first line of the lyrics, he joined in vocally with an eerie contrapuntal melody that told the same story from the Witch's point of view.

"I've never heard that countermelody," I said in amazement when we finished. "I've never even seen a hint that it existed."

"That's a very old song," Gotyr said. "It was old when the Minstrel's College was established at *Calyth*. It doesn't surprise me that parts of it have been forgotten."

"Are you saying that the *Witch* is not an Alomar song?" I asked.

"It's not," he confirmed. "It was sung by the *Eldar* in Canim long before the Alomar came over the mountains."

He rose from where he was sitting.

"It's a beautiful day. Shall we sit outside and play?"

I turned to Élan.

"Do we have time?"

"I'd love to hear more," she said.

Gotyr led us past the racks of wood to a large deck overlooking the river. We took seats and he and I began playing. Soon we were joined by others, drawn by the music. Some sang with us, others just listened. We played until the sun was touching the mountaintops to the west.

As we took our leave, Gotyr said, "*Ol sym masen elested tul seli navoram.* My day was brightened by your presence. Please, come back anytime."

"Gotyr, my thanks to you for your hospitality," Élan said.

I nodded my agreement and added, "I hope to see you again soon."

The household was just sitting down for the evening meal when we arrived back at Alain's house. The entire household, along with me and Ryan, were present, so the places at the table were all full. The food was excellent and there were multiple conversations going on at any one point, most of them in the Elven language. I found it a bit overwhelming. After dinner, Ryan and I joined Alain's family on the terrace.

We sat in companionable silence for a while, watching as the stars came out. The waning quarter moon hung low over the western mountains, providing only a little light. Élan, Réalta, and Alain chatted idly about the events of the day. The moon had dropped below the mountains when one of the cooks brought steaming mugs of tea out to us. The conversation stilled as we gratefully sipped the sweet, warm tea; the night was growing chilly. After a time, Réalta broke the silence.

"Lauren, you were very quiet at dinner, and you've been quiet now, but you seem much less troubled than you did this morning."

"I am, my thanks to you for your concern," I answered. I paused a moment and then continued. "It is strange to me. I am in a place that I never imagined existed amongst people I do not know, and yet today was the first time in a very long time that I have truly felt like myself."

"You were a minstrel today," Ryan observed.

"Word of your visit to Gotyr's shop reached me at court," Alain added. "Those who heard you and Gotyr were quite effusive in their praise. My courtiers were all begging leave to attend."

A pleased little smile slipped out at that; I hoped that it was dark enough that the others couldn't see.

"I am a minstrel," I said, quietly, but with great conviction.

"Remember that, Lauren," Ryan said. "Whatever happens in the future, always remember that."

I was alone on the top of a high tower of a ruined mountain city. I'd been there before. I knew now that it was *Evendim*, the trees uprooted, and the buildings thrown down, the light of the city extinguished. I was aware that I was dreaming, that I'd had this dream before, but I was also in the dream and living it. I raised my eyes to the east, where mountains stood, peak after peak, to a distant plain. Dark clouds massed there, towering over the mountains. I could feel the dark, malevolent intelligence searching for me, reaching for me. A dark wind arose, and tendrils of cloud began streaming toward me, one to the north and one to the south. The part of me that was not the dreamer knew what was coming next.

A wasp skidded in from the wind and managed to gain a hold on the merlon in front of me. Fear enveloped me and I shrank back from the wall. I found myself face down on the stone floor, held there by a being that was at once the wasp, poised to sting, and the black-cloaked figure from Songhaven, its booted foot on my neck.

A hoarse, whispering voice threatened to kill me, threatened to inject poison at the base of my skull.

I struggled to move...

...and woke, sweat-soaked and frightened, in the darkest depths of the night.

Once the beating of my heart had slowed to normal, I tried to get back to sleep, but the dream had hold of my thoughts. The malevolence had reached out for me, and Ambrose had gone down into the darkness. And the people of Cammlin. Many from Cammford as well. The minstrels of Songhaven.

And Peg.

Now I was in *Evendim* amongst the Elves. I'd been taught that they were evil, but I no longer saw them that way. I couldn't. They lived lives not so different from the lives of the Alomar. And now I was with them. Whether I believed it or not, the malevolence, the darkness, whatever it was that was searching for me, that thing believed that I was the Lawbreaker. I had no doubt that what it had done to Ambrose and to Peg, it would do to Ryan, Alain, and Réalta. And Élan.

I couldn't allow that. Not if I could stop it.

I spent the rest of the night listening to the breeze sighing through the trees outside the house and struggling to hold the fragile threads of my determination together in the face of my fear and uncertainty.

CHAPTER SIX

When the stars began to fade from the sky, I rose and dressed. The eastern mountain peaks were painted in dark indigo against a glowing background of pale pink and orange. Ryan and Alain were on the terrace, seated in chairs facing east, conversing quietly while sipping mugs of tea. As I approached, Élan stepped out of the house wrapped in a white robe, her feet bare and her hair disheveled. She noticed me before the others did.

"Lauren, *ol sym en elested tul seli navoram*," she said.

I'd been rehearsing that greeting in private but wasn't ready to attempt it before Ryan and the King.

"And your presence brightens my day, Élan," I replied.

Her pleased smile brought a smile to my own face.

"I was just going to bathe," she told me.

"And I need to speak with your father and Ryan."

She frowned at the seriousness in my tone.

"Lauren, please sit," the King invited. "Tell us what is on your mind."

I joined them. Élan made no move to leave.

"Your Majesty, Master Ryan," I said, looking at each in turn. "I dreamed last night. It's a dream that I've had before. I've told you about the dark power I sense searching for me. In the dream, I'm in a ruined city that I now recognize as *Evendim*. Last night, that power took the shape of a black-cloaked figure like the one I saw at Songhaven. It found me and threatened to kill me."

Neither Ryan nor Alain said anything, but their looks were grim.

"You know that I've struggled to accept that I am the Lawbreaker, the *Endollin*. The dream made me realize that whether I accept it or not doesn't matter. The thing that is seeking me believes that I am the Lawbreaker, and it has killed people to get to me. Some of them were people I loved."

I looked at Élan, standing there in her thin white robe, barefoot, her bare legs below the hem goosebumped in the chill morning air. Something warm stirred in my chest. I couldn't let her be harmed.

"Lorrestian made the ring I bear," I continued. "I do not know if it was meant to do anything other than mark me as the Lawbreaker, but I do know that he made a sword as well. I believe that it will help me stand against the darkness. Will you help me find it?"

Ryan and Alain glanced at each other and then back at me.

"You are the *Endollin*," the King said. "We are fated to follow you whether it be to ruin or to salvation. Whatever you desire, you have but to ask."

That commitment frightened me more than my nightmare had. The King's expression was calm and accepting, as if he had known this was coming and had long resigned himself to the fact. Ryan was frowning slightly. I glanced past them to Élan. She'd wrapped her arms around herself and was shivering but not, I thought, from the cold. The expression on her face told me the truth: she was frightened.

I had to deal with the situation now. I slipped out of my chair and knelt on one knee before the King.

"Your Majesty, you say that you will do whatever I ask?"

"Whatever you command, it shall be done."

"Then let us begin with this."

Ryan was leaning forward, staring at me intently. Élan appeared to be holding her breath.

"If I am indeed the *Endollin*, blind obedience is of no use to me," I said. "That will surely lead us all to ruin. Whatever else I might be, I am only human. As a minstrel, I understand that my knowledge is incomplete and that I may make poor decisions. I need people around me who will help me, who will advise me, people who will tell me when I'm wrong. I don't need people who will simply follow me into foolishness. So, if I am to command you, let this be my first irreversible command to you: Always be the King of th e *Eldar*. Always put your people first. Protect them. Keep them safe."

My gaze flicked to Élan, then back to the King, whose expression was still impassive. For several heartbeats, no one moved. No one spoke. Then Ryan leaned back in his chair, smiling. The King gestured for me to stand as he himself rose. He put his right hand on my shoulder and locked his gaze onto mine. His eyes were sea gray, with just a hint of yellow around the irises.

"I have spent a thousand rounds resigned to the idea that when you came, my people would ride to ruin," he said. "You have just handed me the seed of hope."

He dropped his hand and stepped back.

"Let us decide our next steps as we break our fast," he said. "The morning meal should be ready."

He turned to go, but before I could move, Élan flung her arms around me.

"*Ol gratyl selyn*," she said. "My deepest thanks to you."

Hesitantly, I put my arms around her. A mix of emotions rushed through me: pleasure, uncertainty, guilt. I felt as if I was cheating on Peg. But Élan didn't let go and neither did I. Not until Alain cleared his throat and dryly said, "Daughter, I believe you were going to bathe."

Élan let go and stepped back.

"I was," she said. "I am. I'm going now. I'll join you shortly."

She turned and hurried around the end of the house toward the bath house. I followed Alain and Ryan into the house to the dining room.

Most of the household was at table already. As it had been the night before, there were multiple conversations going on concurrently, with people raising their voices to be heard over other conversations and the clinking of dishes and silverware. The volume dropped notably when Alain entered, but I still found it overwhelming since I couldn't understand any of what was being said.

Alain took his place at the head of the table with Ryan and me on either side. The stable master came to quietly confer with Alain about an ailing mare. Only after they finished did we turn our attention to the food. It seemed that we were somewhat late to the table; as we served ourselves, the other members of the household finished their meals and left to take up their tasks for the day. As the last of them left the room, Élan, dressed now in undyed linen trousers and a deep blue tunic, entered and joined us.

"Mother said to tell you that she ate earlier," she said to Alain. "She's bathing now."

The King nodded in response and then turned to me.

"So, you intend to seek the sword. Where do you plan to begin?"

"I was hoping that you could tell me that. All I know comes from the human translation of *The Book of Kings* and from Ambrose. The book said nothing about where the sword is, and Ambrose claimed not to know."

I paused, remembering my rounds of study with the prophet.

"Of course," I added, "he also never told me that he possessed the ring."

"I am afraid that we do not know where the sword is either," Alain said. "Our scholars have had a thousand rounds to study *The Book of Kings,* and they have been unable to locate either the ring or the sword."

"Lorrestian was your father, Alain," Ryan said. "Did he say nothing to you about the Lawbreaker?"

"Not much," the king replied. "I was in the north, trying to tamp down tensions with the Alomar. From what others have told me, the visions came on him suddenly. He worked like a madman to craft the ring and the sword and then disappeared for nearly half a moon. Then the College of Wizards burned, and we were blamed. The Alomar kingdoms united behind Sorren, and they threw everything they had at us. I fought with the army, trying to slow the Alomar advance, but Sorren was a tactical genius. We were stronger and better equipped, but he beat us every time we stood against him. By the time I saw my father again, *Elsgard* itself was threatened, and he begged me to lead as many of our people as I could into the mountains."

Alain fell silent, his expression haunted, then said softly, "I never saw him again."

"All I know is what we all know, what was recorded in *The Book of Kings,*" Alain continued after a lengthy pause. "He made a ring and sword and hid them away."

"But the account in *The Book of Kings* isn't truly accurate," Élan said.

"What do you mean?" Ryan asked, surprise on his face.

"The book says that Lorrestian hid the ring, but he didn't exactly hide it. He gave it to a minstrel, with–according to Lauren's story–specific instructions to keep it secret and to pass it on only to another minstrel. To me, that says that he knew that the *Endollin* would be a minstrel."

Ryan and Alain glanced at one another and then nodded their agreement.

"Go on," Ryan said.

"That suggests that he saw more than he allowed to be recorded. He put the ring where he knew it would be found. If that's true, perhaps he did the same thing with the sword. Either there is someone out there holding the sword as Ambrose held the ring or the sword is indeed hidden, but there should be clues to its location somewhere, perhaps in Lorrestian's personal writings."

Alain was smiling. Ryan, who was also smiling, leaned back in his chair.

"Well, Lauren," he said. "It looks like your search starts in the library here in *Evendim.*"

"I don't believe that would be worthwhile, Rhion," Élan said.

"Why not?" Ryan asked.

"As father noted, our scholars have had a thousand rounds to study the materials in the library here. There is not a single word there that hasn't been studied, analyzed, and interpreted over and over. If the answer was there, it would have been found long ago."

"Daughter, what are you suggesting?"

"The answer isn't here. If it is anywhere, it's in the ruins of *Elsgard*. We need to go there."

"We?" Alain asked.

"It was my idea."

"And who else would be part of this 'we?'" Alain asked archly.

Élan paused for a moment, considering the question.

"Lauren would have to be," she said. "And Rhion, if he's willing."

Ryan nodded his assent.

"I don't think we three should go alone," Élan continued. "It is possible that there could be scavengers or squatters in the city. I think it would be prudent to take a squad of *Cadwynir*."

"The *Cadwynir* are the *Eldarin* Rangers," Ryan explained to me. Then he turned back to the others. "We'd need to leave soon. The round is waning, and winter will be here soon. Perhaps the day after the Autumn Day of Passages? That would give us a little over a week to prepare."

"I would suggest that you not stay in *Elsgard* too long," Alain said. "Perhaps half a moon? You can collect whatever you find and bring it back here for study. You should take extra mounts to carry whatever materials you find."

The King leaned back in his chair, rested his elbows on the arms and steepled his fingers.

"As much as I mislike sending my daughter and the *Endollin* out with winter bearing down on us, this plan makes too much sense not to pursue it. You three go and begin preparing. I will arrange for the *Cadwynir*. I wish to select the members of the team myself."

"My thanks to you all," I said. "I cannot do this alone."

As we rose from the table, Ryan said, "I do believe that we three should spend a good part of the next week in the library. It would help to refresh our knowledge of what's there and Élan and I can begin to teach Lauren to speak and read the *Eldarin* tongue."

Alain left us to go and recruit *Cadwynir* for the trip. Ryan, Élan, and I walked down into the Westbridge section of the city. The library was a huge building, constructed of native granite. The walls stood perhaps five times the height of a man. The roof was flat, and Élan told me that there was a garden up there, though all that was visible from the ground was the tops of some of the taller trees. The entrance faced the river; the ground before the building was terraced with wide flat steps, paved with the same granite used for the building, from the riverbank up to the front of the building. The massive, arched doors were made of oak. The carved loops and whirls were left in their native golden oak color, but the recesses behind the pattern were painted a deep forest green. The hinges and other door hardware were plated in gold. Despite their size, the doors opened easily and noiselessly when Ryan took hold of the ring-shaped door pulls.

The vast interior of the building was filled with row upon row of shelves, interrupted here and there by small clusters of tables. High up near the top of the stone walls were multitudes of arched windows which let in a great deal of sunlight. The atmosphere was hushed, but I could just make out the sounds of several quiet conversations in the distance.

A small man—the top of his head came only to my shoulder—stepped up as we entered. He was terribly thin, and the skeletal look of his face was emphasized by the fact that his golden hair was very tightly tied back. He spared me only a glance before he said.

"*Elnyr* Élan, *Elmaen* Rhion," he said in a high-pitched voice that sounded vaguely feminine to me. "*Orron tel se arrint sel?*"

"Master Leonyr," Élan answered, "this is Lauren, Minstrel of Alomar and the *Endollin*. Lauren, this is Master Librarian Leonyr."

The Master Librarian's deep-set gray eyes widened, enhancing the skull-like appearance.

"It is an honor to meet you Master Librarian," I said.

"*Se en manana tul seli navoram, Endollin,*" he answered. "I am honored by your presence. How may I assist you?"

"We need to do some research," Élan said. "I think we should begin with *The Book of Kings.*"

"Of course," Leonyr responded. "The original or will a copy suffice?"

"That depends on the copy."

"I was thinking the Arris."

"That should be fine. Current thinking is that he made fewer transcription errors than most."

"If you will accompany me, I will take you to it."

Élan turned to me and Ryan.

"I'll meet you at one of those tables," she said, pointing at a nearby group that was unoccupied. Then she turned and followed Leonyr into the stacks.

Ryan and I crossed to the tables and sat down at one.

"Master Ryan, may I ask you something?"

"Always, Lauren. But I'm no longer your Master."

"You will always be my Master."

He shook his head, smiling.

"Go ahead."

"I've noticed that the Elves here all have silver or golden hair, but you have dark hair."

He waited for a moment, then noted, "That's a statement, not a question. But you want to know why I'm different. I'm only half Elven. My mother was human. She lived in Songhaven with her first husband. He left to serve in the High King's army and was killed during a skirmish with the Kelmar. My mother was so distraught that she fled the city. She never said so, but I believe that she intended to die in the mountains. She was found by an *Eldarin* scouting party. The leader of that party was taken with her beauty and brought her here. In time they fell in love."

"So," I said. "Those trips you would never talk about were to come here? You were visiting your parents?"

"Mostly, yes. But did you ever wonder where our guitar strings come from? The Alomar smiths have not yet worked out how to make thin wire from steel. The strings are made here by the *Eldar*. As a rule, the minstrels have been more open-minded than most of the Alomar. So, even though the *Eldar* have been in hiding since the Great War, we have always maintained secret contact with whoever held the position of Master Crafter at Songhaven. We trade strings for information. So, in addition to visiting my parents, I was also carrying information to the *Eldar* and bringing strings to the college."

At that moment, Élan returned, carrying a large scroll.

"This is a copy of the original book," she explained as she sat. "The original was begun onboard the ships before we came to these lands. No one knows for sure how old it is. When it was realized that time and use were taking their toll on it, scholars set themselves to make copies. There are places in the original where the ink has faded badly and others where the scribe was less than meticulous about the clarity of the lettering. It was soon discovered that there were sometimes substantial differences in the copies. It is generally considered that Arris was most true to the original."

She unrolled the scroll and began to read.

"Throughout the Alomar kingdoms," she read, "The *Eldar* were reviled and accused of heinous crimes they did not commit. Many departed those lands rather than suffer at the hands of people they had considered to be friends. And so it came to pass, one hundred and twenty-one rounds into his reign, that King Lorrestian sent his own son, the Prince Alain, north to treat with the Alomar and to try to restore the bonds of friendship that had once existed. It was at that time that Lorrestian began to have visions. In his visions, he saw war, the rise of puissant beings who named themselves the Keepers of the Alomar, beings who intended death for the People of the Stars.

"The King also saw a hope for his People. Far in the future would come a man of great power, a power great enough to shake the very foundations of the world. He would be the *endollin*, for all natural law would be his, to bend to his will. This man would see the *Eldar* returned from exile, and the coming of war to the lands of the Alomar. The *endollin* would end that war, but the King could not see whether that end would be the restoration of peace or the utter destruction of the world.

"Guided by his visions, Lorrestian forged tokens of the *endollin's* power: a ring for the man of peace and a sword for the man of war. The ring was of gold, worked in a wonderous design, and set with a stone of violet hue. The sword bore a pommel stone of the same violet stone. Both jewels were dark and unreflecting of light. They would wake, the King said, when the *endollin* possessed them. Then, before the fires of war swept the Lellarin Plains, the tokens were hidden, to be found by the *endollin* in his need.

"At the end, only I stood by the King's side. Lorrestian stood before his ruined throne. Arrayed against him stood the seven servants of Mar, the Keepers of the Alomar. Cloaked and hooded in black, the Destroyer stood at their head. The King bade me leave, but I would not leave him to face his fate alone. I retreated out of sight and then paused to observe.

"The King spoke, his voice yet defiant. 'I know who you are Destroyer. I know who all of you are. You may have defeated me and my people, but one day you, too, shall fall. Know this: I have seen the coming of the *endollin*!'

"The figure in black flinched marginally. The others turned toward each other in apparent confusion.

"Lorrestian continued, 'Know this also, for these are the signs of his coming. Watch for them, for they are also the signs of your doom. The Old Ones shall rise and walk again in the hills and on the plains. The People of the Stars will return and come against you. Then fear, Destroyer, for he will then be walking the earth. He will bear the tokens I forged for him: the ring *Elinaur* and the sword *Endolsar*. You, Destroyer, and all those who stand with you, shall fall and your reign will be ended.'

"At that, the black figure raised its arm and clenched its fist. The King's face contorted in agony, and he crumbled to the floor.

"I fled then, seeking to join Prince Alain and the refugees in the mountains. Thus ends my record of the reign of King Lorrestian."

She felt silent, tears welling in her eyes. As remote as those events were to me, Lorrestian was her grandfather, a grandfather she never got to meet. I laid my hand over hers. She turned her tear-filled eyes on me and attempted a small smile.

"My thanks to you for reading that, Élan," Ryan said. "I know that it must be difficult. Lauren, you've now heard both versions. What do you think?"

"There are differences," I said. "Some of them are subtle changes in wording. Others were more substantial and involved additions or deletions of entire phrases. All of the changes to the Alomar version were designed to present the Keepers in the best light and vilify the *Eldar*."

"Agreed," Ryan responded. "There are things we don't understand about this version. For instance, it is not clear how many beings faced the King. It could have been the seven Keepers with the one known as the Destroyer at their head. Alternatively, it may have been eight: the Keepers and the figure in black."

"I noticed that description," I said. "It matches the description of the being that killed the High King and the one I saw at Songhaven."

Ryan nodded.

"Another issue concerns the names *Elinaur* and *Endolsar*," he continued. "Those sound *Eldarin*, but they're not. There is some speculation that they could be words in the True Speech. We have no record of the Old Ones ever using those words, though, so if they are in the language of Making, we do not know what they mean. Lauren, you're frowning. What is it?"

"Could we not ask the scribe?"

Ryan shook his head.

"No. He didn't make it out of *Elsgard*. Several times after the fall, parties of Elves returned in secret to *Elsgard* to search for survivors and to try and recover precious materials. One of those parties found *The Book of Kings* in the kitchen near a rear entrance to the palace."

The Master Librarian stepped out of the stacks, spotted us, and strode purposefully to our table.

"Did you find what you were seeking, Princess Élan?" he asked.

"We did, my thanks to you, Master Leonyr," she answered. "Could you tell me, though, whether any progress has been made on the meaning of *Elinaur* and *Endolsar*?"

He shook his head.

"There has been no progress. We have exhausted all the references we have concerning the True Speech and there has not been even a clue."

"Would you please join us, Master Librarian?" I asked.

His eyes widened again as he answered, "I would be honored, *Endollin*."

"I would prefer Lauren," I said as he pulled out a chair and sat.

"And I am Leonyr," he responded.

"Leonyr, I intend to seek the sword," I told him. "Is there any knowledge that you possess that would assist me?"

I wouldn't have thought that such a skull-like face could be so expressive, but Leonyr's face clearly conveyed every emotion the man was feeling. At my question, the small joy he felt at being asked to join us was replaced by a look of dismay.

"I am afraid not," he said. "I am sure that Élan and Rhion have told you that we have been studying that question for a thousand rounds and we've made little to no progress. If I may, how did you come by the ring?"

"King Lorrestian gave it to a minstrel," I answered, "with instructions to keep it secret and to pass it on only to another minstrel. The last to possess it was Ambrose, who passed it on to me."

"When I heard that," Élan explained to the librarian, "I realized that Lorrestian must have seen more than was recorded in *The Book of Kings*. He knew that the *Endollin* would be a minstrel, and he placed the ring where the *Endollin* would find it. He must have done something similar with the sword. We plan to go to *Elsgard* to search for any surviving personal records the King may have left behind that might give us a clue to the location of the sword. Leonyr, I think that having a librarian with us might help us identify important materials. Is there a librarian who would be willing to ride to *Elsgard*? We leave the day after the Autumn Day of Passages."

"As you know, I was also Master Librarian in *Elsgard,* so I believe that I could do a great deal to assist. If you will have me, I would be honored to ride with you."

Élan smiled.

"My thanks to you, Leonyr. Your presence will increase our chances of finding something useful."

Leonyr rose and said, "I must begin preparations. Is there anything more you require?"

"Yes," she answered. "We need to teach the *Endollin* to read the *Eldarin* tongue. Could you bring us some of the reading primers?"

The Master Librarian nodded and strode off to find the appropriate scrolls. A few moments later, he returned with the scrolls, and we set to work. The day passed quickly and by the time we returned to Alain's home for the evening meal, I had mastered enough of the *Eldarin* tongue to respond appropriately when Alain and Réalta greeted me.

I dreamed of Peg that night.

In my dream, we were lying on Songhaven's stage, surrounded by flames. I was close enough to her that all I could see were her head and the upper part of her body. Her eyes were closed, her face covered in sweat. She made a sound, a sort of hoarse, animal grunt, as if she was in pain but refused to cry out.

For days afterwards, in quiet times when I was alone, I could hear that sound echoing in my mind.

There was a quiet knock at my door.

"*Aduné*?" came Truel's voice. "It is time."

I quickly crossed to the door and opened it.

"I'm ready," I said. "My thanks to you, Truel."

I stepped out onto the terrace. Most of Alain's household was already gathered there. Ryan came around the end of the house, his hair still damp from the bath house. A moment later, Alain, Réalta, and Élan exited the house. Alain paused and took in the gathered household.

"Come," he said. "Let us ascend *Creagalt* to greet the sun on this Autumn Day of Passages."

As he turned to lead the way, Élan motioned for Ryan and me to join them. We quickened our pace to catch up. The walk to the summit of *Creagalt*, the mountain on which Alain's house was built, did not take long. *Creagalt* was the *Eldarin* term for "round top" and round top accurately described the summit of the mountain. There were no trees at the summit, just a broad open meadow that allowed an unobstructed view of the sky in all directions. I'd come up here one night with Élan and Ryan to begin learning the *Eldarin* names for the stars. All the families with homes on the mountain were there, several hundred people in all, waiting for the sunrise.

Alain took up a place in the center of the meadow, facing east. Réalta, and Élan stood to his right. Ryan had been asked to lead the chant; he stood to the King's left. As the sky brightened, people began to move to the western side of the meadow behind the King. I moved to join them, but Élan signed for me to join her and asked the person next to her to step to the side to make room for me. As the edge of the rising sun cleared the horizon, Ryan began the chant:

> We open our hearts this day
> To give thanks to the Old Ones.

At the same time, Élan and the person to my right took my hands. All over the meadow, people were joining hands. As one, we answered Ryan's call:

> We give thanks for the earth and all upon it.

Ryan continued:

> We give thanks to *Aenn*
> Who feeds us in her love.
> Thanks to she who makes the land fruitful.

We responded:

> Thanks and praise to *Aenn*.

I felt my awareness expanding. My feet became roots stretching down into the depths of the earth. At the same time, I was a leaf, letting go of the tree that had been my life to drift to the earth below and I was a hawk, folding my wings to dive on an unsuspecting mouse. I was the swirling wind itself, holding the hawk aloft. I felt a part of everything around me. I heard gasps from those around me, felt Élan's hand tighten on mine, and I knew that they were feeling it, too.

Then the chant was done, and I was myself again. The man on my right let go of my hand, but Élan clung tight and turned to me, her face alight with wonder.

"I..." she started and paused, searching for words. "I was the whole world. I..."

Her eyes searched my face.

"Lauren, did you do that?"

I could hear exclamations of wonder and hushed conversations all around us. Alain, Réalta, and Ryan stepped up to join Élan and me. Élan let go of my hand then.

"I think that perhaps it was Lauren," Ryan said quietly. "I've only ever experienced that once before, the first time we ever celebrated a Day of Passage together. I've never forgotten it."

"I didn't consciously do anything," I said, shaking my head.

"We should discuss this further later," Alain said. "I must be King now."

He turned away from us to the crowd of people.

"My people," he said, pitching his voice to carry. "We are grateful indeed for the lives we have been given. Let us go down now and celebrate."

Alain took Réalta's hand and started for the path back down. I took a step to follow, but Élan grabbed my hand.

"Lauren, wait," she said. "You, too, Rhion."

Ryan nodded and said, "I was wondering when we'd do this."

Some small part of me wondered idly what it was we were about to do but that part of me said nothing. I was focused on the fact that Élan and I were holding hands again. Hers felt so warm in mine and some ache I wasn't even aware that I was feeling seemed eased by the contact. I felt a pang of disappointment when she let go, followed almost immediately by a thought of Peg and a flaring of guilt. My cheeks felt like they were flushed.

Once most of the people had left the meadow, Élan said, "Follow me."

She set off for the north side of the meadow. At the edge of the grass stood an outcropping of gneiss, the top of which had been carved into the form of a falcon in flight. The sculptor had used quartz crystals for the eyes and those caught the early morning light making the sculpture seem aware of us. It was a lesser one of the Old Ones, one I did not recognize.

Élan knelt and brushed some fallen leaves and debris out of a cleared area in front of the formation. The ground there seemed to be covered in ash. Élan took out a small pouch and dumped a small pile of red cedar shavings onto the cleared ground.

"Lauren, this is *Tyth*," she explained. "Journeys are his domain, and he watches over travelers. We give thanks for his protection with an offering of aromatic wood."

She used a small flint to strike a spark, and we watched in reverent silence as the smoke from the cedar shavings drifted skyward. When the pile was completely consumed, Élan stood.

"May *Tyth* smile on our journey," she said. "Now, let's go celebrate."

The *Eldar* celebrated the turn of the seasons by throwing open their homes and visiting as many other homes as they could. Each family arranged for someone to be home throughout the day to welcome guests, but everyone else went from house to house, renewing old friendships and becoming acquainted with new people. Because the weather was unseasonably warm, much of the celebrating spilled out of doors and by the time we reached Alain's home, the terrace was already full of people standing in small groups talking and sampling treats that had been prepared by Alain's cooks.

Sooner or later, music was going to be called for, so Ryan and I went to our rooms to fetch our guitars. By the time I returned, the terrace was even more crowded, and I didn't see anyone I knew. I began making my way through the crowd, trying to keep my guitar from being damaged. I spotted Élan some distance away. She was standing with a tall, golden-haired male Elf, who had his arm around her. She was laughing and smiling. I just stopped where I was and stared, not sure what I was feeling, until an *Eldarin* couple–they introduced themselves as friends of Alain and Réalta–stopped to ask me how I had found my way to *Evendim*.

The rest of the day was like that. I was swept along by currents in the crowds, barely proficient enough in the language to answer the questions put to me by people curious about the *Endollin*. At one point, I wandered into a garden where a group of *Eldarin* musicians were playing lively dance music; across the room I saw Élan dancing with another *Eldarin* man. Late in the afternoon, Ryan, Gotyr, and I ended up in the same place and the crowd there all but demanded that we play. For over an hour we entertained them, until Ryan and Gotyr pointed out that to keep to the spirit of the day we needed to move on. Just before we finished, I saw Élan at the back of the audience. She threw her arms around the man she was with, kissed him, and disappeared into the crowd.

Several hours after sunset, I was down in Westbridge when an eddy in the crowd left me standing by myself in a relatively open spot. All around me, the happy voices of people I didn't know were engaged in conversations I could barely understand. I thought of the few times that I'd seen Élan that day and my mood went gray and sour. I felt lost and alone. I took one last look around me, not sure what I was looking for. When I didn't see it, I turned and began making my way back up the mountain to Alain's house.

It took some time to work my way back to my room. Though I tried to avoid it, several times I was stopped by people who wanted to meet the *Endollin*. I'd been feeling out of sorts most of the day; by the time I got back to my room I was almost in tears. I didn't really understand why. The ring caught my eye. The only reason, I thought, that anyone was interested in me was because I bore Lorrestian's ring. If I didn't have that, would the hunters have brought me to *Evendim*? Would people want to meet me? Would I be staying at the King's home? Would I have met Élan?

Élan. Since the ceremony that morning, I'd only seen her in the company of other men. *Eldarin* men. I felt lost and a little broken and I didn't know why. She'd only known me for a little over a quarter moon. She was my age; she must have had a life before I showed up. I thought she liked me, but why would she? And why should that matter because I had Peg. Guilt flared again followed almost immediately by grief; I'd lost Peg. I sat in the dark in my room, confused, idly picking at the strings of my guitar, searching for a song to express how I felt or to give me an answer. After a time, I heard people outside calling final farewells, so I set my guitar back on its stand and flung myself into bed where I eventually drifted into an uneasy sleep.

I woke well before dawn feeling tense and worn. I thought that a warm bath might help, so I slipped on a robe and a pair of sandals and walked to the bath house. I was the first into the place that day, so I spent a few moments lighting the oil lamps and then put my folded robe on a shelf and slipped into the pool. The warmth was soothing. I closed my eyes and felt the tension in my neck and shoulders relax. The nauseating headache I'd been feeling faded.

The door to the bath house opened and someone entered. I opened my eyes to find Alain and Réalta slipping out of robes.

"Lauren, *nul sym en elested tul seli navoram*," Réalta said as she entered the pool.

"*Na olin en elested tul sely*," I responded.

Alain finished folding their robes and joined us.

"This is a fortunate meeting," he said, settling in beside Réalta. "We had hoped to speak with you in private before your departure this morning."

"How might I be of assistance?" I asked.

They glanced at one another.

"We're not speaking as King and King's Consort now," Réalta said. "We're speaking as parents and, we hope, as friends."

I nodded.

"As friends," I agreed.

"This mission that you are undertaking, it is important," Alain said, speaking slowly as if weighing each word carefully. "Even if you do not find the location of the sword, you will be bringing back important books and other materials that we have longed for but have not dared to try and retrieve."

He paused, as if uncomfortable with what he was about to say.

"There is no one more competent to lead the mission than Élan," he continued finally. "In addition, I have selected the most accomplished of the *Cadwynir* to accompany you."

He paused again.

"But..." I said, when it became clear that he did not know how to continue.

"But she is our daughter," Réalta said. "And she has never been out of *Evendim*. She has never met anyone who intended to harm her. We do not know what you may face. We do not know what eyes may be on *Elsgard*. We occasionally spot Kelmar scouts or squads of soldiers in *Seldenawé*. It is possible that the Keepers themselves may be watching *Elsgard* for signs of our return."

"It is clear that you care for Élan," Alain said. "It would mean a great deal to us if you would keep special watch over her."

They fell silent, watching me expectantly. I had no idea what to say.

"Alain, Réalta, I appreciate your confidence in me," I said finally. "And I would do anything to prevent harm to Élan. But I am not trained to arms. I am not a warrior. I'm a minstrel. Why do you think my protection would matter?"

"Because *you* are the *Endollin*," Alain answered. I caught the emphasis on the word "you."

"I don't understand. What do your histories say about me that gives you such faith in me?"

"It is not what our histories say," Alain responded. "They say simply that the *Endollin* will save the world or destroy it. I only spoke to my father once after he had his visions, the time that he urged me to lead our people away from *Elsgard*. But he told me that what he had seen gave him hope."

"And..."

"Did you have to have that resized?" Alain asked, gesturing to the ring on my right hand.

"No. It fits perfectly."

"Exactly," Alain said. "Lauren, Lorrestian did not see some faceless man who he happened to call the *Endollin*. He saw *you*. Élan was correct. He knew that you would be a minstrel. He knew what kind of person you would be, and that vision gave him hope. And now that I have met you, you give me hope."

"And me as well," Réalta added.

I wasn't sure what I thought about what Alain had said but–despite my feelings the night before–I did consider them to be my friends. I wanted to leave them with what comfort I could.

"If I can possibly prevent harm to Élan, I will," I promised.

They smiled.

"Our thanks to you," they said in unison. "Shall we break our fast together?"

CHAPTER SEVEN

Several hours later, Ryan, Élan, and I made our way down into the city together. We were dressed for the journey in the clothing of the *Cadwynir*, dull green tunics and trousers with a hooded cloak of the same dull green. At the request of the *Cadwynir* Captain, Ryan and I were not wearing our blue minstrel's sashes. We entered the square in front of the palace to find Leonyr, the Master Librarian, there before us. Like us, he was wearing the dull green *Cadwynir* uniform. We had just finished greeting each other when King Alain stepped out onto the wide portico of the palace with Réalta on his arm. As they descended the stairs, we heard the sharp, syncopated rhythm of hooves on the pavement and our escort rounded a corner and entered the square opposite us.

Each of the *Cadwynir* was dressed as we were, but each of them carried a long sword hanging from a broad leather belt. Each was also equipped with a bow and a quiver of arrows. They were mounted on...

"Unicorns," I said breathlessly, not believing what I was seeing.

The animals were somewhat taller and thinner than the horses I was used to. There was something about their shape and the grace of their motion that reminded me of deer. Their movements gave a sense of restrained power, and their large dark eyes displayed a preternatural intelligence. All of them were white or light bay in color and each had a long, dagger-like horn protruding from its forehead.

Élan laughed.

"*Aynekahrn*," she corrected me.

"Whatever you call them," I started.

"Look closely, Lauren," Ryan suggested.

I glanced at him and then back at the *aynekahrn*. Now that I was taking a careful look, I could see that the "horns" were strapped on.

"The *aynekahrn* are different from the horses you are familiar with," Élan told me. "They tend to be taller, and they look like they'd be more fragile, but they are actually hardier than horses and they are far more intelligent. The horns might be strapped on, but the *aynekahrn* easily learn to use them in battle and they are formidable allies."

The *Cadwynir* drew their mounts to a halt before us and dismounted. The King and Réalta joined us. As one, the *Cadwynir* bowed to the King and his wife. The captain stepped forward.

"*Elmar, selé il manana tul seli navoram,*" she said.

"*Selé il manana tul seli wealtyr,*" Alain responded and glanced at me. "We are honored by your service."

Alain turned to us.

"Lauren, Élan, this is Pyrett, Captain of the *Cadwynir*. She will be in command of your escort."

"I am honored to serve," she said. She gestured and one of the other *Cadwynir* stepped forward. "This is Keiler, my second."

"Pyrett, Keiler," Alain continued, "this is my daughter Élan and Lauren, the *Endollin*. With them is Rhion of the Minstrels and Leonyr, Master Librarian."

The two *Cadwynir* bowed to us.

"Élan, you will be in command of the mission," Alain said, his tone clearly indicating that he was giving orders. "You are charged with locating materials that may aid the *Endollin* in his quest for the sword. Captain, you are charged with the safety of the Princess and the *Endollin*. In matters of safety, your decisions are paramount. Do you both understand your charges?"

"We understand, Your Majesty," they replied in unison.

"Then may *Tyth* smile on your journey," the King said. Then he and Réalta stepped forward and embraced Élan.

"Be safe, daughter," Réalta said. She glanced quickly at me and then leaned in to say something only Élan could hear. Élan blushed and nodded and then gave her mother one final hug.

"We should go," she said.

The *Cadwynir* brought four of the *aynekahrn* forward for us. Our personal belongings had been sent down earlier in the morning and had been stowed on our mounts.

The *Cadwynir* leading my mount handed me the reins.

"His name is *Yrtenstal, aduné,*" he told me. "In your tongue, that is Wind's foal."

I laughed. The *Eldarin* ranger cocked his head at me with a puzzled expression on his face.

"The horse I learned to ride on was named Windsfoal," I explained.

He smiled and said, "An odd coincidence, *aduné.*"

The weather was still warmer than normal for the season, so before mounting we removed our cloaks. *Yrtenstal* was taller than I was accustomed to, so it took me several tries to mount, while all around me the *Eldar* seemed to leap into their saddles with little need for the stirrups. I glanced around in embarrassment, hoping that no one had noticed my clumsiness, though my gaze lingered on Élan. It might have just been my imagination, but the sunlight seemed to gather around her, and in that moment, she looked every bit the princess that she was.

Ryan guided his mount alongside mine.

"The *aynekahrn* are trained the same as horses," he told me. "Though you may find that they need less guidance than a typical horse. They also have a far greater endurance, so we'll most likely be riding longer each day."

There were no stirring words to announce our departure. Élan simply urged her *aynekahrn* into motion and the rest of us fell in behind her. She led us west along the south bank of the *Kivin*. Once we passed Westbridge, the paving ended, and we rode on a hard-packed dirt trail that wound its way up into the mountains alongside the river. Several times that morning we forded smaller tributaries of the *Kivin* until our way turned away from the river. By midday, we were deep in the mountains following a barely discernable ridgetop trail. We halted only briefly to eat our midday meal. When we remounted, I guided *Yrtenstal* alongside Élan and her *aynekahrn*.

We hadn't spoken much since the offering to *Tyth* the day before, just a few pleasantries as we walked down the mountain that morning with Ryan. Part of me felt that I needed to tell her about my conversation with her parents that morning, but I realized that mostly I just wanted to hear her voice. She glanced over at me as I drew alongside, though, and then turned back to the trail ahead. I wasn't sure, but I thought she smiled. She didn't say anything, and we rode in silence for a bit. Now that I was beside her, I wasn't sure how to b egin.

"Your parents talked to me this morning," I told her.

She didn't reply but she did glance my way again.

"They asked me to do something," I volunteered, but stopped at that, hoping to draw her into the conversation.

"And?" she asked after a while.

"Élan, did I do something wrong?" I asked. I didn't mean for that to come out, but I couldn't seem to stop myself. "You've hardly spoken to me all day."

All day she'd been holding herself rigidly upright. Now she seemed to slump down in her saddle.

"Lauren, I had to spend yesterday making nice with all the eligible young men from families with close ties to mine. I had to dance with them and drink with them and allow them to believe that I might be interested in them. I didn't get any time with my family or friends, and I missed hearing you and Rhion and Gotyr play. Now I'm tired, my head hurts, and I'm going to have to spend the day in the saddle instead of sleeping."

"Élan, I'm sorry," I said.

"Please just tell me what you want to tell me."

"First, they told me that there's no one better to lead this mission," I hedged. "I agree with them about that."

"Lauren."

"They're worried about your safety. They asked me to watch over you."

She halted her *aynekahrn* and twisted in the saddle to face me.

"I don't need anyone to watch over me," she said.

"I know that," I replied. "I told them that I'm no warrior. If anything, I need someone to watch over me. But they made me promise because I'm the *Endollin*."

She spurred her mount back into motion.

"Well, now I feel so much safer," she said, the sarcasm in her tone spiked with anger.

"I don't intend to treat you like you need my protection," I said. "I just wanted you to know."

She didn't reply. We were riding up a slight rise. When we reached the top our *aynekahrn* stopped before we could rein them in. As the rest of our party joined us, we heard slight gasps of dismay.

Below us, a broad swath of the forest was stricken. Everything was blackened and broken, but not from a fire. There was no ash, no scent of burned wood, but the sweet, sickly smell of rot hung in the air. Little remained of the trees but broken, falling apart stumps about the height of a person. The underbrush was almost completely gone and what was left was twisted, black, and rotting. There were animal remains there as well. Squirrels, rabbits, deer, birds, all twisted and bloated, their fur and feathers blackened.

"What happened here?" Élan asked, sounding suddenly small and vulnerable.

"I've seen places like this before," Keiler said. "A couple of times in the past my patrols have come across spots where the forest had died like this. Those places were small, though. I've never seen one this large."

"I've seen something like this before as well," I said. "It struck a farming village called Cammlin. According to the people there, all their crops and animals simply died overnight. What was left looked just like this."

Not sure why, I slipped off my *aynekahrn* and walked slowly toward the blighted area. There was a clear line of demarcation between the normal and the dead areas. When I reached that line, I squatted and held my hands palm down just above the blackened ground. I closed my eyes and opened myself to whatever sensations presented themselves. After a moment, I could sense it: the malevolent intelligence I'd felt hunting me. The traces were there, faint but unmistakable. That being had touched this place, blighted it.

I stood and turned back to the group. Ryan had dismounted as well.

"Lauren?" he asked.

"The thing that is hunting me did this," I told them. "I'm sure of it."

"Why?" Élan asked.

"Why am I sure or why would any being do this?"

"The latter. This feels…" she paused, obviously struggling for words. "It feels wrong or sick."

"I mislike this," Pyrett cut in. "I do not know whether the blocking of our path was intentional or not, but we should move in case whatever caused this returns. I wish to be well away from here before nightfall."

"Agreed," Élan responded.

As Ryan and I mounted, several of the *Cadwynir* spurred their *aynekahrn* forward, but the mounts refused to set a hoof on the blighted ground. The riders tried several more times, but their *aynekahrn* were clearly becoming agitated and they finally desisted.

"We must go around, then," Pyrett concluded and led the group to the south, staying well away from the edge of the blackened ground.

I settled in beside Élan, putting myself between her and the blighted area without saying that's what I was doing. Sometime later, Élan looked at me and smiled slightly. She pulled her mount closer to mine and said quietly, "My thanks to you."

It took us several hours to work our way around the blight and return to the trail. The sun had sunk below the mountains to the west and the light was going gray when Pyrett finally felt comfortable stopping and making camp for the night.

The next day passed uneventfully and late in the afternoon we worked our way down the western face of the mountains into the foothills. We forded the *Glaess* River and set up camp a short distance from the west bank. Élan and Pyrett were pleased at our pace; another five days would put us in *Elsgard*.

I rose early the next morning. Only a few others in the camp were stirring. To the east, the sun was just showing above the mountains, a thin sliver of red coloring the edge of the sky. Overhead, the sky was full of dark clouds that were slowly spreading to the east. The weather was still quite warm, so I decided to bathe. I rounded up a change of clothes and made my way slightly upstream from camp. I found a break in the underbrush where it was clear that animals made their way to the water and followed the path down to the riverbank. Someone was there before me.

It was Élan. She was neck deep in the water with her back to the shore. I froze where I was. For a moment I stood, unsure what to do. Then I took a step backwards intending to retreat and my foot came down on a fallen tree branch. At the crack, Élan turned and spotted me. I froze again and we locked eyes.

My world narrowed to Élan. She filled my vision. My breath was ragged and shallow, and I was suddenly very aware of the wildly irregular beating of my heart, which felt like it was trying to block my windpipe. Élan's expression never changed. She simply stood from the crouching position she had been in and slowly walked toward the shore, her eyes never leaving mine. I don't think I ever shifted my gaze, but somehow I was aware of every rivulet of water running down the curves of her body and how they caught the light of the rising sun and became shimmering lines of diamonds and pale rubies.

She took her gaze from me as she stepped onto the shore and retrieved her towel from where it hung over a bush. Without looking at me again, she began drying herself. I was still too entranced to move.

"You seem to be taking your promise to watch me quite seriously," she said, still without looking at me.

That broke the spell.

"I just came to bathe," I stammered out. "I didn't know that you were here."

"You don't seem to be bathing," Élan observed as she set aside her towel and picked up her dull green tunic.

In reply, I took a couple of steps forward and hung my towel over a bush. I began to pull my tunic off over my head, but I'd forgotten to remove my belt and got stuck with my tunic half on and half off. By the time I got myself untangled and could see again, Élan was gone.

Though the weather was warm, the water was cold, and I didn't linger overly long in the river. I dressed quickly and headed back toward the camp. In my mind, I could still see Élan rising from the water and the image brought a smile to my face. At the same time, I felt guilty; I'd promised myself to Peg. She was waiting for… But she wasn't waiting for me. Not anymore. My thoughts were a tangled mess, and I had no idea how Élan would react when I reached the camp. For all I knew, she'd have the *Cadwynir* clap me in chains.

No one said anything as I ducked into my small tent to stow my clothing and towel. One of the *Cadwynir* had a large pot of farina ready and served me a bowl. As I sat to begin eating, Élan exited her tent, fetched a bowl of farina, and sat down beside me.

"I think the weather is going to change today," she said. Then she leaned closer to me, smiling. "I snuck back and watched you for a minute," she confided, so quietly only I could hear.

I'm pretty sure that I blushed, but I also laughed.

"Maybe we should agree to watch out for each other," I said.

"Maybe we should," she replied.

Overhead, there was a long rolling rumble of thunder that echoed back from the mountains.

Élan turned out to be right about the weather. By midday, we'd left the foothills and were riding across the Lellarin Plains. As we left the hills, a stiff wind blew up from the north and within an hour we could see our breath in between gusts. All of us wrapped ourselves in our cloaks. Midway through the afternoon, a cold rain began to fall. It wasn't a heavy or a driving rain, but it was constant and–even with the protection afforded by the *Eldarin* cloaks–we were soon all wet and miserable. Only the *aynekahrn* seemed unaffected; they kept up a steady pace that was faster than even the fastest horse.

But even the *aynekahrn* couldn't run forever. Long after dark we stopped. There were no hills or trees, nothing to act as a windbreak or to provide shelter from the rain. We ate a cold, damp meal and then decided to walk; no one was going to be able to sleep. Several hours later the rain stopped and shortly after that, we reached dry ground.

"We should try to get a little sleep," Élan said.

"That makes sense," Pyrett agreed, and began to make arrangements for sentries and for someone to prepare the morning meal. The rest of us saw to our mounts and then wrapped ourselves in our cloaks and laid down to get what rest we could.

By the time the sun rose, the cloud cover was gone, and the day was bright and sunny, so I got my first good look at the Lellarin Plains. To be honest, there wasn't much to see. Stands of trees were rare and the few we came across were small. The plains appeared to be little more than an ocean of grass. Late in the morning the north wind finally died away, allowing the sun to warm us somewhat. I found myself wondering what had led the *Eldar* to establish their capitol city in the middle of the plains.

That night, I found out. The sun went down, and the stars became visible in all directions, with nothing at all to obstruct the view. I walked a short distance away from the camp and spent long moments simply watching the sky. I started in the north, where the North Star, the Keystone, shimmered red-violet into blue-violet and back far above the horizon. I turned to the east and found the cluster known as the Seven Sisters. Beyond that, in the southeast, was the broad band of light that the *Eldar* called *Elalhynn*, the River of Stars. A little south of west I found Dartem, the Huntress and then the Hound. My gaze returned to the north, and I stood there gazing at the North Star, simply enjoying a feeling of peace. Then I felt someone beside me. It was Élan.

"I've never been out of the mountains," she said. "The openness is a little overwhelming." She was silent for a moment and then continued. "The sky is so huge. I feel like I can see forever. I've never seen anything so beautiful."

I turned my head to look at her.

"I have," I said before I could stop myself. I quickly turned back to the North Star, glad that in the dark she couldn't see my face flush. She didn't reply and after a while we returned to camp.

Three days later, in the afternoon, we reached *Elsgard*, the City of Stars. The Lellarin Plains are generally considered to be flat, but from the *Glaess* River to the east and the *Mordel* River on the west the land gently rises toward the center. In the center of the plains, the terrain becomes more varied, with low, rounded hills separated by broad, shallow valleys. The central plains don't have any more trees than the outer plains, but the valleys often contain small ponds or marshes. In the midst of all that, *Hollinskye* Hill stands like a recumbent colossus with *Elsgard* built on and around it.

When I first saw the top of the Hill on the horizon, I thought I was seeing things. The *Eldar*, though, noticed it and quickened our pace slightly. As we approached, the hill and the city seemed to slowly rise from the grass. When the entire city was in view, we reined in as Keiler and a pair of scouts rode back to join us. Pyrett, Élan, Ryan, and I met them.

"We don't see any signs of anyone outside the city," Keiler reported. "We should check inside though, to make sure that no one is waiting for us inside. Where do we plan to stay?"

Pyrett turned to address Élan.

"For tonight, I recommend that we camp together as a group in the Great Hall of the palace," the captain said. "It's big enough for all of us, it's defensible, and it will put us close to the library. As we have a chance to check out other locations, we can begin to split up into smaller groups."

"Whatever you think is best," Élan replied. "I've read about the city, but I've never been here."

The captain turned back to her second.

"We'll wait here, Keiler. Check the quickest route to the palace and then come back for us."

As the scouts rode off, the rest of us settled in to wait. I took the opportunity to examine the city.

Hollinskye Hill stood entirely within the walls of the city. The Hill was roughly elliptical in shape with the long axis running north and south. The sides sloped up somewhat steeply to a broad flat top that the *Eldar* called *Ellaurellin*, the Field of Stars. The sides of *Hollinskye* were dotted with houses; most of the city's population had lived on the hill. A stairway–known as the Thousand Stairs–had been built into the northern end of the hill leading from ground level up to *Ellaurellin*. Halfway up, the stairway was flanked to the west by a concert hall and to the east by a college. Further up, the palace stood on the west side of the stairs and the library on the east. I could easily make out those four buildings from where we waited; all were constructed of the opalescent Elfstone.

The walls of the city circled the hill, generally about a quarter of a mile from the base. The walls were pierced by six gates–one at each of the cardinal and ordinal directions–and each gate was warded by two towers. The walls and towers were all constructed of Elfs-tone. *Elsgard* gleamed in the afternoon sunlight and from our vantage point we could see no signs that the city had been abandoned for a thousand rounds of the seasons.

By the time the scouts returned, the sun was low on the horizon, and we'd eaten a cold evening meal. As soon as the scouts were spotted, we began mounting up and the squad was ready to go when the scouts reached us.

"We saw no signs that anyone has been here recently," Keiler reported. "We startled some animals living in the parks but saw no tracks and no indications that any of the buildings we passed had been occupied in the near past."

"Excellent," Pyrett replied. "What route would you recommend?"

"I'd suggest that we enter through the northeast gate and follow the Wall Road around to the northwest gate. That will give us some options for escape should we have missed any surprises inside. From the northwest gate we can use Cook's Road to access the palace."

"Very well. Let's go."

I looked around at my companions as we began moving. All the *Eldar* looked eager, as if they were coming home. I guess that for many of them, they were. Élan and Ryan, though, looked like starving people who had been offered a banquet. For the first time in their lives, they were seeing the ancient home of their people, a place of myth and legend that they'd never hoped to see. I smiled; I was pretty sure that I'd had that same look when I first saw Songhaven.

We gave the *aynekahrn* free rein and it didn't take them long to reach the northeast gate of the city. Up close, the walls seemed massive. They stood over five times the height of a man, but even up close they were dwarfed by the bulk of *Hollinskye*. The gates–what was left of them–hung open. Lack of care and exposure to the weather for a thousand rounds had allowed the thick wooden doors to rot away and now only shreds of weathered gray wood clung to the metal hinges. Metal straps and the massive ring-shaped pulls lay rusting on the ground in the center of the opening.

The *Cadwynir* formed a protective circle around me, Élan, Ryan, and Leonyr. We cautiously entered the city, all eyes scanning our surroundings for any signs that we were not alone. Except for Wall Road, which circled the entire city just inside the walls, the streets of *Elsgard* were laid out very much like those in *Evendim*; they twisted and flowed and followed the original contours of the land as much as possible. The city buildings were all made of stone: granite or marble or limestone. Doors and windows and many of the roofs–anything that had been made of wood–had mostly rotted away. As in *Evendim*, the buildings and streets had been arranged to allow for a great deal of natural greenspace, but the gardens had long since gone wild. Most of the gardens and street corners contained statues. Some were of *Eldarin* men or women, some were of animals, and some depicted the Old Ones. The statues were carved out of various types of stone; the ancient *Eldarin* artists didn't seem to have a strong preference. Many of the figures in the gardens had been overgrown with brambles and vines and many of those on the street corners had been toppled or defaced. Sorrow washed through my chest; *Elsgard* must have been a place of beauty before the *Eldar* had been murdered or driven out.

We entered the intersection inside the north gate, and I couldn't help but to stare. All traces of the wooden gates were gone, and the arched opening was scorched and blackened. Some unnatural force had blown through the gates, leaving horizontal scorch marks in its wake. In places within the arch, large chunks of the Elfstone walls were gone.

Élan noticed the direction of my gaze.

"In the final assault, the Keepers used magic to blow down the gates," she explained. "At that point, the Alomar soldiers poured through the opening. According to the histories, there was nothing but chaos in the city for days afterwards."

I opened my mouth to try and say something, some words of comfort or atonement, but nothing came. My people had done this. I looked at the gaping wound where the gates had stood, the defaced statues, saw in my mind the terror and the deaths of innocent men, women, and children whose only crime was that they had been born *Eldar*. The Alomar histories said that the *Eldar* had murdered all of the students and the Masters at the Wizards' College. That act was the final provocation that led to the war and, ultimately, the slaughter of the innocents here. Even if the histories were correct that the *Eldar* had destroyed the Wizards' College, I couldn't find it in my heart to say that the retribution that had been exacted was just.

I was still lost in thought when we reached the northwest gate and turned toward *Hollinskye* on the Cook's Road, so called because it provided easy access for wagons hauling food and other supplies to the palace and the concert hall. Halfway up the hill we turned off the road onto the wide paved terrace in front of the palace.

The palace was a squared-off c-shaped building, two stories tall, and flat-roofed. The courtyard between the arms was covered, the roof supported by two rows of four columns. At each corner of the building was a tower that stood twice the height of the main building. The ends of the arms were lined with tall, arched-top windows. Even after a thousand rounds of abandonment, the palace was magnificent.

"There is a grassy area out back," Keiler said. "I suggest we leave the *aynekahrn* there to graze, under guard of course. The rest of us can camp inside in the Great Hall."

Pyrett nodded and we dismounted. Each of us pulled our saddlebags off our mounts and then four of the *Cadwynir* led the *aynekahrn* back the way we had come and around the end of the building. The rest of us headed toward the palace with the *Cadwynir* in the lead. They all had their hands on the hilts of their swords.

Like the north gate, the doors of the palace had been blasted away. As we entered, the import of that hit me. Just inside the doorway we stopped, and I stepped forward to speak to Pyrett.

"Is there nowhere else we could camp?" I asked quietly. "Élan's grandfather died here."

"I am aware of that, *Endollin*," the captain answered, just as quietly. "The Princess and I spoke about that several times this afternoon. She agrees that, at least for now, this is the best place for us to bunk."

I nodded and looked around the Great Hall. It was a large space, twice as wide as it was deep and two stories in height, though there was a wide walkway around the sides and front wall at the level of the second floor. Fifty feet across the room from where we stood was a raised dais upon which stood the *Eldarin* throne, carved from single block of Elfstone. The back of the throne extended well above where the head of the monarch would be when seated and a large six-pointed star with the top and bottom points longer than the other four was inlaid in the upper half in gold. Seven stained glass windows on that wall allowed light into the room. Huge fireplaces occupied the walls to the left and right and beside them were doorways leading to the wings of the palace. The floor was made of polished black marble and the same six-pointed star, this time done in Elfstone, was inlaid in the center of the room.

"*El an Arastalon*," Ryan said reverently.

"The Star of *Arastalon*," Élan translated for me. "The symbol of our people."

"Who was *Arastalon*?" I asked.

"We do not know," Leonyr answered. "The Star came to these lands with our people, blazoned on the sails of their ships and shining from the banners they carried. So many of those ancient travelers died in the Great War that no one living remembers whether *Arastalon* was a person, a place, or a thing."

"Since the War," Ryan said, "we have not been who were once were and so the banners have remained furled. Never have I seen the Star so openly displayed."

We stood in reverent silence for a few moments, but then began to settle in for the night. Some of the *Cadwynir* left to find wood for a fire while others began cleaning out one of the fireplaces. The rest of us worked to clear away dust and debris from the section of the floor where we planned to sleep. Soon, we had a small fire going and a warm meal to eat. While we ate, Pyrett and the *Cadwynir* set shifts to maintain watch for the night and Ryan, Élan, Leonyr, and I discussed plans for exploring the library. When the sun set, the only light we had was from our little fire and it did little to illuminate the huge space we were in. One by one, our company settled into their blankets to sleep. The marble floor was hard, but we were all so weary from the road that no one had trouble falling to sleep.

By morning, however, we were all uncomfortable. The marble was unyielding and, even with our thick blankets, it leached the warmth from us. We were all up before the sun.

As we were breaking our fast, the last shift of sentries came in and tried to settle themselves down to sleep. Two of the *Cadwynir* went out to keep watch over the *aynekahrn*. I was sitting with Élan and Leonyr, each of us silently nibbling at bread and apples and sipping warm tea from metal cups. A small group of the *Cadwynir* rose from where they were eating and headed out the door of the palace. Pyrett herself rose and came over to us.

"I've sent people to the library to walk through the place and ensure that there are no threats," she said. "Once they're back, you can go over anytime you wish."

"My thanks to you, Captain," Élan replied. "I'm assuming that you'll be sending people with us when we go."

"Of course. I'm guessing that you also plan to search the palace, so the rest of us will begin sweeping the residential and staff wings." She stretched by rolling her shoulders and rubbed her neck. "I'm hoping that we'll find a more comfortable place to sleep."

I smiled and Élan gave a short little laugh.

"That would be nice."

A short time later, the group from the library returned and reported that there was no evidence of threats in the library. Pyrett assigned them to accompany us and so Élan, Leonyr, Ryan, and I headed for the library in the company of four of the *Cadwynir*. As we approached, I experienced a quick surprise; the library was a twin to the one in *Evendim*. When I mentioned that, Leonyr smiled and said, "I was Master Librarian here for a very long time. When I was asked to help build the library in *Evendim*, I chose a design that was familiar."

Surprisingly, the massive door of the library was still intact with only a slight fading of the paint to indicate its age. Inside, the air was stale and musty smelling, and a thick layer of dust covered everything. Other than the tracks of the *Cadwynir*, there was no evidence that anyone had been in the library for a very long time. Again, I found myself surprised; even from where we stood, it was clear that most of the books and other materials were remarkably well preserved.

"You look puzzled, *aduné*," one of the *Cadwynir*, a man named Jorith, asked. "Is something amiss?"

"No, nothing's wrong. I'm just surprised at how well-preserved the books are."

"Our intent in assembling the materials here," Leonyr explained, "was to preserve them. In the times before the Great War, there was much virtue in our workings. I am glad to see that our efforts here have not failed entirely."

That comment puzzled me, but Leonyr was already moving forward, closely followed by Élan. Two of the *Cadwynir* stationed themselves inside the doors and the other two began to patrol the interior of the library. That left me alone with Ryan.

"Ryan, what did Leonyr mean? Did he and the other librarians use magic to preserve the books?"

"Yes and no," Ryan answered. "The *Eldar* do not work magic as humans do. There has never been an *Eldarin* wizard; wizardry is the province of humans. That's why the burning of the Wizard's College was such a provocation." He paused for a moment, a slight frown on his face as if he was considering how to continue. "The *Eldar* don't *do* magic," he said finally. "They *are* magic. Our very essence is magic. Some of that essence finds its way into everything we do and enhances our skills. For instance, you're now using an *Eldarin* knife to shave. Have you noticed a difference compared to human-made blades?"

I nodded.

"The *Eldarin* one is sharper than any blade I've ever seen before." A sudden thought occurred to me. "Is that why *Evendim* seemed different, seemed more real than anyplace I'd ever been before? I thought I was imagining it."

Ryan nodded.

"It is. *Elsgard* was once like that. Perhaps more so. As Leonyr said, things were different before the Great War. Since then, the *Eldar* have been diminished, less than what they were. *Evendim* is great, but *Elsgard* when the *Eldarin* lived here..."

At that moment, Élan returned.

"We've checked the section that houses the royal records," she said. "It is still intact. We're going to start going through what's there. Would you join us?"

Ryan and I followed her to a section of the library toward the right rear of the building. Leonyr had cleared the dust from a couple of the tables and already had several boxes of papers and scrolls stacked on each. Ryan, Leonyr and Élan began pulling materials out and spreading them out on the tables, discussing what they found in each. I pulled a scroll from one of the boxes and partially unrolled it. I could make out a word here and there, but most of it was incomprehensible to me; a week had not been long enough to truly learn the *Eldarin* tongue. I listened to my three companions for a time, but finally drifted off and began to wander the library. Dispirited at my inability to help, I finally sat at one of the tables and watched the play of sunlight coming in the windows on the dusty surface. Idly, I began tracing out some of the few simple *Eldarin* words I knew in the dust.

Jorith found me there.

"Are you well, *aduné*," he asked. "Is there anything I can do for you?"

"Give me your knowledge of the *Eldarin* language," I said sourly.

A muffled gasp escaped him.

"You can do that?" he asked. "You can take my language skills? How?"

Surprised, I looked up at him. His face clearly displayed his apprehension, but he held himself stiffy, ready to do whatever the *Endollin* needed.

I smiled at him, but inwardly I sighed.

"I have no idea," I admitted, shaking my head. "I don't know if I could read your knowledge or how to go about it if I could. But please know this. I would never do anything to harm you."

He relaxed a little.

"I'm just feeling a little useless right now," I said. "We need to review records, but I can't read them. Élan might have been better off bringing a child of eight rounds in my place."

Jorith looked uncomfortable.

"Thank you for checking on me, Jorith," I said. "I should not task you with my problems. Please, don't let me keep you from what you were doing."

"As you wish, *aduné*," he said and turned away.

I returned to the palace after the midday meal and spent several hours practicing. Because we wished to avoid attracting attention while travelling, Ryan and I had refrained from playing. The acoustics in the Great Hall were excellent and it felt good to be playing music. Several hours later, Élan returned from the library, her face and clothes smudged with dust.

"We didn't find anything that would help locate the sword," she told me. "We've gone over most of the records from Lorrestian's reign that had been sent to the library, but there was nothing that would help us. Leonyr and Rhion are still going through the last of it and then they'll start searching the rest of the library. Pyrett said that the residential wing has been cleared, so I'd like to start searching the rooms on the second floor. Those were my family's bedrooms. Lauren, would you search them with me?"

"Of course," I answered as I rose and began packing my guitar into its case.

We spent the rest of that afternoon and the whole next day searching the bedrooms but found nothing that would help us find the sword. We did, however, find a small painting of Alain when he was a child and a formal portrait of Lorrestian and his wife Genaine; Élan added them to the things that we would take back to *Evendim*. Like the library, everything was covered in a thick layer of dust and cobwebs hung in the corners of the rooms, but whatever power had preserved the materials in the library had been less strong here. A scroll on the bedside table in what must have been Lorrestian's room had almost completely decayed to dust. Though it was in ruins, it was clear that the bed was unmade; the attack on the city must have come fairly early in the day, before the staff had completed their morning tasks. Small details like that made the search difficult for Élan, made the story of the loss of her grandfather real and personal. Several times the pain and sorrow overwhelmed her, and I found myself trying awkwardly to comfort her, searching desperately for something to say but in the end just holding her until she pulled away and returned to sifting through the dust that was all that remained of a part of her family she would never know. As the sun set on our second day in the city, we decided to give up the search of the personal quarters and move to the King's library and office on the first floor.

The next morning, Élan, Ryan, and I began searching the first floor of the residential wing. The north end of that wing was devoted to a library; the *Eldarin* Kings had maintained their own library housed in the palace. Next to the library was the King's private office and we began our search there.

As we entered from the hallway, I saw that Lorrestian's office was a large rectangular room. The door we entered by was near the end of one of the long walls and directly across the room from us a set of double doors opened onto the palace courtyard. The walls were lined with oak, very similar to Alain's home in *Evendim*. On the same wall as the double doors was a large fireplace made of fieldstones with a marble hearth and mantle. To our left, the wall was covered in shelves as was the adjacent short wall. The shelves were full of objects, small statues, several miniature portraits, and a great many books in various states of decay. The room was dominated, though, by a large desk. It didn't seem to fit the room; it seemed just a bit too large, and it was made of some dark wood–mahogany I thought–that seemed out of place with the light oak walls and floors. Behind the desk was a large oaken chair.

Élan slowly walked around the room, glancing at the objects on the shelves. She circled around the desk once, then pulled out the chair and sat down. She sat silent for a moment. I thought I saw a tear slide down her cheek and stepped forward to stand before the desk. At my movement, she looked up.

"I'll look through the desk drawers," she said. You two search the rest of the room."

I just stood looking at her for a moment. She returned my gaze and attempted a crooked smile.

"I'll take care of the desk," she said.

I nodded and ran my gaze over the top of the desk. It was littered with objects, scraps of paper, a sealing stamp, the remains of quills, and an inkpot, the contents of which had long since dried up. I was about to turn away, but one object caught my eye.

It was a ten-sided wooden object. Bright colors were visible through the dust covering it. I picked it up and brushed the dust away. Under the filth, the colors were as bright and vibrant as if they had been painted the day before. Half of the sides of the object depicted dragons, red, green, blue, white, and gray. The other five sides contained markings, all of them different, but following a pattern: a dot inside a partial circle above patterns of lines and dots.

"What is this?" I asked.

"I don't know," Élan replied.

"I do," Ryan replied, joining us at the desk. "Beside their buildings, it is the only Lost artifact that has ever been found. I've never seen it before, but I found descriptions of it in the library at *Evendim*."

"What is it?" I asked, turning it over in my hands to examine each face.

"No one knows for sure," Ryan answered. "Most people think it was a child's toy."

"It's curious that the colors haven't faded or been chipped at all," I observed.

"May I see it?" Ryan asked.

I handed it over, feeling a slight sense of reluctance as I did so. Ryan spent a few moments examining the object, then set it back on the desk and returned to examining the objects on the shelves. I picked the thing up and placed it in a small bag I'd brought in case I found anything useful and then turned to the shelves myself. Élan began opening desk drawers and examining their contents.

Some time later she sat back and sighed.

"I never realized that actually ruling as king was so boring," she complained. "These drawers are full of reports of farm yields and amounts of goods sent to and received from the various Alomar Kingdoms and Altiera. There are endless accounts of disputes between people over the most ridiculous things. I saw a report of a man who dragged his daughter before the king because she kissed a boy he didn't approve of."

"So, there was nothing of use?" I asked.

She shook her head.

"Not so far, but I have one drawer left to go. It's one of the big bottom drawers, so I may be a while yet."

She leaned forward and I heard the drawer slide open.

"That's odd," she said, mostly to herself.

"What's odd?" Ryan asked.

"The face of this drawer matches the one on the other side of the desk. It looks like it should be the same size. The drawer itself seems less deep, though. Wait a moment."

She turned to the other side of the desk, and I heard the other drawer slide open.

"It is less deep," she concluded. "I don't think anyone would notice if they weren't looking for it and especially if they didn't open both drawers. This one is less deep but was made to look the same to casual inspection."

At that point, Ryan and I had joined her behind the desk. Élan slid out of the chair, laid down on the floor next to the desk, and slid her arm up underneath the smaller drawer.

"There's a catch here," she told us.

There was a faint click and the scraping of wood and Élan sat up holding a stack of individual sheets of paper that were bound together with a faded red ribbon. She examined the top sheet and looked up at us, smiling.

"The top page is written in grandfather's hand," she said. "It's dated and seems to be an account of what he'd done that day. I think this might be a journal."

I exchanged glances with Ryan and we both smiled down at her.

"Would you like help reading those?" Ryan asked.

Élan shook her head.

"I don't think so," she answered. "If this is my grandfather's journal, I think family should have the first look at it."

"Very well," Ryan replied. "Lauren, why don't we go fetch something for the midday meal. Can we bring you anything, Élan?"

"Yes, my thanks to you, Rhion. I'll eat while I'm reading."

When we returned from the Great Hall with a plateful of fruit, bread, and cheese, Élan was smiling.

"Fortunately, the pages were in order by date," she explained. "So, I skipped to the entries toward the end. They cover the time when grandfather would have been having his visions and forging the sword. There aren't any specific mentions of the sword, the ring, or even of the visions, but there was one thing of interest."

She paused, picked up a piece of bread, and bit off a mouthful. Ryan looked at me and then back to Élan.

"And?" he asked.

Élan just smiled sweetly as she continued chewing. Finally, she swallowed and said, "There was really only one passage that might be helpful. Grandfather was growing increasingly weary as time went on. In the last of the entries, he wrote 'the walk to the workshop was tiring.' That suggests that the place where he forged the sword wasn't here in the palace or even nearby. We haven't found clues to the location of the sword here, but they might be wherever it was that he made it. We need to locate his workshop."

"Nothing in here hinted at where that might be," I noted. "Should we move to the King's library?"

"We should, but I'd like to finish eating first. Rhion, there's nothing too personal in these entries if you'd care to take a look at them."

We spent the rest of the afternoon and all the next day going through materials in the King's library. Early in the day we happened on a large box of maps. I couldn't read most of what was written on them, but Ryan provided me a list containing the *Eldarin* words for sword and other related terms and I spent a fruitless day examining the maps looking for those words. It took us two days to decide that there was no useful information in the library. We then spent another four days searching the staff wing of the palace. Élan was growing increasingly frustrated at the lack of progress; she didn't want to return to *Evendim* in failure and she feared that she would disappoint her father. Moreover, the daily reminders of what her family–and her people–had lost were taking their toll. I spent hours listening and holding her hand as the tension and the pain came pouring out. Oddly, as the one who had set the whole search in motion, I felt at peace, as if I was waiting, but I wasn't sure what I was waiting for. I was sure, without knowing how I knew, that we were doing exactly what we needed to do, and I tried to convey that to Élan.

On the morning of our tenth day in *Elsgard*, Élan and I were standing on the Thousand Stairs near the palace, looking out over the city. She'd announced the night before that we needed to start searching the city for Lorrestian's workshop and we were trying to decide where to begin.

"It's huge," she said, sounding dismayed.

"It is," I agreed. I wanted to help Élan, but I was feeling odd and distracted as if some sound just below the level of my hearing was drawing my attention.

"I guess we should start in the northwest," she suggested. "According to what I've read, there were a large number of crafters located there."

For some reason, I found myself thinking of the morning I met Ryan. I'd heard music that morning, music that guided me...

I was hearing it now. With a small shock of surprise, I realized that it sounded very like the *Arimë Daelyr*. Without thinking, I took Élan's hand. She looked surprised and didn't move when I took a step to follow the music.

"Lauren?" she said, puzzlement in her voice.

"Trust me," was all I could say.

She came with me then. We crossed the plaza in front of the palace and headed down the Cook's Road. Halfway down the hill, the music took us down a winding side road that wound its way toward the southwest part of the city. We reached level ground, and the music led us south. I saw the southwest gate in the distance to our right and then we turned back toward the hill. The music began to fade as we neared a large building that looked as if it had once been an inn. Around back, we found a large shed and there the music fell silent.

Élan looked questioningly at me, and I nodded. Together, we pushed open the double doors–something had preserved much of the wood from decay–and stepped into the shadowed interior. In the center of the floor was a large anvil. On the back wall was the forge, the leather parts of its bellows long gone. The walls were lined with hanging tools. To our right was a large workbench.

Élan turned to me.

"Lauren, how..."

I just shook my head once. She turned and walked over to the workbench. She rummaged through the detritus on the bench for a time, then turned her attention to the materials stored on a shelf below it. I heard her moving things around and several objects made of metal fell clanging to the floor. Élan gave a short gasp of surprise and then she rose and turned to me. In her hands was a leather satchel. Embossed in its surface was the king's sigil.

She turned back the flap and we peered inside. It was stuffed full of papers, and it was clear that mice had been into it; the visible edges had all been chewed.

"The writing I can see," Élan said, peering inside, "looks like it's in grandfather's hand. I can't be certain, though, without a better look and I'm afraid to pull any of the papers out given the condition they're in."

"Then we should get them back to Leonyr," I replied. "I'm sure that he'll know the best way to handle them."

When we entered the palace, Pyrett was shouting at a group of the *Cadwynir*. One of them saw us and pointed. Pyrett turned and–when she saw us–broke off railing at the *Cadwynir* and stormed across the Great Hall as if we were wanted criminals.

"I think we're in trouble," Élan whispered to me, just before the captain reached us.

"Where in *Aenn's*..." Pyrett started, suddenly remembered who she was speaking to, and choked back what was obviously going to be a very colorful expression. She simply glared at us for a long moment.

"Princess," she started again, her voice now ice cold. "*Endollin*. Where have you two been?"

"We found Lorrestian's workshop," Élan said. "This satchel is full of papers in his handwriting. I think we've found what we came for."

That seemed to mollify Pyrett somewhat, but her face was still flushed with anger.

"You went out into the city alone?" she demanded. "Why did you not take some of my people with you. I thought I was clear that no one–especially you two–was to wander the city alone. Your safety is my responsibility, but I cannot fulfill that responsibility if you ignore me."

"But Pyrett..." Élan started, but the captain cut her off.

"Princess, you heard your father's charge to me. You agreed to his terms."

"I did," Élan said, sounding contrite.

Some of the anger faded from Pyrett's eyes at Élan's tone.

"Élan, I do not wish to have to return to *Evendim* and tell the King that I lost you," she said softly.

"I understand, Pyrett," Élan answered, just as softly. "I, too, did not want to return to my father a failure."

In response, the *Cadwynir* captain stood regarding us with ice gray eyes for a moment. Then she said, "Well, it seems that you will not be. What have you found?"

Élan showed her the satchel, and the captain accompanied us to the library to show it to Leonyr. The Master Librarian gingerly took the satchel from Élan, turned back the flap closing it, and spent several minutes peering in at the contents. He tilted his head this way and that and several times carefully inserted his hand to try and open space to see the documents a little better.

"These do appear to be in Lorrestian's hand," he announced finally. "I can't be sure, but I think I saw drawings of the ring. If the information we seek is anywhere, I believe it will be on the documents in this satchel."

"Can we remove them to get a better look?" I asked.

"I do not believe that we should try, *aduné*," the Master Librarian replied. "The documents have been badly damaged by rodents and insects. We would be better served to wait until we are back in *Evendim*, and I have access to all the tools and materials I use to preserve precious documents."

Élan shook her head, clearly frustrated.

"To be so close," she said.

"I understand, *Elnyr*," Leonyr said. "But we would not wish to have the information we seek crumble in our hands because we did not take every precaution. It will not be long. I have located everything I think we need here and have begun packing it up for transport. I should be ready to depart within two days."

"Very well, Master Librarian. I'll leave the satchel in your care."

We returned to the palace and Élan spent the afternoon going through Lorrestian's office looking for small keepsakes that she could bring back to *Evendim*. Ryan and I spent the afternoon practicing; several times Pyrett came back to chase the *Cadwynir* gathered around us back to their duties. Several of the *Cadwynir* had found a deep pond not far from the city and had returned with nearly a dozen large fish; the evening meal that night had the air of a celebration. Everyone was in a good mood; we'd found what we were looking for and they would soon be returning home.

When it was full dark outside, Élan sought me out.

"Lauren, I wanted to climb up to *Ellaurellin*. I'd like it if you'd go with me."

Jorith was sitting nearby, running a whetstone over the edge of his knife. When he heard what Élan said, he looked up at us in surprise, saw me notice him, and returned quickly to sharpening his knife.

"Is there some significance to that?" I asked Élan.

"*Ellaurellin* is revered among my people," she said. "The field has been considered hallowed ground since before my people came to these lands. Most of the others have already visited. I would like to go tonight, and I would like to share the experience with you."

Jorith was very pointedly not looking at us. Élan saw the direction of my gaze and a pained expression flitted across her face.

"When the *Eldar* lived here, couples who wished to plight their troth would demonstrate their commitment to one another by climbing the Thousand Stairs together," she explained. "That is not what I was asking you to do. A person's first visit to *Ellaurellin* is a meaningful experience, one that none of my friends has ever had. I wanted to share it with you."

She was looking at me expectantly, with just a hint of anxiety. I realized suddenly that this was important to her, more important than I realized.

"*Se condi er manana*," I said. "I would be honored."

Her smile caused my heart to skip a beat.

"We should talk to Pyrett before we go," she said.

"I do think that would be wise," I agreed.

Together, we went to find the *Cadwynir* captain. As we approached, Pyrett looked up and asked, "Élan. Lauren. What can I do for you?"

"I wanted to go up to *Ellaurellin*," Élan answered. "Lauren was going to go with me. We wanted to clear that with you before we did."

"My thanks to you," Pyrett replied. "I would prefer that you not go alone. I will accompany you, but I shall wait at the top of the stairs to allow you some privacy in the experience."

"My thanks to you," Élan said.

The three of us stepped out of the palace and waited several moments for our eyes to acclimate to the darkness. Climbing nearly five hundred stairs didn't take as long as I thought it would, but I was beginning to breathe hard by the time we reached the top. Pyrett stopped at the top of the stairs.

"I shall be here if you should need me," she said quietly.

"Our thanks to you, captain," Élan said just as quietly.

The captain eased herself down to sit on the top step and Élan and I walked side by side toward the center of the hilltop.

"It is tradition to avoid looking up until we reach the center," Élan told me.

Ellaurellin covered the entire top of *Hollinskye* Hill. The night was very quiet, but not silent. A gentle breeze whispered softly, and crickets were chirping nearby. Occasionally, I could hear far off nightbirds calling. There were no birds nearby; no trees grew in *Ellaurellin* to shelter them. The grass was no more than ankle deep, though no one had taken a scythe to it in more than a thousand rounds. As we walked, we passed several backless benches made of stone. The center of the field was marked with a circle of the stone benches. Each bench was made of two upright stones capped with a slab and the circle was perhaps four paces in diameter. It struck me that in daylight, the place would look like some kind of miniature stone monument, but just then the dark and the hush and Élan's subdued attitude evoked a deep sense of reverence. When we'd reached the near part of the circle, we stopped and turned back toward the north.

"Now we can look," Élan said, so quietly that I could hardly hear her.

We both let out short gasps of surprise. I do not know why it was so, but it seemed as if the stars hung right over our heads, just barely beyond our touch. To the north, the Keystone glittered, looking more blue-violet than red-violet. Élan was whispering something. It sounded like a prayer, and I did not interrupt her. When she finished, she took my hand and we slowly walked around the circle, pausing only to regard *Elalhynn*, so clear here that we could begin to make out the individual stars forming it. When we reached the north again, Élan patted the bench, and we sat.

For a quarter of an hour or so, neither of us spoke. Awe kept us silent. I'd seen the stars before, had been entranced and calmed by their beauty. But that night, I felt small, all my pain and desires insignificant in the face of such vast peace and beauty. Élan broke our silence.

"Lauren, how did you find grandfather's workshop? You led us directly there."

I didn't answer for a moment, and she didn't press.

"I was guided," I said finally. "I have never told anyone this. Twice before today when I needed to find someone or something, I heard music that guided me. I heard it again today."

She was looking at me with an awed expression.

"You used magic," she said.

I shook my head.

"Not consciously, no. I really wanted to help you find the forge and the next thing I knew, I was hearing the music in my head."

"Could you not have done so before today? Why wait?"

"Waiting wasn't by choice," I explained. "I don't call up the music; its appearance is always unexpected."

"And you say that it has happened before?"

"Yes. Twice. The first time, my father was forcing me to train as a warrior. Some of the other boys deliberately injured me during the training. I couldn't train, but I loved to explore the forest, so I was out walking and heard the music. It led me to Ryan. The second time was in Amersford. I was there with Ryan and Ambrose to determine what was happening. I was heading to one place to try and find someone who would talk to me, but the music led me to another place and someone who gave me the answer."

Neither of us spoke for a few moments, but then more came out. I told her more about the attack by Denny and his brothers, and about the tree and my father's attack on me. And I told her about the soldiers I had killed after Ambrose's death. When I finished, I hung my head, fully expecting her to walk away from me in fear and disgust. Instead, she took my hand.

"Lauren, if they had taken your hand, do you think they would have bothered to stop the bleeding? I don't. You would have died there."

I didn't say anything and a moment later, she continued.

"The first night we met, you said that you hadn't willed what happened. Something inside you acted to protect you. Even if you had willed it, there is no crime in saving your own life."

Some of the guilt faded at her words. Ryan had said something similar to me, but somehow it mattered more coming from Élan. We sat in silence for a time, still holding hands. Then she let go and twisted to look around us.

"Things are different here," she said, speaking very softly, reverently. "No trees have ever grown here. The grass never gets higher. In spring and summer, *Ellaurellin* is dotted with starflowers. They're the only flowers that grow here. On summer nights the air is full of fireflies. I'd love to see that."

"So would I," I replied.

She was quiet for a few moments.

"This was all here when the *Eldar* came," she said. "The benches and the Thousand Stairs. We didn't build them. We're not sure who did; they don't seem like Lost constructions."

Again, she fell silent for a time. I didn't feel the need to fill that silence. She'd asked me to be there; this time was hers.

"I promised you once that I'd tell you this story. Now seems like the time..."

She paused, and when she spoke again her tone was even more reverent than it had been.

"Among the most ancient of our stories is the one that tells of the coming of the *Eldar* to these lands," she began.

"They came in three ships: the Fortune, the Endeavor, and the Shadow. Driven by the need to explore, they left their homes to find new lands and bring new knowledge back to their people. When they reached the lands at the very edge of their people's territory, their thirst for new knowledge drove them to go further. Much time passed and they saw no land. Supplies were running low. The crews debated whether to turn back or to press on, and the decision was made to continue ahead as they knew that there was no land for a long way behind them. Within days they found a small group of uninhabited islands and were able to replenish their stocks of fresh water and fruits. The islands were too small to support them, however, and so they continued.

"One evening as the sun set those who were watching saw a blaze of green on the horizon. The next morning brought great puzzlement. The crews woke to find that every person on board all three ships had been asleep. No one had been at the helm and no lookouts had kept watch. The sails were all furled. The seas were dead calm and there was no wind. When night fell, the wind began to blow, and the navigators looked to the heavens to chart a course. They found that the stars were strange to them and that none of their charts showed where they were. Some claimed that they had somehow crossed a boundary into a new world. Others pointed to the fact that, among the strange stars, the great guide star still hung in the northern sky. With that fixed point, they unfurled the sails and continued.

"And one morning as the sun cleared the horizon, the lookout on the Fortune cried out that she saw land. By midmorning they made landfall. As luck would have it, a great natural harbor lay before them. They anchored the ships and sent scouting parties ashore. When the scouts returned, they reported that, as far as they could determine, the region was uninhabited and that much fresh water and arable land was available. The decision was made to go ashore and begin construction of a settlement. They called the land *Orismë*, which means Journey's End.

"Construction of homes began. Scouts were sent out to the north, south, and east, to go as far as possible and to determine whether other people inhabited the new land. They returned to report that the new land was actually a large island and that no other people had been seen. The scouts who had gone east, however, reported the most surprising news: from the eastern beaches they could see a larger landmass to the east.

"The crews of the Endeavor and the Fortune made the decision to sail to that land, leaving Shadow's crew to continue work on the settlement. The trip was less than a day's sailing. Upon landfall they sent out scouts. It took two weeks to determine that this was a new continent and that the lands within their survey were seemingly uninhabited. The Endeavor was sent back to *Orismë* to inform the people there of the new land.

"They found the settlement empty. The buildings appeared to have been abandoned in haste; meals were left uneaten on the tables; farming tools lay where they had been dropped in new fields. Gradually they became aware of a growing sense of dread, an unshakable feeling of being watched. Endeavor's crew searched the island but found no trace of their comrades. Some began to report seeing movement out of the corners of their eyes and the sense of dread increased. Fear spread amongst Endeavor's crew, and they fled the island, renaming it *Ech Numen*, Shades Isle. They never returned."

Élan paused only a moment before continuing.

"My people set out to explore the vast new land they'd found. As they did, the memory of their previous home began to fade. Married men and women on the crews forgot the spouses they had left behind and took new husbands and wives from among their crewmates. In time, children were born. Near the place where they came ashore, they found the remains of a city. They named the place *Ervenschal*, which means earth-fall. They followed the river upstream and found the remains of another city at what is now *Aennsrhyd*. They built their capitol city here in the heart of the Lellarin Plains, where the view of the stars they loved was unobstructed in all directions. Eventually, their explorations led them into the mountains to the east and they discovered *Calyth*. And so things were for many rounds of the seasons until the coming of the Alomar."

She turned her head to look at me. I couldn't read her expression, but the light of the stars was in her eyes and my heart broke at the beauty in her face.

"Élan..." I started to say.

All at once, the night fell completely silent. Chill air seemed to slip past, though the breeze had died away and the air was still. Deep within me, something stilled, went into hiding. I tore my gaze from Élan to look up. Overhead, the stars were dimming. Élan cried out in alarm and in the distance, I could hear fearful neighs from the *aynekahrn*. Élan and I stood; she clung to me, and I wrapped my arms around her while the vast malevolent intelligence swept past us overhead, searching...

I heard footsteps pounding toward us and Pyrett ran up, her sword drawn.

"Élan, Lauren, are you unharmed?"

"Yes," I answered as I watched the haze over the stars spread toward the western horizon.

"What is that?" the captain asked.

"I do not know," I replied. "But whatever it is, the power behind it seeks me."

Élan and Pyrett both looked at me, fear on their faces.

"Is this what blighted the forest?" Élan asked.

"Yes," I answered.

"I can feel it deep inside," she told me. "It feels so wrong."

We stood frozen, silent, until the faint, sickly haze between us and the stars began to dissipate. When the sky had cleared completely, Pyrett turned to me.

"*Endollin*," she said. "We need to speak."

CHAPTER EIGHT

I felt Élan stiffen and realized that we were still clinging to one another. We let go in the same instant and turned to face the *Cadwynir* captain. Pyrett's face was stern, but I saw hints of fear around her eyes. Her sword was still out, and she held it protectively across her body, though the tip was pointed at the ground.

"Of course, Captain" I answered, matching her suddenly formal mode of address.

"May I be frank?"

"Always."

"I find myself in a difficult position."

"How so?"

"As you know, I was assigned to protect you and the Princess."

I nodded in response.

"If whatever caused that is hunting you, I am no longer sure that it is safe for the Princess to be around you."

I heard a sharp intake of breath from Élan who said, "Pyrett, I don't believe Lauren would harm me."

Pyrett nodded her agreement.

"Nor do I. But that thing that is hunting him probably would. If it finds him and you happened to be near..."

She left that thought hanging for a moment before she continued.

"Whatever that was, I do not believe that I could stand against it. I do not believe my entire squad could stand against it. I couldn't protect you from that."

The *Cadwynir* captain looked pained at the admission. The *Cadwynir* were the elite of the *Eldarin* military and Pyrett and her squad–hand-picked by the King himself–were the elite of the elite. The captain had a point and Élan had no response.

"What do you suggest that we do, Captain," I asked.

"I do not know, *aduné*" she replied. "I am conflicted. Logic and instinct say that I should keep the Princess as far away from you as possible. A small, quiet voice inside, however, suggests that doing so might not be wise."

At that moment, we heard several sets of footsteps approaching at a run. Pyrett pivoted to face them, sword at the ready, but relaxed when she saw that it was several of her comrades. The approaching trio of *Cadwynir* all had their own swords drawn. At their head was a woman named Iseabail.

"Captain, are you all well?" Iseabail asked.

"We are," Pyrett answered. "How are the rest of the party?"

"The Master Librarian was sickened by the phenomenon, but he is now recovering. The *aynekahrn* were also quite disturbed. Jorith and two others are with them calming them." She looked up at the now clear sky. "What was that?"

"Let us discuss that back in the palace. We will need to make some changes for our remaining time in the city."

No one spoke as we returned to the palace. The *Cadwynir* spread out to surround me and Élan. Once in the Great Hall, Pyrett called for everyone except those with the *aynekahrn* to assemble. We gathered around in semicircle in front of her.

"We do not know exactly what that was that we all witnessed," she began. "The *Endollin* is sure, though, that whatever caused it is seeking him. I have no reason to doubt him on that point."

She paused to look around the group.

"Given that whatever is seeking the *Endollin* now seems to have a general idea where he is, I do not believe it is wise for us to linger here. Master Librarian, how soon can you be ready to depart?"

Leonyr had obviously been ready for the question.

"I believe we've located everything that may be useful and several items of great value that have long been lost to us. I can have it all packed for safe transport in two days."

Pyrett nodded her acknowledgment.

"*Cadwynir*," she continued. "I want an extra sentry on each night shift. And I never want the Princess or the *Endollin* left without an escort."

I could see the *Cadwynir* looking around at each other, obviously considering the changes they would have to make to fulfill their captain's orders.

"I do not wish to make shift rotation more difficult than it needs to be, but I want two of you to leave at first light to scout our route west. Go as far out as you can in one day and then return."

Ryan, Élan, and I were standing together and Pyrett directed her attention to us next.

"I would like you three to stay close, preferably here in the palace. In addition, as my people will be taking on a greater load of safety duties, it would help if you could take on preparing our meals and caring for the *aynekahrn*."

Élan and I nodded. Ryan, however, spoke up.

"Captain," he said. "I believe I might be of more use assisting Leonyr in his packing."

"I could be ready somewhat sooner with assistance," the librarian noted.

"Very well," Pyrett said. "Rhion is with Leonyr. Does anyone have any questions?"

No one said anything, so Pyrett nodded.

"Then we all know what needs to be done. I need to meet with the *Cadwynir* to set duty rotations before we turn in for the night. Princess, *Endollin*, if you will excuse me."

Ryan, Leonyr, Élan and I watched for a moment as our escort moved off to discuss the night watch, then began preparing for another night on the cold marble floor of the Great Hall.

The next two days passed quickly. Élan and I were almost constantly busy. Both of us had some experience cooking, but not for fourteen people. We suffered some good-natured kidding about the scorched taste of the farina the next morning, but the *Cadwynir* watching over us gave us a few pointers and our remaining meals were ... acceptable. Our escorts also assisted us in caring for the *aynekahrn*, though truly there was little enough to do there beyond making sure that they were in a field with enough grass to graze and that they were secure.

After we had cleaned and stored the dishes on our last night in *Elsgard*, Élan and I–accompanied by Pyrett and Jorith–stepped out onto the plaza in front of the palace. The night was cool, and a slight chill breeze from the north was refreshing after two days spent mostly indoors. A waning gibbous moon hung in the southwest and tiny scraps of cloud sailed across the star-filled sky, driven by that breeze from the north. The *Cadwynir* kept their distance, giving us some degree of privacy. Élan had been unusually quiet all afternoon.

"You've been very quiet today," I said.

She didn't answer at first, so I just waited.

"Tonight is our last night here," she said finally, her speech halting and sorrowful. "I was just thinking about what happened on *Ellaurellin*. It was my first time there, the first time that anyone I know who is not from my parents' generation was there, and it ended with…" Her voice trailed off. "I don't know if I'll ever be able to go back."

Her eyes were filled with unshed tears and my heart ached to see her so sad. I turned to our escorts and raised my voice slightly.

"Captain, may I speak with you?" I called.

Pyrett and Jorith both joined us.

"What can I do for you, *Endollin*?" Pyrett asked.

"I would like to request a favor," I replied. "I would like to go back to *Ellaurellin* with Élan. There is no telling when either of us will return to *Elsgard*. Our first time to the field was spoiled and I'd like to replace that memory with a better one."

Pyrett looked from me to Élan. Her stern look softened as she noted Élan's tear-filled eyes.

"Do you expect that that thing will come seeking you again?" she asked.

"I don't believe so," I answered. I'd been thinking about that question. As far as I could remember, the only time that the gaze of that dark power returned repeatedly to the same area was after the attack on Songhaven when the figure in black had sensed me near. "That wouldn't fit the pattern that I've observed."

Pyrett considered for a moment.

"I do not see significant risk in it," she said. "I would like to visit *Ellaurellin* again myself. Let us go."

The look Élan gave me nearly broke my heart. Her eyes were still full of tears, and she looked as if she was about to smile and cry at the same time.

"*Ol gratyl selyn*," she said.

"*Se condi mun pürdonnen tol sel*," I replied. She did smile then.

We climbed the stairs without speaking. At the top, Pyrett and Jorith halted while Élan and I continued to the center of the field. We sat on the ground near the bench we'd occupied before and leaned back against the bench so that we could look almost straight up. The stars hung above us, seeming almost close enough to touch, flaming jewels of red, orange, yellow, white, and blue. The night was hushed; nothing near us made a sound except for the breeze whispering faintly through the grass. After a time, Élan scooted closer to me and laid her head on my shoulder. After a moment, I slipped my arm around her, and we sat together like that for a long while.

We saw it at the same time. The star streaked across the northern sky from west to east, trailing a line of white fire. I'd seen falling stars before, but they had disappeared as quickly as they had appeared. This one crossed the entire sky without diminishing and was as bright when we lost sight of it as it had been when we first saw it. Élan twisted to face me.

"Seeing a falling star while on *Ellaurellin* is considered lucky," she said quietly. "Seeing one like that must be doubly so. Lauren, my thanks to you."

"*Pürdonnen tol sel*," I replied.

She just looked at me, her eyes searching my face. I felt something building between us, but then she leaned back and said, "We should go back now."

I stood and gave her a hand up. Once standing, she didn't let go and we walked hand and hand until we were almost close enough for Pyrett and Jorith to see us. Only then did she let go.

I stood on a sandy patch of land, an iron-grey sea to the left and right. White-capped waves crashed on either side, growing stronger and more violent with each passing second. All around, the sky boiled with lightning-laced black clouds, and thunder growled like some massive animal, searching for something–or someone–on which to vent its rage. Wind battered me from all directions, and it was all I could do to remain standing. The grief and anguish inside me were building, every bit as violent and turbulent as the storm outside, an aching sense of loss that ripped my heart asunder and threatened to steal my breath a way.

"I lost her, Ryan," I said, knowing that I had said those words before, but knowing now that I was talking about Peg. "I tried but I lost her."

I turned then to find no one there. I was utterly alone at the heart of the storm. I didn't mean to, but I couldn't help myself: an inarticulate cry of despair tore itself out of me...

...and I woke to find tears streaming down my face and Élan crouched over me, her hand on my shoulder where she had shaken me awake.

"Lauren," she said gently. "You cried out. Are you well?"

I felt like I was struggling to breathe. I put my hand over hers and nodded, trying to catch my breath. Some of the others were beginning to gather around, curious and concerned looks on their faces.

"It was a nightmare," I managed to get out finally. "I..." My voice trailed off. I was reluctant to tell her what I'd dreamed. "I'm... I'll be fine. My thanks to you for your concern."

She watched me, doubt and concern on her face, as I sat up.

"Are you sure?" she asked.

I nodded, stood, and began storing my blanket in my saddlebags.

"I'm fine," I repeated. The terror and the pain of the dream still had hold of me. I couldn't talk about them, couldn't even admit their existence. "It was..." I struggled to find a word to describe it. "It was disturbing. Give me some time."

She simply nodded and together we went to break our fast. An hour later we rode out of *Elsgard*. Six days later, with the first snowfall of the season falling softly on our shoulders and lightly dusting the land, we worked our way down the bank of the *Kivin* and into *Evendim*.

The first quarter moon after we returned to *Evendim* was difficult for me. Élan convinced Leonyr to set aside the other treasures he'd brought back to focus on the satchel full of Lorrestian's papers. She left the house most days before the morning meal and didn't return until after the evening meal. We talked briefly in the evenings; she was by turns excited and disappointed by what she and the Master Librarian had found during the day. Lorrestian had recorded in exquisite detail the mix of metals he used in the ring and had experimented with many designs for the ornamentation before deciding on the final design. The unused designs were mostly variations on a theme of opposites. The final design, however, was an adaptation of the flowing loops and circles that the *Eldar* carved around doors, the bright gold of the raised lines standing out in stark contrast to black paint in the recesses.

At Alain's request, Ryan left the day after we returned to go to Songhaven. They both wished to know what had happened at the minstrels' college in the aftermath of the attack and were hoping to also get some word of what had been happening in the Federated Kingdoms. The king himself spent his days with his advisors and the leaders of the military, preparing for the *Eldarin* army to march; he was convinced that the fulfilment of Lorrestian's prophecy was near.

That left me on my own for most of the day. I had no duties within Alain's household and no obligations anywhere in the city. Many people were working very hard to help me, but as a person I seemed to have been forgotten. So, I spent a great deal of time alone in my room practicing. The weather, which had stayed unusually warm for the fall, had suddenly turned bitter cold. Too cold to go out without a cloak. The one I had worn on the trip to *Elsgard* was part of the regulation *Cadwynir* gear and had been returned to them when we reached *Evendim*. I had no other. The few clothes that I did have had all been given to me by Alain.

I felt lost. People were working to locate Lorrestian's sword for me. I had asked them to do that. Remembering my conversation with Élan in *Elsgard*, I tried to reach out myself to find the sword. I stood on the terrace in the freezing cold and opened myself to the music, but nothing came. Only when I could no longer control my shivering did I give up and go back inside. As I sat warming myself beside the small fire in my room, I considered what I had just done. I had deliberately sought out a weapon. But I was a minstrel and the thought of carrying a sword, of wielding a sword, and intentionally killing disturbed me to my core. I had picked up a sword in the fight that claimed Ambrose's life and I still flushed with shame every time I thought of that. I remembered the conversation I'd been part of the night I met Peg...

Peg. I'd dreamt of her several times on the trip back from *Elsgard* and again after we reached *Evendim*. In most, I was just sitting with her, knowing somehow that she shouldn't be there, and that she was going to be gone again soon. I woke from those dreams heartbroken, with tears rolling down my face. Then I'd join Alain's family for the morning meal and make small talk until they all left to attend to their tasks, and I'd return to my room alone.

I realized after eight days that sitting alone in my room wasn't doing me any good. Peg had once told me that sitting alone in the dark could wither your heart and that was exactly what I'd been doing since we returned. With that realization came another: the *Eldar* were not going to ask me for anything. I was the *Endollin*. They weren't ignoring me; they were waiting for me to tell them what I wanted. The question was, what should I be doing? I thought I knew the answer, I just didn't want to face it.

Eventually, though, I decided that I had to face it. People were going to be counting on me. To do what I needed to do would require help from the King. Because it was several hours past the morning meal, I knew that Alain would be in the palace in the center of the city. I steeled myself for a long walk in the cold, but I really wasn't prepared for how bitterly cold the weather was. By the time I reached the palace—which I now knew was built to the same plan as the one in *Elsgard* but constructed of granite instead of Elfstone—I was shivering continuously. As I approached the palace door, I was challenged by a pair of guards in the midnight blue and gold livery of the King's Guard.

"*Endollin*," one of them said. "*Selé il manana tul seli navoram.* How may we be of service?"

"I would like to request an audience with the King," I said. I was shivering so badly that it took me three tries to get the sentence out.

"At once," the man said.

He opened the door, and we stepped inside. It was warm inside; there were fires in all four of the massive fireplaces. The dark granite walls made *Evendim's* Great Hall seem smaller than the one in *Elsgard*. The space was populated with many small groups of people, all in deep conversation with one another. Several individuals stood at the foot of the dais, conversing with Alain, who sat upon a huge wooden throne. The guard spoke briefly to the Warden of the Door, nodded to me, and returned to his post.

The Warden was holding a tall oak staff with an ornamental head fashioned after the head of a mace. He rapped its iron foot three times on the marble floor and announced in a loud voice, "Lauren, son of Dalach, Minstrel of Alomar and *Endollin*, requests an audience with Alain, son of Lorrestian, King of the *Eldar*."

I briefly wondered how it was that the Warden knew my father's name, but then the hall fell silent, and all eyes turned toward me.

The King looked up from his conversation, saw me, and nodded.

"I will hear you, *Endollin*," he said, pitching his voice to carry.

I walked slowly across the hall to kneel before the King, still shivering despite the warmth of the room. The King noticed.

"You are not wearing a cloak," he observed.

"Your Majesty, I do not own a cloak and have not yet learned how I might go about earning enough to purchase one," I replied.

"It would be poor hospitality indeed, to have a minstrel visit my realm and suffer for the lack of a cloak."

He glanced at one of the men with whom he had been conversing and nodded and the man hurried off.

"Sire, I do not come before you today as a minstrel," I said.

The King cocked his head and simply looked at me expectantly.

"Sire, many of your people are working diligently to locate Lorrestian's sword. They do so at my request. However, as a minstrel, I am not trained to arms. If I am to use the sword effectively, if I am to protect your people and mine, I need training. Thus, my request: if it pleases Your Majesty, I'd like someone to train me."

The King spent a moment staring at me impassively and then said, "*Endollin*, I would have a word with you in private. Approach, please."

I rose and climbed the three steps to the top of the dais.

"Lauren, could you not have asked me this tonight at the house? You had to freeze yourself half to death to ask me in front of all my courtiers?"

"I think I did, Alain. On the journey to *Elsgard*, I only interacted directly with a few of the *Cadwynir*, but they were uneasy around me, and I saw the occasional looks from all of them. You said yourself that until you met me, you were sure that the *Endollin* was going to doom your people. I thought that they should hear that I respect you as their king, that I intend them no harm, and that I will do whatever I can to protect them."

He nodded.

"Very well. Step down and I will announce my decision."

I stepped down off the dais and turned to face the King. As I started to kneel, he gestured for me to remain standing.

"*Endollin*," he said, pitching his voice so that all could hear. "I have heard your request. I know that as a Minstrel of Alomar, training and tradition forbids you to carry arms. Your willingness to set aside your training and the traditions of your people to aid the *Eldar* means much to me. I, therefore, grant your request. I will consider whom to appoint overnight and will inform you of my choice on the morrow."

"Your Majesty," said a familiar voice and Pyrett stepped out of the crowd. "If I may be so bold, I would offer my services. I would be honored to train the *Endollin*."

Alain nodded to her and turned to me.

"*Endollin*?"

"*Se condi er manana tul masyl wealtyr*," I replied. "I would be honored by her service."

"Then it is settled," the King replied. "I shall leave it to you two to make the arrangements."

Alain turned back to the men he'd been speaking with when I arrived, and I turned to Pyrett.

"Captain," I said, "Thank you for agreeing to train me."

"As I said, it will be an honor," she replied. She ran her eyes over me, assessing. "Have you ever trained before?"

At that moment, the man who had left earlier returned with a hooded cloak. It was dyed a deep blue and was lined with rabbit fur.

"*Sel cali ol selyn, aduné*, I said as he handed it to me. "You have my thanks, sir."

He simply nodded his acknowledgment and then returned to the conversation with Alain.

"I trained for a couple of moons when I had fourteen rounds," I told Pyrett in answer to her question.

"So, not much. When do you wish to begin?"

"Could we begin tomorrow?" I asked.

"We certainly could. I have a *shynsen* at my home. We can work there."

"*Shynsen*? I do not know that word."

"A *shynsen* is a large room specifically designed as a personal space for practicing the skills of a warrior."

Something in her tone told me that the offer to train in her *shynsen* was unusual and not made lightly.

"My thanks to you, Pyrett," I said. "I am grateful for your offer to allow me to train in your personal *shynsen*."

"A *shynsen* is a personal space, so adding personal is unnecessary," she said, but she was smiling as she said it. She then taught me the way from Alain's home on *Creagalt* to her home in Westbridge. Then she returned to her duties and I, wrapped in my new cloak, returned to Alain's home.

Later that evening, I was sitting in the front room of Alain's home with Alain, Réalta, and Élan. We had drawn our chairs up in a semicircle facing the fireplace. Élan was telling us about her work with Lorrestian's notes.

"All of the intact documents concerned the ring," she said, "I've told you about those. They were all on the top of the stack. The documents on the bottom are in very bad shape. At some point, water got into the satchel and caused the ink to run. It also fused many of the pages together. In addition, those pages are the ones that mice and insects dug into. Most of them are beyond hope of recovery, but I've got hundreds of small scraps and pieces with legible writing on them. None of those pieces has more than a couple of words on them, but I'm hoping to be able to piece some of them together. If I can, maybe we'll learn something about the sword."

"Even if you cannot," Alain said, "I want you to know how proud I am of what you have accomplished so far. You have truly put your heart into this effort."

He stood and Réalta joined him.

"We are going to retire," she said. "May the night bring you pleasant dreams."

That left Élan and me alone, each of us staring into the fire.

"I've been so busy since we got back," she said after a time. "We haven't had much time to talk."

I didn't say anything but glanced at her and nodded.

"I hear that you are going to begin training to use a sword," she said softly. "Lauren, that must have been a difficult decision. How are you?"

I turned to look at her. Part of me still felt as if she had been ignoring me, but the look of concern on her face seemed truly genuine.

"Resigned," I answered. "Afraid. Ill. Élan, when I had but fourteen rounds, I left my home to avoid training to be a warrior. I ran from the training because I didn't wish to kill. But that thing that is hunting me has already killed the High King of the Alomar, it has killed people I loved..."

I broke off then, a confused knot of emotions clogging my throat.

"It killed Peg," she said, some strong emotion straining her voice.

I nodded.

"And now I'm here in *Evendim*. I can't let it hurt your people. I can't let it hurt..." I swallowed hard and looked directly at her, "you."

She didn't respond and I didn't continue. We sat regarding one another until a loud snap from the fire broke the spell. I dropped my gaze to the floor.

"Élan, whatever it is that is hunting me feels huge and powerful. I don't know whether I can stand against it. Even if I can, I don't know how. But if picking up a sword–the sword–gives me a chance to stop it from hurting you or anyone else, then I have to take that chance, no matter what it does to me."

We didn't talk much after that, but she moved to the chair next to mine and took my hand in hers. We sat like that until the fire burned down to embers. Then Élan rose to bank the fire for the night, and I left to go to my room.

The next morning, I set out early to meet with Pyrett. Her home was on the very western edge of the city and beyond it was nothing but unsettled foothills. My walk there took me through the Westbridge section of town, and the air was full of the smell of fresh baked bread and pastries from the *tybith* I passed. Pyrett's house was one of the few that I had seen in *Evendim* that had a second story. The walls of the first story were built of stone, but the second story was of wood construction. Pyrett answered the door as soon as I began to knock, and she immediately took me up a narrow flight of stairs to the upper floor.

The entire second story was one large room, rectangular in shape, perhaps 6 paces wide by 8 paces long. The western and eastern walls–the long walls–each contained nine windows. The windows to the west offered an amazing view of the mountains while the eastern ones looked out over *Evendim*. The walls were painted a pale blue, and the floor was polished wood. The north wall held several large wooden cabinets that I assumed contained weapons. The walls were also adorned with tapestries and paintings, all depicting natural landscapes. I was pretty sure that one or two of the paintings had been created by Réalta. Altogether, the effect was calming and peaceful.

"Pyrett, your *shynsen* is a very beautiful and peaceful place," I said. "That surprises me."

She looked at me quizzically.

"Why is that," she asked.

"You practice fighting here," I answered. "The man who trained me before always seemed angry. He always seemed to try and get us worked up."

"I have endeavored to eliminate emotion from this place," Pyrett replied. "In battle, fear clouds your thinking. Elation clouds your thinking. In a fight, emotions are an enemy. In battle, shun them. Love, fear, joy, hatred, those are for life. In life, feel them, revel in them. They give meaning to life, and they give us something to fight for. But when fighting, strive to remain calm. The goal is to outthink your opponent and that is difficult to do if you are afraid or angry."

"Do you have any idea what Lorrestian's sword is like?" she asked.

"No," I replied. "So far, Élan has been unsuccessful in retrieving information from Lorrestian's notes. So, all that I know is that it exists, and that it has a stone like the one in this ring somewhere on it."

"That is unfortunate," she said. "It would be best to train with something as much like the weapon you will be using as possible. Until we know more, we will have to make do."

She gestured for me to follow as she started across the room.

"To truly be effective, your sword should be an extension of your arm," she told me. "You need to be comfortable holding it and moving it should be as natural to you as moving any other part of your body. But beyond that, you should use whatever is in your environment to aid you. Objects around you can serve many purposes, from small things that you can throw at your opponent to large objects that you can use to limit your opponent's movements."

I nodded and she continued.

"You also need to read your opponent, the slight shifts of stance or grip that signal a forthcoming movement, the furtive glances that reveal intent, or the physical signs in breathing and posture that signal confidence, weariness, or defeat."

"I understand," I said.

We'd reached the cabinets, and she opened one and pulled out a pair of wooden training swords.

"Let us begin," she said as she handed one of them to me.

One day several weeks later, a palace messenger arrived at Pyrett's home just as we were finishing for the day.

"*Endollin*," he said. "The King requests your presence at the palace as soon as possible."

"That's all of the message?" I asked.

"It is, *aduné*," he answered. "I can add, however, that the request was issued shortly after *Elnyr* Élan arrived and spoke with the King."

I exchanged glances with Pyrett. I'm sure that we were thinking the same thing: Élan must have learned something about the sword.

"Go," the *Cadwynir* captain said. "I will see you tomorrow."

When we arrived at the palace, the messenger took me to what had been the residential wing in the *Elsgard* palace and to the King's personal office. Alain was seated behind the desk, which was smaller than his father's and made of a much lighter colored wood. Élan was sitting in a chair before the desk, a look of impatience on her face. The King looked up as we entered and smiled.

"My thanks to you, Trevith, for locating the *Endollin*," he said. "And my thanks to you, Lauren, for coming so quickly."

Trevith bowed to the king, nodded to me, and left the room, closing the door behind him.

"Lauren, please sit. Élan has news."

I took the other chair before the desk, and Alain and I turned to Élan.

She leaned forward in her chair.

"I've done everything with grandfather's notes that I can," she said. "As you know, most of what could be read dealt with the ring. I've told you about most of that. I will add this now: Lauren, you once said that you didn't know whether the ring did anything other than mark you as the *Endollin*. From studying grandfather's notes, I'm fairly certain that is all that it was ever intended to do. Nothing in what he recorded even hinted at some other purpose."

"My thanks to you," I replied. "I'm glad to know that."

She smiled and then continued.

"The materials in the bottom of the satchel were all badly damaged. Water and pests destroyed most of it. I had hundreds of scraps with writing on them and I've spent hours trying to piece together what I could. Too much was missing, though. I was on the final pile of scraps and seriously considered giving up and throwing them out. I decided, though, to go ahead and finish. I'm glad that I did. I found almost a dozen small scraps that all fit together. Much is missing, but they all seem to come from the same sentence. It says 'sword of law' and then there are some missing words, the word 'cave', and then 'locked in ice and warded by fire.'"

She looked at Alain and then me and then turned back to her father as if waiting for one of us to speak. Neither of us did.

"Based on that," she continued, "If the sword of law is *Endolsar*–and I think it is–then we now know that *Endolsar* means sword of law. And if that's true, then *Endolsar* is a word in the True Speech, a word that comes from the same root as *Endollin*."

"That's all I have, though," she said, sounding a little defeated. "In all that we brought back from *Elsgard*, that's all I have been able to find."

I started to speak, but Alain cut me off.

"Élan, it is only part of a sentence, but it is a part of a sentence that we did not have before. Your analysis of the meaning of *Endolsar* is sound; I believe that you are correct. Further, there is more information in what you found than you seem to recognize."

Élan looked at her father, a puzzled frown on her face.

"What do you mean?"

"My reading of the sentence," Alain explained, "is that the sword is in a cave. Caves are most often found in hilly or mountainous terrain. That means that we do not need to search the cities or the plains. We also know from the historical record how long Lorrestian was gone from *Elsgard*. Combining those, we can calculate how far he could have gone which will allow us to narrow our search to only those hills and mountains that he could have reached in the time he was absent from *Elsgard*."

Élan nodded, smiling.

"I cannot even speculate about the meaning of 'locked in ice and warded by fire'," Alain admitted. "Perhaps our scholars could offer a theory. You should share this with them as soon as you can."

"I will," Élan said. "I wanted you two to be the first to hear."

I slipped out of my chair and knelt on one knee before Élan.

"*Ol gratyl selyn*," I said. "You have worked so hard and have provided the only information that we have about the sword. I am in your debt."

She leaned back in her chair and smiled.

"Well, then," she said. "Tonight, after the evening meal, I would like you to sing for me."

"As you wish," I replied and bowed my head.

Our initial elation over Élan's findings died down quickly. Though the sentence fragment narrowed the search, the remaining area to be searched was still huge. Mounted on an *aynekahrn*, Lorrestian could have reached anywhere in the Corun Hills, the eastern slopes of the Breton Mountains south of the Corun Hills, or the northernmost slopes of the Gray Mountains. Leonyr noted that the Great South Road through the Corun Hills had been rerouted at about the time that Lorrestian hid the sword and suggested that perhaps the change was due to something Lorrestian had done, but teams sent to the old routing found that over much of its length the ancient road had been cut by massive landslides. They found no evidence of a cave.

The search was also hampered by the weather. Early in the second moon of *Tymnahaef*, temperatures dropped to well below freezing and stayed there. The *Kivin* began to freeze over for the first time in history and even a brief time outside with exposed skin risked severe frostbite. Nonetheless, I wrapped myself up each morning and reported to Pyrett's home to train. I had improved somewhat, but seemed to have hit a level of competence that I couldn't surpass no matter how I tried. Near the middle of the third moon, I was working with Pyrett when she disarmed me again. I was feeling somewhat proud; I had managed to last almost ten minutes, far longer than usual. As I started to retrieve my sword, Pyrett spoke.

"Lauren, stop. We need to talk."

I turned to her, puzzled.

"We've been training for well over a moon now. You're better than you were when we began, but you're no longer improving."

"Pyrett, I'm trying..." I began, but she cut me off.

"Let me speak my piece," she said. "I know that you think you're trying. But I have been sparring with you and I've watched you when you've sparred with other partners. You're holding back. You're a minstrel and you do not wish to harm another person and so you're holding back. I understand that."

She paused to pick up a cloth and wipe the sweat from her face.

"Lauren, there will always be disagreements among people and fighting should never be the first choice for resolving those disagreements. Killing your opponent doesn't resolve the disagreement, it merely postpones it until the next person with that point of view comes along. You would be better served by converting that person to your point of view or–if warranted–recognizing that the other person is correct and adopting their point of view.

"Sometimes, however, you will encounter someone who will not listen to you, someone who will refuse to discuss with you, someone who will endeavor to harm you or kill you. Then–like it or not–you must fight. Even then, you should do no more than you must. Do not kill if incapacitating your opponent will suffice."

She went to retrieve a glass of water from a small table at the end of the *shynsen*. I followed.

"Pyrett," I said. "I understand that. But when Marc and his men attempted to take me, I killed seven of them. I didn't mean to, and I didn't will it, but I killed them. I do not want to do that again and I especially do not want to accidently kill you."

In a flash, she turned and struck my arm with the flat of her wooden sword, hard. As I reached to cover the spot, she smacked my hand, not hard enough to break anything, but hard enough that it brought tears to my eyes. I stared at her, dumbfounded.

"Lauren, I've listened to what you've told me about that. Whatever power resides in you seems to recognize the difference between a simple hurt and a life-threatening attack. If it were otherwise, I would have been dead a number of times over in the last moon."

I shook my head, rubbing my sore hand.

"You couldn't have just told me that?"

She smiled.

"This was, I think, more effective. Still, I do believe that it would be wise to continue practicing with wooden swords and avoid live steel."

I laughed at that as she continued.

"As I said, you've been holding back. You ignore obvious openings and fail to press clear advantages. Lauren, you cannot win fighting defensively only. I've felt that thing that's hunting you. If it can kill you, it will. And if you just try to defend against it, it will prevail. Defense cannot last against a determined opponent. In fighting defensively, you must prevail every single time. Your opponent, however, only has to succeed once. Sooner or later, it will find a weakness, or you'll make a mistake..."

She stopped, turned toward me, and searched my face, perhaps for signs of understanding or acceptance. What she saw clearly didn't satisfy her.

"People are counting on you," she said. "The Alomar do not know it, but they are counting on you. The *Eldar* are counting on you. Lauren, the entire world is counting on you. And, if all of that is not enough, consider Élan."

My heart lurched.

"Élan?"

She shook her head slightly.

"Do you think I am blind? I have seen the way you two look at each other. You obviously love her, and she just as obviously loves you. The only two people who have not yet admitted that are the two of you."

Ignoring my stunned look, she returned to the center of the *shynsen*.

"Well," she said. "Pick up your sword. We must get back to work."

I was sitting beside Élan. She smiled at me and leaned in as if to kiss me. Then she stopped. I wasn't sure how to react. I wasn't sure whether she really wanted me to kiss her or not, so I leaned towards her. We'd move closer, then back a little. Then our lips met in a quick, light kiss. Then again. Then we kissed for real...

...and I woke alone in my bed. I felt snug and content, too warm and too comfortable to move, and reveling in the feel Élan's lips on mine. Slowly it dawned on me that it had only been a dream, and I found myself faintly puzzled that I would dream such a thing. Then I remembered the morning's conversation with Pyrett. And then I remembered Peg and I felt my face flush. I did sleep again that night, but my sleep was troubled by desire and shame and longing and guilt.

I rose early the next morning and–bundled up against the cold–went to soak in the bathhouse. I could not get the dream images out of my head, and I could still feel Élan's lips pressed against mine. Then thoughts of Peg would arise: how she looked lying in the sunlight the first time we'd made love, the way she felt when she snuggled up against me on cold winter nights. The sound she'd made in my nightmares...

My training session with Pyrett that day went reasonably well. I made it clear that I'd heard what she'd said the day before, so even though I was quieter than normal, she didn't push me, but limited the conversation to what I could do to improve.

That afternoon–like most afternoons–I was on my own. Though Élan had finished her work with Lorrestian's notes, she still had other obligations that kept her busy most of the day. I had mentioned once that I was looking for a quiet, out-of-the-way place to practice and Alain offered the use of his personal study, a small, one-room building that stood a short distance from his house. I stopped in the kitchen for a light midday meal, retrieved my guitar from my room, and went to Alain's study.

The study was a single medium-sized room, with the light oak walls that Alain preferred. The space was dominated by a huge window that overlooked *Evendim*. The metal framework of the window was as small and thin as it could be and still securely hold the panes of glass. The glass in that window was the clearest I'd ever seen; the *Eldarin* crafters had done superb work and there was little or no distortion of the view. Even in winter, the view of the city and the valley was spectacular.

I spent a few minutes lighting the fire and warming myself and then perched on an armless chair facing the window. I had intended to run scales and bass runs, but instead I just sat and stared out the window and allowed my hands to play gentle, melancholy chords while in my mind I once again leaned forward to kiss Élan. I heard Pyrett's voice saying, "You obviously love her..." and I told myself that I couldn't love her, that it wouldn't be fair to her since I loved Peg. I didn't want to betray Peg's love for me, but Peg was gone, and Élan seemed to like me. Pyrett said that Élan loved me. My thoughts were confused, colored with longing and pain. My hands found a chord sequence and I sa ng:

> It's altogether the saddest thing
> I think I've ever done.
> To be all alone and loving you
> In the early morning sun.
> To wonder who you're knowing
> And where you're going to
> And is there time and is there space
> For me and love and you.

A tear slid down my face. I wasn't sure who I was singing for...
I felt a hand on my shoulder and Élan said, "You are not alone."
I hadn't heard her come in and I jumped slightly. But then I put my hand over hers.
"My thanks to you, Élan."

The next half moon–the days leading up to Rounds End Day–were a confusion of emotions and activities. For the Alomar, Rounds End Day was the Day of Atonement, a day of penance and deprivation. We were taught to use the days leading up to it to reflect on the previous round and our sins against Mar and to plan how we could better worship her in the new round of the seasons. Fasting in those days was encouraged and no one ate at all on Rounds End Day. For the *Eldar*, however, Rounds End Day was a day of celebration and thanksgiving, a day to appreciate all that you had and to share your bounty with family and friends.

I had been asked to perform at a large gathering of the King's family and friends and I wanted to learn a few traditional *Eldarin* songs to honor my hosts. I was thinking that I could work with Gotyr to learn a few songs. The morning after I was asked to play, however, Réalta suggested as we broke our fast that Élan could help me and that we could even sing together on those songs. My thoughts immediately went to all the time that I'd spent singing with Peg and my heart nearly shattered, but Élan looked so happy that I couldn't refuse.

After we ate, I wrapped a scarf around my face, pulled on my hooded cloak, wrapped cloths around my hands and went down to Pyrett's to train. I had been taking her lessons to heart and that morning for the first time I had pierced her defenses and landed a blow. So, I was feeling fairly good as I began my climb back toward Alain's home.

Halfway there, a couple of men fell in behind me. Wrapped as I was against the cold, they didn't recognize me. They were speaking the *Eldarin* tongue, but I'd learned enough by then to follow what they were saying.

"*I hear that the* Endollin *has been asked to play at the celebration,*" one said.

"*Yes, he has,*" the other replied. I recognized his voice. It was Davan, the head of one of the other ruling families. "*Did you hear as well what Alain has done?*"

That piqued my interest, and I slowed my pace just a little so that I could hear them better.

"*No,*" the first speaker said. "*What has he done?*"

"*He has his daughter singing with the* Endollin *at the celebration.*"

"*Truly? Or are you jesting?*"

"*No, I do not jest,*" Davan said. "*Is it not enough that he's had the* Endollin *living in his home all these moons and that he sent the two of them off to* Elsgard *together?*"

"*I do not exactly like it,*" the first man said. "*But can you blame him though? A match between Élan and the* Endollin *would offer many advantages.*"

"I understand that," Davan said, irritation in his voice. *"But to throw her so blatantly at him? It strikes me as terribly gauche."*

"Truly, Davan? Or are you simply upset that you haven't had a chance to make the case for your own daughter?"

At that point, their path diverged from mine, and I heard no more of the conversation. The uncertainty that I felt about singing with Élan, however, had been replaced with shame and sadness.

That afternoon, I sat alone before the fire in the front room of Alain's house. My guitar was resting in a stand in front of me and I watched the flickering light of the fire dancing on the silver strings. I didn't look up when Élan entered.

"Lauren, *ol sym en elested tul seli navoram,*" she said as she sat.

I didn't answer but continued to watch the firelight playing on the strings of my guitar.

"Lauren?" Élan said, sounding puzzled.

My heart felt as if it was struggling to beat while buried in gray ash. I finally turned to face her.

"Élan, were we fated to be together? Is our relationship–whatever there is between us–just the fulfillment of some prophecy that no one has told me about? Or is it all just political expediency?"

She looked shocked and hurt and some part of me immediately felt bad for hurting her. She didn't answer at first, but I could see her scanning my face, trying to understand. Then she slumped back in her chair and a tear slid down her cheek.

"After all this time, after all we've done together, that's what you think of my family? That's what you think of me?"

I didn't respond. I was sad that I'd hurt her, but I couldn't see past my own hurt and confusion.

"There is no prophecy concerning you and me. And I have no idea what political gain you think I or my family would get from you and I having a relationship. When his term ends, my father will step down from being King. Were we together, it would not add even one minute to his reign. And you and I being together would not win him more votes in his Council. His policies have always been popular; no one has argued against anything that he has proposed, not even in preparing to march out to war for you."

She paused, tears flowing freely now.

"Why would you think my family is trying to put us together?"

She waited for me to answer, but I still couldn't bring myself to speak.

"Do you know what my mother told me before we left for *Elsgard*?"

I shook my head, feeling my anger begin to drain away to be replaced by chagrin.

"She told me to stay away from you. My parents do not want us to get close."

"Why?" I asked, my voice hoarse with emotion.

"You may be the *Endollin*," she answered. "And they like you. They respect you. They counted on you to protect me. But you are still a mortal. They don't want to see me give my heart to you only to see it shattered when you die."

She wiped the tears off her face.

"Rhion's mother is mortal," she said very quietly. "She has sixty-nine rounds of the seasons now. She hasn't recognized anyone–not even Rhion–for more than a round of the seasons. She is emaciated, her hair has gone thin and white, and she is wasting away a little more every day. Rhion's father is still devoted to her, but he now has to care for the great passion of his life as if she were a newborn child. She is fading away while he is still as hale and strong as he was when they first met nearly fifty rounds ago. His heart is broken–perhaps beyond healing–and he is already deep in grief. We fear what he may do when she finally dies."

Tears were streaming down her face again. I felt terrible, but I couldn't find words to say.

"Lauren, I know that you are still grieving for Peg. I have tried to respect that, to allow you time to heal, and so I did not speak even when realized how I was beginning to feel about you. Why would you think that my interest in you was only political?"

In a strained monotone, I told her what I'd heard as I returned from my training that morning. The hurt look on her face faded somewhat, replaced by puzzlement.

"I do not know why Davan would say such a thing. Political marriages have never been the way of our people. Could he possibly have known it was you and was jesting with you?"

"I don't believe so," I said. I stood, intending to go and kneel before her and beg her to forgive me, but she stood and met me halfway.

"Élan, I am so sorry," I said.

In reply, she put her arms around my neck, pulled me to her, and kissed me. And after a stunned instant, I kissed her back. I put my arms around her and tried to pull her even closer. We pressed up against each other as if we were trying to merge with one another. After a few moments, she broke the kiss, laid her head on my shoulder, and whispered, "Did that feel political?"

"Not at all," I whispered back.

A short time later, we were singing together. We began with *The Cylin Witch*. Élan had a beautiful voice, and she could vary the intonation to express everything from a warm, inviting, sing-around-the-kitchen-table feeling to a haunting, aching loneliness that made me wonder exactly what her early life had been like. She was perfectly capable of carrying a song on her own but could also weave a light, ethereal harmony around even my most complex melodies. Her interpretation of the countermelody for the *Witch* managed to convey–just through the tonal qualities of her voice–a sense of a lonely woman, misunderstood and driven out of her society who nonetheless chooses to aid a member of that society despite the consequences to herself.

After that, we sang together every afternoon. If Réalta had intended to keep us apart, asking us to sing together undermined that intent. I felt as if we were growing closer every day. As we practiced, I found myself learning to anticipate what Élan would do from subtle changes in her voice or expression. Réalta's original plan had been for Élan to sing only a few *Eldarin* songs with me, but we so enjoyed singing together that she learned all the other songs that I planned to play as well. Singing with Élan elicited the first true joy that I had felt since I earned my minstrel's sash.

That half moon was not entirely joyful. My nights were full of tortured dreams. The odd dreams that I had of Peg–the ones in which we were simply together but in which I knew that she would soon be gone–increased in frequency. Interspersed with those were nightmares in which I was hunted by the dark thing, watching as it consumed the people and places that I loved. Once, I dreamed that I had found the sword. I never saw it but was holding it as the dark thing enveloped me, swallowed me, and then used me to tear the world apart.

The rumors that Alain was somehow unfairly benefiting from my relationship with Élan persisted and spread beyond Davan. By Round's End Day, a third of Alain's Council had expressed concerns that the King had used his daughter to gain some unnamed advantage. Members of Alain's household reported that even people on the street were beginning to complain. We were all puzzled; there were no benefits to Alain and the rumors never said what they were supposed to be. But discontent–rare among the *Eldar*–seemed to be growing.

Alain's Round's End Day celebration was a joyous event, well enjoyed by those in attendance. Davan and several others of the King's Council refused to attend, but those who were there sang and danced and laughed and ate and rewarded Élan and me with ovation after ovation. It was well past midnight when the last of the guests departed to get some rest before the sunrise start to the Winter Day of Passages atop *Creagalt*. Élan and I walked back to Alain's home together. At the door, I paused.

"Lauren, *tel seli saft wydd er awl an elnir nal sharit nal gwenfed*," she said. "May your next round be full of light and love and joy."

"*Tel seli saft wydd er awl an elnir nal sharit nal gwenfed*," I replied.

We kissed then, the first time we'd done so since our first kiss.

"We should get some rest," she said. "You still have one more song to sing."

Dawn found us on the summit of *Creagalt*, wrapped in the heaviest cloaks we could find to fend off the bitter cold. I was standing alone to the King's left; for the first time I would lead the sunrise chant. As the rising sun lifted clear of the horizon, I took a deep breath and sang:

> We open our hearts this day
> To give thanks to the Old Ones.

Twice before I had participated in the ancient rites honoring the Old Ones and twice before my awareness had expanded to include all the world. This time was different; the effect was immediate and profound. I was every slumbering tree, bare of the leaves that made my food, my life slowed almost to a standstill. I was the water in the *Kivin*, icy hard but waiting for the warmth that would set me free. I was a black bear, curled up in my den and I was a deer searching the frozen forest for something green to fill my empty stomach. I could sense the people around me, could see the bright lights of their spirits. All at once I became aware of subtle lines of light linking all of them to some power that lived in the core of every particle of the world and, climbing up some of those gossamer bonds, thin tendrils of darkness, of wrong.

Without thinking and without understanding how I did so, I pushed back against the darkness. It resisted at first, but then melted away. As it faded, I briefly sensed the dark presence, full of malevolence, but also of fear. Then it was gone, and I was myself again, singing the final notes of the rite. I fell silent, feeling drained.

There was a disturbance behind me. I turned and found a dozen or so people pushing their way through the crowd toward me. Davan was at the head of the group and my heart sank, fearing an ugly confrontation that would spoil the day's celebration. The group stopped in front of me; Davan stood face-to-face with me. He was a tall man, half a head taller than me, with long golden hair held back from his face by a thin gold circlet. His eyes were an icy grey-blue. His expression was unreadable.

Then to my surprise, he knelt. He and the entire group dropped to one knee and bowed their heads. They stayed like that for a long moment and then Davan looked up at me, his face suddenly full of emotion.

"*Endollin. Ol gratyl selyn*," he said. "I saw it. I saw the thing that was darkening my spirit. I felt you drive it out. I owe you my life." He looked at the others in his group and they nodded their agreement. "We all do."

"I also owe an apology to you and to my Princess and to my King. I behaved as a fool, and I beg your forgiveness."

Alain stepped forward then.

"I do not believe that an apology is necessary," he said. "I too saw. You were under the influence of some dark power that assailed our very lifeforce. I believe we have all been saved by the *Endollin*. Rise, my friends, and let us celebrate together."

The King raised his voice to address the crowd.

"My people, we are grateful indeed for the lives we have been given. Today, we are also grateful for the actions of the *Endollin*, who drove back a darkness assailing us. Let us go down now and celebrate."

CHAPTER NINE

There was an immediate change in the weather, obvious even as we left the summit of *Creagalt*. The bitterness was gone from the cold and by early afternoon the temperature had warmed to the point that people traded their heavy, fur-lined cloaks for lighter weight ones.

Alain's family had chosen Élan to remain at home to serve as the family's host on the Winter Day of Passages. I elected to stay with her. We spent the day greeting people as they arrived, offering welcome and food and drink to a steady stream of guests. Stories from our trip to *Elsgard* were told, discussed, marveled over, and then told again. We were frequently asked to sing, and before we knew it, we were singing almost continuously. We quickly ran through the entire repertoire that we had prepared for the celebration the night before, but the requests to sing did not cease and so we began to improvise. Early in the evening, Gotyr arrived with his guitar and the three of us entertained the crowd together. The guests so enjoyed our music that–despite the custom–they came, and they stayed. Soon, Alain's home was so full of people that it became difficult to move.

It was well past midnight when we felt it. I was singing *The White Dolphin*, a rousing, somewhat bawdy sea chanty about the ship that was the long-time winner of the annual sailing race from Cha Peraluda to Meren. Élan was improvising a harmony and Gotyr, a *kahill* wrapped around the neck of his guitar, was playing along using different chord forms. I saw a few people gasp and double over and glanced at Élan. She raised one eyebrow, but then the room was suddenly filled with cries of alarm. Élan and Gotyr faltered and fell silent, both obviously afraid. Deep inside me, something went still and silent and I knew that outside the stars were dimming as the dark power reached out, seeking me.

It didn't last long. Within minutes, the sense of that malevolent presence faded and was gone. The celebratory mood was broken, though, and the suddenly somber crowd began to break up and leave for their own homes.

When enough of the guests had departed that it was possible to move in the house, Alain and Réalta entered. Their faces were pale, their expressions guarded, though I thought I saw signs of fear in their eyes.

"We've been back for some time," Alain said. "The house was so full of guests that we couldn't get in. Then..." He gestured awkwardly skyward. "Was that what you experienced in *Elsgard*?"

"Yes," Élan answered.

"It was searching," Réalta said, her voice strained. "I could sense that it was looking for something."

"It was seeking me," I responded. "It must have felt what I did this morning."

I had been considering all the times that I had sensed the dark power seeking me and struggled to form my thoughts into words.

"When I do something like I did this morning, I think it gets a vague sense of where I am," I said. "But it can never quite find me."

Alain was staring at me intently.

"And if it does?" he asked.

"I hope I've found the sword before then."

Alain didn't respond to that but stood regarding me thoughtfully.

"What was that?" Réalta asked.

"I do not know," I answered. "I dreamed of it as a child, and I have sensed it searching for me ever since."

Alain was looking thoughtful.

"Lauren, I have given this much thought since you and Élan described what happened in *Elsgard*," he said. "The *Book of Kings* says only that the *Endollin* will battle the Keepers, but oral tradition amongst my people—and yours, I believe—has always said that the *Endollin* will battle the Keepers and Mar. As I'm sure that Rhion and Élan have told you, there is some ambiguity about whether there were seven or eight beings in the throne room when my father was killed. The potential eighth—the figure in plain black—sounds like the being that killed Aerman Sorren and that you saw orchestrating the attack on Songhaven. You said that the one at Songhaven is the one that is seeking you. There was a Keeper present at the attack, and they are always associated with Mar. So, I must ask: could the figure in black be Mar? Could Mar herself be the power searching for you?"

I should have been surprised or shocked, but what I felt instead was a sense of relief or satisfaction, the feeling you get when you finally see the answer to a vexing puzzle. It made perfect sense that the powerful being that hunted me, that both hated and feared me, was the goddess Mar. I should have been terrified, but the idea was simply too big, too enormous for me to even begin to grasp it. My heart was hammering in my chest. It was all suddenly too real. I'd lost Ambrose. I'd lost Peg. I'd lost even my life as a minstrel; how could they ever accept me back when I had killed seven men... No, it was eight. I'd forgotten the Meren soldier. I had the *Endollin's*–the Lawbreaker's–ring. I had no doubt that I would eventually come to possess the sword. And then–whether I willed it or not–I was going to face the Keepers and the goddess.

I felt my face go pale and I swayed on my feet. It was all too much, and I was exhausted from two days of continual celebration combined with far too little sleep.

"Alain, I think–no, I am sure–that you are correct. But right now, I am too tired to think, so I have no idea what to do with that information."

He nodded.

"We, too, are weary. Let us all get what rest we can and discuss this further after we rise."

I retrieved my guitar from the stand it was resting in, slipped it into its case, slung it over my shoulder, and headed for the door. With a quick glance at her parents, Élan walked out with me. At the door to my room, I paused and turned to face her.

There was no moon, but–as always–a gentle light seemed to play around Élan's features, as if she somehow took in the starlight and then reflected it back. I just stood there, drinking in every line of her face. I couldn't believe how much she had come to mean to me, how much I treasured her.

"Lauren, are you well?" she asked.

"I'm afraid," I said softly. "Mar has already taken one person I loved. I'm afraid that she'll take you."

She didn't say anything. She just tilted her head slightly to one side and watched me expectantly with steady gray-green eyes.

"I love you, Élan," I whispered.

"And I love you," she answered.

We wrapped our arms around each other then and clung to each other while I tried to quell the dread growing in my heart.

I slept late the next morning. Pyrett had given me the day off from training, so there was no need to rise early. By the time I reached the dining room to break my fast, only Réalta was still at the table.

"Lauren, *ol sym en elested tul seli navoram*," she said as I entered.

"*Na olin en elested tul sely, Elmyr* Réalta," I replied.

She nodded, a slight smile on her lips.

"Your use of the *Eldarin* tongue has much improved," she said. "But I am not a queen."

"I don't understand. You're married to the king. Doesn't that make you queen?"

"I am married to the king, yes. But marrying a ruler does not make me a ruler. Had Alain become incapacitated before Élan reached her majority, I might have been considered to serve as regent. More likely, it would have been someone from one of the other ruling families or another member of Alain's Council."

"So, what makes someone a ruler?" I asked.

She gave a short, delighted laugh.

"We *Eldarin* have been trying very hard not to answer that question for an exceedingly long time," she replied. "We no longer remember why the five families were selected or whether there were once rules for adding more. To us, the king is a servant of the people and the members of the five families have been willing to fill that role for a long time. Others who wish to serve find other roles within our society."

We paused our conversation while I served myself some fried eggs and sausage. They were not very warm, but as the last one to the table, I couldn't be choosy.

"Réalta, may I ask you a question?"

"Certainly," she replied. She looked at me over the rim of her teacup as she took a sip.

"What do the *Eldar* know of Mar? I know that you do not worship her, but can you tell me anything about her?"

"Do you not know the scriptures?"

"I do," I replied. "But the *Torun Mar* is, when you really study it, a paradoxical work. A great many of its words are devoted to saying that Mar loves the Alomar, but a great many more are devoted to recounting the sinfulness of the Alomar and laying out the extreme penance that they owe to Mar for those sins. Further, it was written by Mar or by people devoted to Mar. Neither of those is likely to be unbiased."

"You do not trust your goddess or her servants?"

"She *is* trying to kill me," I observed. "And her servants are the ones who taught me that she loves me. They also taught me that the *Eldar* are evil, but I have recently come to doubt that teaching."

She looked at me as if she wasn't quite sure what to make of that last remark. Then she nodded, took another sip of tea, and said, "Unless Alain is correct that the being who killed Lorrestian was Mar, our last direct interaction with her was many hundreds of rounds before the Great War. At that time, several of the Old Ones–particularly *Aenn*–were regular visitors to our cities and towns. They offered wise counsel and taught us many things. Then one day, Mar appeared. At first, she professed a desire for friendship, but it soon became clear that what she truly wanted of us was worship. Some who were there reported that she stopped just short of demanding worship from us. When we questioned the Old Ones about her, they refused to answer and seemed uncomfortable even mentioning her name. It was clear to us, however, that they did not trust her. As a result, though we treated her with respect, for in some ways she seemed like the Old Ones, we did not worship her, and she soon lost interest and left us. We believe that's when she first discovered the humans to the east of the Breton Mountains."

I poured myself a cup of tea and wrapped my hands around the mug to warm them. Réalta was watching me intently. Several times I thought that she was going to speak, but she didn't. Finally, I asked, "Réalta, is there something that you wish to say?"

Again, she looked as if she were about to speak, but just then several of the staff came in from the kitchen to clear away the dishes from the morning meal. Réalta excused herself and left the room, leaving me wondering what it was that she couldn't bring herself to say to me.

The weather stayed mild and late in the afternoon six days after the new round began, Ryan rode in from Songhaven. After the evening meal, we all gathered before the fire in the front room to sip mulled wine and hear what Ryan had learned.

"Both the city and the college were in complete disarray after the attack," he reported. "Most of the students and all of the teaching Masters had been murdered. Kayne, the

Warder of the city, had also been killed, so there was no one to take charge. The Kelmar had also taken all the horses, so there was no quick way for them to send for help."

Ryan paused a moment to blow gently on his wine, took a small sip, and then continued.

"It was Ambor who took over. He wasn't at the concert because of his gout and the Kelmar didn't search the Rillian Tower well enough to find him. Almost everyone in Songhaven knew him and they were all willing to listen to him. By the time I arrived, he had already sent several of the older students to Durning to purchase horses and to send out the word that help was needed. They also sent out the message that all minstrels should come in. Under Ambor's guidance, the residents had buried the dead and elected a new Warder, so the city was beginning to function again. Ambor was in the process of reorganizing the College. He was personally teaching the few remaining students. He asked me to stay, but I told him that I had pressing personal affairs to tend to. Then the weather turned bitter cold, and it was too dangerous to leave."

We sat in silence a moment. I was thinking about all my friends and colleagues who had died in the attack on Songhaven. I felt my eyes beginning to water and Élan, who was sitting next to me, took my hand. I smiled a crooked smile at her and squeezed her hand. Ryan noticed the exchange and raised an eyebrow. I said nothing and after a moment he began to speak again.

"Just before the weather got bad, Amergin rode in. She'd been at Durning when the students arrived. I had several long talks with her. She told me that Anders has been crowned High King and the Alomar are generally hopeful that he will lead them well. The reward for you is still on offer, Lauren, but the High King's men are no longer involved in the search. The Kelmar are still building up their forces outside of Han. According to Amergin, they occasionally mount an attack on the city, but back off as soon as there is resistance. Still, most of the Alomar forces have moved north to defend the city or–failing that–to keep the Kelmar from pouring through the pass into the Federation."

He leaned back in his chair.

"Amergin also told me something that I find quite puzzling. She said that one evening she was performing at an inn in Amersford when suddenly, right in the middle of a song, she could neither sing nor play. The lyrics and the skills were just gone. She felt like she still knew the songs, but they simply would not come. There were several other minstrels present, but they had the same problem. When she told me that, I recalled that I had had a similar problem one evening. I was practicing and suddenly I could no longer play. All my knowledge felt locked away; still there but completely inaccessible."

"That was the night of the attack on Songhaven," I said quietly.

They all turned to look at me.

"Garth said that our gifts had been rescinded. I felt something inside me change. Then the next morning, when I found Rachel, she said that she couldn't sing. She begged me to sing *The Parting Song* for her and when I tried, I couldn't. I'm not sure why, but it occurred to me to play the *Arimë Daelyr*. That seemed to break whatever it was that bound the music, and I was able to sing again."

Ryan nodded.

"And I found that I could suddenly play again the next morning," he said. "You say that Garth did something?"

"He said that he did. I am convinced that it was the figure in black. Mar."

"And what is the *Arimë Daelyr*? How did you play it if you couldn't play your guitar?"

"The *Arimë Daelyr* is an instrumental song that I learned from a man in Noweth," I answered. "He taught me to play it on a flute. It is a beautiful song."

"I would like to hear it sometime," Ryan said.

"I too, would like to hear it," Alain agreed and leaned forward in his chair. "Lauren, with what happened at Songhaven and then on *Creagalt*, you have twice overcome Mar's power. I choose to see that as a hopeful thing."

I tried to smile, but I don't think I managed it.

"Those were simply skirmishes," I said. "I have yet to face her directly."

We were all silent for a time. Then Ryan spoke up.

"You have now heard my news. What has been happening here?"

"Élan," Alain said. "Why don't you share what you found."

Élan let go of my hand and leaned forward.

"Not very much," she admitted. "I was only able to recover part of a single sentence. But from that fragment we learned that *Endolsar* means 'sword of law' in the True Speech. We also know that it is in a cave, 'locked in ice and warded by fire.'"

"In a cave?" Ryan asked. "No hint of where?"

"I am afraid not," Alain answered. "I sent some parties out to search, but they found nothing. Then the cold set in and, like you, we were trapped inside. Now that it is warmer, I am thinking of sending more searchers out."

I shook my head and said, "I don't think that will be necessary."

They all turned to look at me.

"I've been thinking," I said. "I don't believe that we took Élan's ideas far enough."

"What do you mean?" Élan asked.

"Lorrestian put the ring where he knew it would come to me. I didn't have to go looking for it. I suspect that he did the same thing with the sword. Wherever it is, I will come upon it. I must. He saw me facing Mar and the Keepers with it."

"You don't seem as conflicted about that as I would expect," Ryan observed.

I paused a moment before answering.

"Ryan, we've been talking about everything that has happened and we're reasonably sure about this. The dark thing that has been seeking me. It's Mar."

"I wondered why you identified the being at Songhaven as Mar," Ryan said. He looked thoughtful for a moment. "Perhaps," he said finally. "Once word got out that you were a minstrel, I can see why a punitive being such as Mar would have ordered an attack on the minstrels. Why, though, would she murder the High King?"

"The assassination occurred right before the Kelmar attacked Han," I reminded him. "That can't be a coincidence."

"True," he replied. "And Larsen was meant to kill Anders. It could be that the intent was to prevent the Alomar from making an effective defense against the attack. You and Ambrose forestalled that."

"But what about the Kelmar behavior since then?" Alain asked. "Why are they just sitting outside Han?"

"Something more is going on," Réalta said. "Something bigger than we imagine. Mar has long desired to return the Alomar to her dominion and she knows that the *Endollin* now lives. I feel that she may be trying to both subjugate the Alomar and neutralize the *Endollin*. That will require a far larger plan than simply taking Han. We must be vigilant."

"I believe you are correct, my love," Alain said. "I have had our military preparing. Our smiths have increased our stock of swords, shields, and armor. We have thousands of arrows already finished, with more to come, but our fletchers have run out of fletching material. When the weather broke, I sent parties out further than normal to try and round up enough material to at least finish the arrows we have. Our warriors have been training nearly every day." He looked at me. "As has the *Endollin*."

Ryan glanced at me, a slight frown on his face, but then he turned back to Alain.

"So, we will be marching to war soon?"

"I believe so," Alain answered.

"Have you given any thought to who will be in charge during your absence?"

Alain nodded.

"There is really only one choice," he said. "Élan will serve as regent in my absence."

I felt Élan stiffen beside me and her eyes locked on her father's face.

"Me?" she asked. "I thought I would be riding out with you."

"We are one of the ruling families," Alain replied. "Many rounds remain in my term, our family's term. I, or another of my family, must fulfill our obligations to our people. Daughter, you are my only living kin. You have been preparing for this moment your entire life. There is no one else who can serve and, frankly, no one I would trust more to safeguard our people. *Evendim* will be vulnerable. I do not believe that Mar's forces will strike here, but you will need to be prepared to defend the city or to evacuate it as need be."

Élan looked as if she was about to leap to her feet in protest. I put my hand on her arm. Her head whipped around as if she were going snap at me, but something in my face stopped her. She put her hand over mine and turned back to face her father.

"*Se condi er manana yn weal*," she said. "I would be honored to serve."

Ryan looked from me to Élan, a quizzical expression on his face. Then his eyes widened slightly, and he smiled.

"And just what have you two been up to while I was gone?" he asked.

Élan blushed. I'm sure that I did, too.

"We sang together at Alain's Round's End Day celebration," I said. "And again, the next day."

"We've been getting requests to sing from all over the city," Élan added. She turned to me. "I really think we should begin accepting at least some of them."

Ryan raised one eyebrow.

"They seem to have become quite affectionate toward one another," he said, glancing at Alain and Réalta.

"They have indeed," Réalta said sternly, but then she caught my eye and smiled.

Élan and I did begin to accept invitations to perform together. We played first at her cousin's *tybith*. Then came an invitation to play at a special event at the library. Soon, our days were almost completely occupied. I spent mornings training with Pyrett and

Élan worked with her father learning the daily routines of governing the city. Then we'd spend the afternoon rehearsing and the evenings performing in one venue or another. Sometimes Ryan or Gotyr joined us. The pace was demanding, but I was relishing the increased amount of time I got to spend with Élan. Singing together–learning to read what another person will do from subtle gestures or shifts in expression, melding your voices into one–is its own kind of intimacy and I loved having that intimacy with Élan. And when we weren't singing, we talked. We shared the tales of our childhoods, told the stories of our families, wondered what our futures held, or we just talked about the mundane events of the day. And almost every night, we sang.

I believe that part of the reason we were so in demand and part of the reason that we were willing to accede to that demand was that we knew it wouldn't last. It was a time of peace and joy, but we all knew that it was coming to an end. The smiths were busy forging new weapons and quartermasters were acquiring food, tents, clothing, and medical supplies and packing it all so that the army could leave on a moment's notice. Soldiers spent their days training; they and their families waiting for the moment that the orders would come to march. The people of *Evendim* were stressed and nightly performances by their Princess and the *Endollin* relieved some of that stress. And so, we performed.

The weather stayed mild for a few days after Ryan's return, but then winter returned, and the temperatures dropped to near freezing and stayed there. One night in the middle part of the first moon of *Tymnahunoch*, a heavy snow began to fall while Élan and I performed, and we had to force our way home in the early hours of the morning through calf-high snow. We paused just inside the door to the front room to remove our snow-covered cloaks and boots and then we sat side by side on the small sofa and stretched our feet to the banked fire in the fireplace.

Élan snuggled close. I put my arm around her, and she laid her head on my shoulder.

"I'm exhausted," she whispered.

"So am I," I whispered back. I intended to say that we should go to our rooms before we passed out where we were, but sleep claimed me before the words left my mouth.

I woke the next morning to the sounds of preparations for the morning meal drifting in from the kitchen. Élan was still in my arms. I knew that I should wake her, that it would be awkward for us to be found as we were, but I couldn't bring myself to give up having her so close. A moment later, though, she stirred, looked up at me with sleepy eyes, and smiled.

"I could do this for the rest of my life," she said quietly.

"Me, too," I replied, just as quietly.

"We should get up now, though," she said glancing to the hallway that led to her parents' room, "or the rest of our lives is not likely to be long."

I got up and went to build up the fire. I was in the middle of that when Alain, already dressed for the day, entered the room. He saw us, then noticed our cloaks and boots by the door. He raised one eyebrow, but all he said was, "Élan, Lauren, *ol sym en elested tul seli navoram.*"

"*Na olin en elested tul sely,*" we answered together.

Élan watched her father as he left the front room for the dining room. Then she turned back to me.

"You, sir, have sullied my reputation," she said quietly.

I put on my best most evil villain smirk.

"Well, you did take up with the most evil person in the world," I replied.

Her laughter was a joy to hear.

Tensions in *Evendim* grew as the second moon of *Tymnahunoch* passed. Spring was coming and, with it, the likelihood that the Kelmar–in the service of Mar–would make some move, and almost everyone expected that move to be a full-scale attack on Han. Élan was taking on more of the day-to-day tasks of governing so that Alain could spend time training with his troops. I still spent my mornings training, but in the afternoons, I met with Alain, Ryan, Pyrett, and other military leaders trying to determine our best course of action. It seemed clear that the Kelmar attack would come through Han, but what role the *Eldar* could play in turning back that assault was unclear. Thus, coming up with a plan was almost impossible. Further, hanging over all those discussions were two troublesome facts: I was still a wanted man in the Federation and the *Eldar* were seen by most of the Alomar as evil oppressors of humans. We weren't going to be able to just ride up to the Alomar and offer our services; the Alomar leaders would be more likely to attack us than talk to us.

Late one afternoon near the end of the second moon of *Tymnahunoch*, Alain, Élan, Ryan, and I were gathered in the king's private office in the palace. We had spent the afternoon talking in circles about how we could possibly get the *Eldarin* army through the Federation to Han without provoking a battle and were seated in front of a roaring fire wearily sipping mulled wine. None of us spoke; we'd run out of things to say. We all turned at a polite knock at the door and Trevith stepped into the room.

"Your Majesty, *Elnyr* Élan," he said. "Pardon me for interrupting, but Master Librarian Leonyr is here and is requesting to speak with you."

Alain glanced around at us, a puzzled look on his face.

"Send him in," he instructed Trevith.

A moment later, Leonyr walked in, carefully cradling a small leather tube in his hands. He bowed to the king and said, "Your Majesty, I have made a small discovery, but one that I believed you would wish to know of, or else I would not have troubled you."

Alain nodded his acknowledgment.

"Ever since *Elnyr* Élan recovered the fragment of Lorrestian's notes, I've had it in my mind that I had read those words before. I did not wish to speak of it before now on the chance that I was simply misremembering. Today, however, I discovered that I was not."

He pulled a cap off one end of the tube and very carefully removed an obviously ancient scroll.

"This is *Dor Kareth an Scrifail*," he explained. "The Book of Ruin. It was written by Evam, the son of one of Lorrestian's chief councilors. It is Evam's personal account of the Great War. It is unfinished because Evam died in the assault on *Elsgard*, but it was mixed in with his father's papers when the councilor fled the city. The father himself died when his group was ambushed by the Alomar before they were out of sight of the city walls. The rest of the party survived and brought the papers here."

"An all-too-common story," the king said.

"Indeed," the librarian agreed. "Evam's account has been of interest before now because it is highly personal and gives a sense of what it was like living through those times. I have read it several times when I feel a need to remind myself of how it felt to be an ordinary citizen waiting in the city as the war moved ever closer."

Leonyr paused, the ghost of old memories visible in his haunted expression.

"Near the end of the account, Evam wrote that he had overhead part of a conversation between his father and King Lorrestian. According to Evam, the king said, 'I found a cave in the hills and laid it to rest there, locked in ice and warded by fire.' Evam did not hear his father's reply, and he did not understand what the king's words meant, but I believe that we can be sure that Lorrestian was speaking of the sword *Endolsar*."

We all sat up at that, our weariness suddenly gone.

Alain spoke first.

"The wording of that passage sounds as if the king knew that his listener would understand which hills were meant," he observed. "Is there anything in the book that would indicate which hills those were?"

"There is not," Leonyr answered.

Alain sighed and sank back into his chair, his disappointment plain to see.

"As interesting as that passage is in terms of validating what Élan found, it doesn't help narrow our search. Given what we already know, he could have meant the Corun Hills or the foothills of either the Breton or the Gray Mountains."

"How about the phrase 'locked in ice and warded by fire'?" Ryan asked. "Do we know what that means? Could it tell us something that could narrow the search?"

"I am afraid that I can shed little light there," Leonyr replied. "It suggests that the sword has been in ice for the last thousand rounds, but I know of no persistent source of ice south of the Northern Wilderness. There is certainly no such source within the distance that King Lorrestian could have travelled."

Alain looked around at the rest of us.

"Any other thoughts?" he asked. Élan and I shook our heads. Ryan shrugged.

"Leonyr, my thanks to you for bringing this to our attention. Would you care to join us for some mulled wine?"

Leonyr shook his skull-like head.

"My thanks to you for the offer, Your Majesty," he replied. "But I should return the book to the library."

He turned and left the room, and we all settled back in our chairs and went back to sipping our wine while staring wearily into the fire.

One morning half a moon later, I was at Pyrett's home training. She had brought in one of her *Cadwynir* colleagues, a wiry, medium height *Eldar* named Kalin, to spar with me. Kalin was known as an expert swordsman–one of the best in the *Cadwynir*–and I was somewhat apprehensive about facing off with him. From what I'd heard, he was blindingly fast and very good at misdirection. He also prided himself on his control and he insisted that we train with live steel. He backed down on that request, though, when Pyrett pulled him aside and explained what had happened to the last person who had fought me with a true weapon.

Kalin tied his long silver hair back and picked up his wooden training weapon. At Pyrett's signal, we began. Kalin took a couple of quick, exploratory swings at me that I countered with as little motion as possible. I was watching Kalin intently, looking for some hint of what he would do, but his reputation was well-earned; I could perceive nothing of what he intended. I was nervous, but I'd managed to wall it off to one side. I knew it was there, but it had no more importance than one of the posts holding up the ceiling.

Suddenly, with no signal that it was coming, Kalin struck. I managed to block a rapid series of strikes that seemed to come at me from all sides. As I parried the last of those, I twisted my wrist in just the right way and Kalin's stroke went wide, leaving him wide open, and my sword point touched his chest. I heard Pyrett suck in a breath and Kalin grinned at me. I was stunned.

"Boy," he said. "No one has touched me in a very long time. Was that skill or beginner's luck?"

"Would you believe it was a miracle?" I asked.

He laughed and Pyrett said, "I think you should..."

Just then, someone began pounding loudly on the door to the house. Pyrett, followed closely by me and Kalin, hurried down to the front door. When the captain opened it, we found Trevith waiting on the other side. Three *aynekahrn* waited on the road.

"*Endollin*," Trevith said, bowing slightly. "Captain. You are asked to report to the palace immediately. Scouts have come in with urgent news."

Pyrett and I exchanged glances. We both knew what this summons meant: there was information on the Kelmar.

"Kalin, my thanks for your time this morning," Pyrett said. "We must forego the rest of the session."

"I understand, Captain," he replied. "I think I should go begin preparations to march."

"You may want to delay that until we know for sure what the scouts have to say."

He nodded and turned to go.

"Kalin," I said. "My thanks to you for being willing to spar with me. I wish that we had more time; I could learn a great deal from you."

"Perhaps," he replied. "As I said, no one else has touched me in a great while. I am still curious about how you managed to do so."

"I'm pretty sure it was simple luck," I answered.

"Perhaps we will have the opportunity to find out someday. Be well, *Endollin*."

As Kalin strode off, Pyrett, Trevith, and I mounted. A short time later, we entered the palace. Alain was seated on the throne in the Great Hall. The room was full of his councilors and generals. Seated before the dais on a pair of wooden chairs were a pair of weary-looking scouts in *Cadwynir* green.

Before the Warden of the Door could announce us, Alain spotted us and called out.

"*Endollin*! Captain! Please, join us."

As we drew nearer, I recognized the scouts as Jorith and Iseabail, two of the *Cadwynir* who had accompanied us on the trip to *Elsgard*. Both looked strained and tired, and both had dark circles around their eyes. They rose and bowed slightly to Pyrett as we approached.

"Now that everyone is here," Alain said, "I would hear what our scouts have to say."

He turned his gaze to Iseabail and nodded his permission for her to begin.

"Your Majesty, Jorith and I were sent south to scout the region around *Seldenawé*. Six days ago, we noticed movement along the valley floor. It was a Kelmar scouting party, but a larger one than any seen this far south in many rounds. Jorith followed them while I waited to see if others would follow."

She paused and looked around the room.

"Others did follow. A Kelmar army was marching through *Seldenawé*."

All around us there were gasps of shock and muttered expressions of disbelief.

"We both independently observed them," Iseabail continued. "Then Jorith rejoined me, and we confirmed what we had seen. By our count, there were approximately four thousand men. They did have horse-drawn wagons of weapons and supplies, but none of the soldiers were mounted. There were two mounted figures, though, one cloaked in gray, one in orange. Those individuals each carried an iron-shod wooden staff."

A shock of recognition ran through me. Those had to be Keepers.

"I did not know that the Kelmar had wizards," one of the generals–a man named Konne–said.

"They do not," someone else answered.

"Those were not wizards," I told them. "Those were two of the Keepers of the Alomar. I've seen one of them before. He led the attack on Songhaven. The one in gray was Cimone, the patron of builders and crafters. The other, the one in orange, was Gorfin, patron of smiths."

There was a moment of silence after that.

"You are sure?" Konne asked.

"I am."

"It was the might of the Keepers that defeated us in the Great War," Konne said, suddenly sounding small. "We might have held our own against the Alomar, but the puissance of the Keepers overcame every defense we had."

A ripple of fear ran through the room and there were quiet expressions of dismay. I saw Alain's eyes sweep the room, seeing the morale of his people beginning to fail. He rose to his feet, his expression resolute.

"My people, a thousand rounds of the seasons ago, we stood alone against the Alomar and the Keepers. Despite the efforts of our king and our greatest heroes, we were defeated. Much was lost and we have been in hiding ever since. Now, the time foretold by Lorrestian has come. The *Endollin* is among us, bearing the ring that Lorrestian forged for him. Many of us feared his coming, believing that he would lead us to ruin. But now we have come to know him, and we know now that he is a man of honor and learning, a man who stood in this very hall and committed himself to stand with us. It is time for us to come out of hiding. We must find a way to renew our ancient friendship with the Alomar. We must face the Kelmar and the Keepers. But this time, we will not stand alone. We will have a champion with us. We will have the *Endollin* with us."

As Alain fell silent, I looked around the room. There were no cheers and many of those present still looked somewhat frightened, but the mood in the Great Hall had palpably shifted. I'm not sure why, but I stepped out of the crowd and mounted the dais. Alain was watching me intently. I came to a stop before him and he nodded very slightly, as if he had discerned my intent. I bowed to him, and, to my surprise, he returned the bow. Then I moved to his left, and he took hold of my right wrist and raised my arm, the back of my hand facing the crowd. I don't know if it was something I did, or something Alain did, or some chance trick of the light, but the great jewel in the ring flashed, a burst of violet light, shot through with spangles of red and blue. There was a brief, stunned moment of silence, and then they all cheered.

A short time later, a small group of us met in Alain's personal office to plan what we would do. The king had cleared his desk, and a large map was spread across the top, its edges held down with various objects from around the room. The king and Élan stood to one side of the desk with Konne and Rolugh, the top two generals in the army, and Pyrett and Iseabail, the two most senior captains of the *Cadwynir*, on the other side. Ryan and I stood at one end of the desk, studying the map, and listening to the others.

"Now we know what the Kelmar have been doing," Rolugh said. "They attacked Han and then sat there to draw the Alomar forces north. All the while, they've had another army marching the long way around to attack from the south."

She looked around the room.

"Could this actually work?" she asked.

Ryan stepped toward the desk.

"Only once before have the Kelmar attacked from both north and south," he said. "That was in 491 as the Alomar count it. The High King Artos and his son Helm divided their army and were able to repel both attacks, but the High King was killed. That time, though, the Alomar were forewarned. Hunters on the Lellarin Plains spotted the southern army and rode their horses to death to get word back to the King of Amersford. This time, the Alomar have no warning."

"And we cannot give them one," Pyrett added. "Any messenger we send would be killed before the message could be delivered."

"There is an answer," Alain said quietly.

Everyone turned to look at him.

"To reach the Alomar, they must cross the *Aennsrhyd* Bridge. *Aennsrhyd* was ours. I say we take it back and we fortify it. We will keep the Kelmar from attacking the Alomar army's undefended rear. That may be enough to get them to listen to us."

"Can we reach *Aennsrhyd* before the Kelmar?" Rolugh asked.

"They are on foot," Iseabail reminded her. "They will not reach *Aennsrhyd* for at least another moon, probably a few days more."

"And we have the *aynekahrn*," Konne said. "If we leave in two days, we could still be there half a moon before them."

"Very well," Alain said. "We ride in two days." He looked around at the rest of us. "Go. Make it happen."

Two days later in the early morning we were gathered in a large field west of the city on the north bank of the *Kivin*. It was cold enough that we could see our breath and nearly everyone was wearing hooded cloaks. Ryan and I were standing with the ten soldiers who formed the King's personal company. All around us, warriors in the deep blue and green of the army or the dull green of the *Cadwynir* stowed supplies in saddlebags, checked saddles and bridles, or simply walked their mounts to keep them warm. Many of the citizens of *Evendim* were there as well, saying their farewells to the husbands and wives, the sons and daughters who were riding off to war.

It was dark, but all across the field torches had been mounted on poles and a great many people also carried torches. I'd lost count of the number of times I'd walked *Yrtenstal* in a wide circle around our group. We were waiting for the king.

Alain and his family arrived mounted on *aynekahrn*, Réalta to his right and Élan to his left. Élan was carrying a long pole with a furled banner at the top. As they reined in, Élan tugged a cord, and the banner unfurled as she raised it up. A murmur of astonishment rippled through the crowd as they saw it. *El an Arastalon*. The star was done in gold on a field of deep blue. As it caught the torchlight, the star seemed to flicker. For a thousand rounds, the *Eldar*, broken and defeated, had kept the star banner furled. Now Élan held it aloft proudly. The soldiers near the king's family began to cheer and the sound spread from that core until two thousand voices shouted their recovered pride and defiance and hope to the stars above. I joined them.

When the shouting had died down, Alain gestured and one of his men rode forward and accepted the banner from Élan. After handing off the banner, Élan dismounted and stepped over to me. Without a word, she flung her arms around me and kissed me deeply. For the briefest of instants, I wondered what her parents would think, but then I gave myself over to her and kissed her back. When she finally broke the kiss and stepped back, I noticed that the people around us were silent; I could clearly hear the guttering of the torches in the slight breeze.

"Go, love," she said. "But come back to me."

The words shredded my heart and sent pain searing along every nerve in my body. In my mind I saw the torchlit Grotto, the serious look on Ryan's face as he brought word that we were summoned to go out with Ambrose, and the sad smile on Peg's face the last time I ever saw her. I felt tears spill out of my eyes to freeze on my cheeks.

"Lauren, what is it?" Élan asked anxiously.

I had to swallow several times to relieve the constriction in my throat before I could answer her.

"What you said," I replied. "Peg said almost exactly those same words to me when we parted. It was very like this, the torchlight and me riding away." Some part of me knew that I was sounding frantic, but I couldn't help myself. "Élan, I love you. I don't want to lose you."

In reply, she embraced me again.

"I will be here when you return," she said quietly, but fiercely. "I love you, too."

She let go, stepped back a single step, then turned and walked back to her family. I didn't see her mount because I noticed that Alain and Réalta were both staring at me. Alain caught my eye and held it, his expression grave. I had a feeling that he and I were going to have a rather uncomfortable talk in the near future. He finally broke the eye contact and turned to the waiting army.

"Mount up," he ordered.

He urged his mount forward and then turned to face Élan and Réalta.

"Citizens of *Evendim*, attend me," he said.

It took a moment, but then everyone was quiet.

"I ride off to war at the side of the *Endollin*. I name my daughter Élan regent. She will serve in my stead while I am gone. Élan?"

"Yes, Your Majesty?"

"Before all the *Eldar*, I name you regent, to serve until my return. I charge you with the care and protection of our people and our home. I do not expect that *Evendim* will be threatened, but if it is, remember this: should an attack come, flee if possible. Fight only if you must. All the things here are not worth even a single life. Do you understand?"

"I do, Your Majesty."

"And do you accept this charge?"

"I do, Your Majesty," Élan confirmed, then added, "*Se en manana yn weal*.

"People of *Evendim*, the charge has been made and accepted. Élan shall rule until my return. I urge you to support her; there is no one I trust more to serve you."

He urged his mount back toward Élan and Réalta. He spoke quietly to them for a few moments, then backed his mount a few steps and turned to face the west.

"Warriors of the *Eldar*," he called. "I ride now to meet our fate. I do not fear to do so. Will you ride with me."

"We will," answered two thousand voices.

Alain urged his *aynekahrn* forward and I climbed into my saddle to follow.

We followed the north bank of the *Kivin* for several hours, climbing up out of the bowl-shaped valley that harbored *Evendim*. Then we turned north for a time, following one of the tributaries of the *Kivin* before turning a bit north of west following a ridgetop trail. Several hours after we set out, Alain sent word that he wished me to join him at the front of the army. I urged *Yrtenstal* forward to join the king. When I reached him, we pushed forward until we were far enough ahead of the group that we could speak without being heard.

At first, Alain said nothing, but then he said, "*Endollin*, Lauren, may we set aside our titles and speak together as two men?"

"Of course, Alain," I answered.

"My thanks to you," he said, but then fell silent for a few moments. Then he turned to me.

"You are not of the *Eldar*," he said finally, cautiously. "Do you appreciate what Élan did this morning."

"She kissed me in front of everyone," I said. "I've seen her kiss other men during celebrations."

"Not like that," he replied. "That was an intimate kiss. Among the *Eldar*, such a kiss given in public is a sign of a deep commitment. My daughter has committed herself to you."

I didn't respond; I'd had no idea.

"Your reaction seemed to be one of pain," he observed.

"Her words of farewell were almost exactly the same as the last words that Peg spoke to me," I told him.

"You still grieve that loss," he said.

"It hasn't been that long," I replied. "What Peg and I had was special. We had planned to marry. I will forever grieve her loss. But I love Élan. How could I not? She is intelligent and thoughtful. She is kind and compassionate. She is possessed of great wisdom and integrity. All that is good and beautiful in the world lives in her. Even if she did not care for me, even if she gave her heart to another, still I would love her."

Until that moment, I had not admitted–even to myself–the depth of my feelings. I glanced toward Alain and found him watching me, a curious expression on his face.

"I would not see her hurt," he said.

"I would will myself from existence before I would knowingly hurt her," I replied.

"But hurt her you will. You are mortal, Lauren. You will eventually die and leave her alone."

I had no reply to that.

The *Eldar* had prepared well for a cold-weather march. We had five hundred *aynekahrn* with us that were merely carrying supplies. Among those supplies were special tents, each large enough to sleep ten soldiers. Those tents were tall enough to allow the occupants to build a fire in the center and they had a vent in the roof peak to allow the smoke to exit. Thus, despite the frigid weather, we all slept reasonably well. Ryan and I were housed with Alain, Konne, Rolugh, Pyrett, and Iseabail. Some nights, Pyrett, Iseabail, or both were absent as they rotated scouting tasks with the other *Cadwynir*. We rose early each morning to have a hot meal, paused long enough at midday for another, and had a third before retiring in the evening.

We spent two days riding westward. Overhead, gray clouds gathered and grew darker. According to Konne and the others, the third day would see us working our way down the west slopes of the Bretons toward the plains. Then we could truly make use of the speed and endurance of the *aynekahrn*.

When we rose on the third morning it was snowing. It was a light snow as we ate the morning meal and broke camp, but as the morning wore on the snowfall grew heavier and a strong wind came howling out of the north. By midday, I could barely make out the riders around me and patches of ice and snow clung to *Yrtenstal's* coat and to my clothing. Even wrapped in a heavy, fur-lined cloak, I was shivering. The wind had increased and was blowing the snow sideways. It stung my face and blew deep into my hood, where it melted and ran down my neck. I squinted against the gale-driven snow, trying to make out the rider I was following, but all I saw was a wall of gray and white. Occasionally, *Yrtenstal* and I brushed against pine trees, their branches accumulating a thick coating of heavy, wet snow.

As we passed one, I heard a loud crack. *Yrtenstal* recognized the danger before I did, and I felt his muscles bunch. Just as he lurched forward, the falling pine branch, laden with snow, struck me in the chest and swept me off my mount. I landed hard, barely cushioned by the snow, and by the time I got to my feet, *Yrtenstal* was lost in the howling storm.

"*Yrtenstal*," I yelled as loudly as I could, but I could barely hear myself. There was no way the *aynekahrn* could hear me. I had no time to look for the animal; I had no idea how late in the day it was, and I couldn't afford to be caught in the open when night fell. I had to find shelter. I turned in a circle, trying to spot another rider or some haven from the wind and snow, but all I could see was the stinging wind-driven snow.

Then I heard it. The quiet music that had guided me in the past. I turned to my left and followed it. The way was uphill and quickly grew steeper and then I was standing before an opening in the hillside. A cave. The music went still, and my heart began to pound as Lorrestian's words echoed in my mind.

I took two steps in and, out of the wind, stopped to take stock. If I stretched out both arms, the walls of the cave were just past the tips of my fingers and the roof was similarly just out of reach overhead. Outside the cave mouth was a wall of swirling, howling white. Deeper in the cave, I thought I saw light, but I wasn't sure. Still, light could mean fire and I was very cold, so I began walking deeper into the cave. Some twenty paces in, the passageway curved to the left and began to narrow. After a few steps, I had to turn sideways to proceed. After another ten paces, I entered a large chamber.

It was well lit, though I saw no source of light. The chamber was roughly circular and straight across from where I stood was another passageway leading to someplace even more brightly lit. To my right was nothing but a bare rock wall. To my left...

To my left was a dragon.

It was maybe thirty feet long from the tip of its nose to the end of its tail. It was predominantly red, but a line of upright scales down its back was black. It was curled up so that its head was resting on the tip of its tail, and it was watching me with yellow eyes.

"*Vorath, Endollin*," it said.

"You know me," I said. It came out somewhere between a statement and a question.

"Indeed," the dragon replied. "I have been waiting for you."

"Waiting for me?"

In reply, the dragon raised its head and looked at the passageway to the other chamber. "You should go in now."

A chill of apprehension ran through me, but I crossed the dragon's chamber and entered the other passageway. A short distance later, I entered another chamber.

This one was somewhat larger than the dragon's chamber and the walls were covered in ice, lit from within with a blue-white glow. Directly across from the entrance was a block of ice in the shape of an altar and, standing upright in the altar was the sword *Endolsar*.

It was a plain weapon, but beautiful in its way. The blade was perhaps thirty inches long, tapered at the end, with a single flat fuller along most of its length. The blade was highly polished; even from where I stood, I could see my reflection in it. The hilt was gold plated, with straight quillons. In the center of the quillon was set an oval moonstone and in the pommel was a dark, unreflective stone. I glanced at the stone glittering in the ring on my finger. No doubt the stone in the sword would wake when I touched it.

I walked across the chamber and stopped before the altar. I stood there and regarded the sword. Everything it meant swirled in my mind–the power, the deaths that had already occurred, the possibility that I could somehow destroy the world. Ryan had told me to remember that I was a minstrel. As a minstrel, I had no business taking up a sword. I lowered my hand and turned away.

I seemed to hear voices whispering just at the threshold of hearing, cries of desperation and despair. All at once images swarmed though my head. Animals dying or twisted, farmers struggling with blighted lands, children starving. All the people of the world living in squalor and deprivation. Behind it all I heard a single flute playing the plaintive, mournful *Arimë Daelyr*. A single tear rolled down my cheek.

I became aware that the dragon was somehow watching me, though it had not moved from where it lay in the other chamber. It didn't speak, but I could hear its voice in my head. "You can stop it. You can stop it all. You are the only one who can."

I turned back to the glittering sword. I reached out my left hand and grasped the hilt that, a thousand rounds before, had been made for me.

Cast of Characters

Adham (AD-ham; pronounced similarly to Adam with a soft "h" sound at the beginning of the second syllable)–a resident of Cammford. Cori's brother.

Brody (BROH-dee)–a resident of Cammlin. Husband of Glynis.

Cori (CORE-ee)–a resident of Cammford. Adham's sister.

Emilie (EM-uh-lee)–a girl living in Willow Bank.

Fergus–a resident of Willow Bank. Rhona's husband.

Fianait (FEE-ah-nye)–a resident of Cammlin. Daughter of Brody and Glynis.

Glynis (GLIN-is)–resident of Cammlin. Wife of Brody.

Imogen (IHM-oh-jen)–a resident of Noweth. Daughter of Nevyn and Shailey.

Jess–a rancher in Keffnael.

Karstyn (car-STUHN)–a resident of Noweth.

Kendal (KEHN-duhl)–a travelling merchant.

Kyle–a boy who lives in Cammford.

Login (low-GIN)–a resident of Noweth. Sloan's husband.

Lorcan (LORE-can)–Tadgh's brother (deceased).

Mitch–a travelling merchant. Works for Ottilie.

Nevyn (neh-VUHN)–a resident of Noweth. Shailey's husband,

Ottilie (OTT-illy)–a traveling merchant.

Owin–an innkeeper in Durning.

Quin–a Healer who lives in Cammford.

Rhona (ROW-nah)–leader in the village of Willow Bank.

Shailey (rhymes with daily)–a resident of Noweth. Nevyn's wife.

Shea (shay)–a resident of Cammlin. Son of Brody and Glynis.

Sloan–a resident of Noweth. Login's husband.

Steafán (stef-ON)– Peg's older brother.

Tadgh (pronounced as "tie" with a g on the end)–a resident of Noweth.

Valeria (vah-LEHR-ee-a)–a Healer in Cammford.

Eldar

Abria (AH-bree-ah)–a resident of Evendim. One of the staff in Alain's household.

Alain (AL-ane)–King of the Eldar. Son of Lorrestian

Arris (AR-ris)–a scribe who copied the Book of Kings (deceased).

Élan (AY-lahn)–daughter of Alain and Réalta

Evam (ehv-am)–son of one of Lorrestian's councilors (deceased).

Gotyr (goh-TUHR)–a luthier in Evendim.

Iseabail (IHZ-eh-bale)–one of the *Cadwynir*

Jorith – one of the *Cadwynir*

Kalin (KAH-lin)–one of the *Cadwynir*

Keiler (KAYE-luhr; the first syllable rhymes with the English "eye") – one of the *Cadwynir*

Konne – a general.

Leonyr (LAY-oh-nuhr)–Master Librarian in Evendim.

Lorrestian (LORE-es-tee-an)–a king of the Eldar and a prophet (deceased).

Pyrett (PUH-ret)–First Captain of the *Cadwynir*

Réalta (RAY-all-ta)–Alain's wife.

Rolugh (ROW-loo)–a general.

Trevith (TREH-vith)–a messenger for the King.

Truel (TRUE-el)–a resident of Evendim. One of the staff in Alain's household.

The Kings of the Alomar

Aerman Sorren (The ae is pronounced as a long "i" sound as in "aye", so ayer-MAN SOAR-in)–High King of the Federated Kingdoms of Alomar.

Anders Sorren–Aerman's son. Ascended to the throne after his father's death.

Helm Sorren–the twenty-ninth High King of the Federated Kingdoms.

Marc–petty king of Amersford.

Minstrels

Ambor (am-BOAR)–a Minstrel of Alomar.

Ambrose (AM-broz)–a Minstrel of Alomar. Master of the College of Minstrels and a prophet.

Amergin–a Minstrel of Alomar.

Avery–one of Lauren's fellow students.

Colin–a Minstrel of Alomar (deceased).

Denys–one of Lauren's fellow students. Sings duets with Rachel.

Elissa (eh-LIS-ah)–a Minstrel of Alomar. She teaches at Songhaven.

Pegara (pe-GAHR-a)–a Minstrel of Alomar. Daughter of Houl of Han. Usually called Peg.

Rachel–one of Lauren's fellow students. Sings duets with Denys.

Ryan / Rhion (RYE-on)–a Minstrel of Alomar. Lauren's Master at Songhaven.

Tavis (TAH-vis)–one of Lauren's fellow students.

Old Ones

Aenn (eyenn)–one of the major Old Ones. Associated with the earth.

Tyth (tuhth)–One of the minor Old Ones. Associated with journeys. Watches over travelers.

Keepers

Cimone (SIH-moan)–The patron of builders and crafters. He wears a gray robe.

Garth–The patron of the minstrels and protector of travelers. He wears a blue robe. Garth is second only to the Destroyer in Mar's favor.

Gorfin (GORF-in)–The patron of smiths. He wears an orange robe.

A Note on Languages

The Andol tongue spoken by the Alomar was originally shared amongst all the people of what is now the Kelmar Empire. Its current form came about when the Alomar crossed into the lands west of the Breton Mountains. There they encountered the Eldar and the Altierans and an entirely new environment: the ocean. All three shaped the language spoken by the exiled Alomar.

Though Andol was once a single tongue, thousands of rounds of antagonism and isolation resulted in shifts in pronunciation and idiom in both the Alomar Kingdoms and the Kelmar Empire. Further, the Alomar freely borrowed words from the Eldar and the Altierans and invented some of their own to describe their new world. Thus, though the Alomar and Kelmar could understand one another, the speech of one sounded odd to the other.

Throughout the books, Andol is rendered as English. Words from other tongues are printed in italics, including a small number of words from the unknown old Andol tongue.

Old Andol

The origin of some words in the Andol tongue have been lost to time. Amongst those are the names of the seasons. Minstrels, noting the similarities in the initial syllables, suggest that the names may once have been phrases rather than single words, phrases that–perhaps–began with "season of..." of "time of..." What the original language may have been, however, is unclear as those initial syllables are not cognates of words in any known language.

Tymnagena–spring.

Tymnacynn–summer.

Tymnahaef–fall.

Tymnahunoch–winter.

The Eldarin Tongue

The Eldar revered the stars and words and imagery concerning stars permeated Eldarin culture. In the Eldarin language, this is seen in the fact that in compound words, star (el) was always the first word in the compound. Thus, Elsgard is literally StarCity, but is more properly translated as City of Stars.

Like English, the Eldarin tongue signals the function of a word in a sentence by its location in the sentence and like English, the preferred order is Subject-Verb-Object (SVO).

Some notes on pronunciation:

a is pronounced as in "at" (IPA /æ/), except when preceding an "r" or an "l" sound, then it is pronounced as in "father" (IPA /aː/)

ae is pronounced as a long "i" sound as in "my". So *Aenn* is pronounced like the English "eye" with the extended n sound on the end.

c is always pronounced as a hard "k" sound as in "cat." The one exception is the word "ciel"–a word borrowed from the True Speech–in which the "c" has a soft "s" sound.

ch is pronounced as a combination of the hard "k" and softer "tch" sounds, somewhere between the ch sounds in "character" and "church."

dd is pronounced "th" as in "though."

e is the short /e/ sound as in "head."

The acute accent (é) is used over the letter e to indicate that the vowel should be pronounced as ay as in "hay."

ea is pronounced as a long e as in "see"

i is pronounced as in "kit" or "hit."

ie is pronounced as a long e, as in "brief".

A doubled nn at the end of a word is slightly longer and receives just a little more emphasis than a single n. The difference is similar to the difference in the English but and butt.

o is pronounced as in "horse" (IPA /ɔː/)

u is pronounced as in "blue" (IPA /uː/)

ü is pronounced like the long umlauted u in German, roughly like the "ew" sound you make when you smell something bad.

y is the unstressed schwa sound (roughly uh).

Eldarin Dictionary

aduné (ah-doo-NAY)–sir

Aeldar Singu (aisle-DAR sin-goo)–Old Ones

aenn (eyenn)–earth

Aenn (eyenn)–one of the major Old Ones; a major river named for the Old One

Aennsrhyd (eyenns-RUHD)–crossing of the river Aenn

alhynn (AL-huhnn)–river

an (rhymes with the English "can")–of

arrint (sounds very similar to the English word aren't with the stress on the first syllable)–assist

Arth (areth; sounds like the English "are" with a th on the end) - world

astolé (as-toe-LAY)–greetings

awl (sounds like the English owl)–full

aynekahrn (aye-NUH-carn) – a horse-like creature,taller and thinner than a typical horse, but much more intelligent and hardy.The word "aynekahrn" was learned from the Old Ones, but does not appear to be aword in the True Speech.

calyth (cah-LUTH)–haven

cali (cah-LIH)–have

ciel (see-EL)–roof (borrowed from the True Speech)

condi (con-DIH)–would

Creagalt (cree-GALT)–round top

dar (rhymes with the English "car")–people

dolgin - shared

dor (rhymes with the English "for")–the

ech (similar to the English "etch")–shade's

el–star

elmaen (el-MINE)–master, as in an expert in some field

Eldar–(from el–star and dar–people)–People of the Stars.

elested (el-LES-ted)–brightened

elmar (EL-mar)–king (pl. elmaren)

elmyr (EL-muhr)–queen (pl. elmyren)

elnir (EL-nir)–light

elnar (EL-nar)–prince

elnyr (EL-nuhr)–princess (pl. elnyren)

Elsgard–City of Stars (from el–star and gard city)

en (pronounced the same as the letter "n." IPA /'en/)–am, is

er (rhymes with the English "her")–be

erven (er-VENN)–earth

Ervenschal–literally, earth-fall. The Eldar name for Landfall.

Evendim (EH-ven-dim)–twilight

gard (rhymes with the English "hard")–city

gorthin (GORE-thin)–gathering

gwenfed (gwen-FED)–joy

grat/gratyn/gratyl (grat/grat-UHN/grat-UHL)–deep/deeper/deepest

hyda (HUH-dah) - with

il (similar to the English "ill", but the "L" sound is shorter)–are

kahill (KAH-hill)–a capo

kalyn (CALL-uhn)–cute

kareth (CAR-eth)–book

Lellarin (lehl-LAR-in)

manana (MAH-nah-nah)–honored

masyl (MAHS-uhl)–her

mear (meer)–lake

Mordel–(MORE-del)

morosin (MORE-oh-sin)–lost

mun (rhymes with the English "moon")–do

myl (muhl)–this

na (nah)–as

nal (rhymes with the English "wall")–and

navoram (nah-VOOR-um)–presence

nul (nool)–our

numen (NEW-men)–isle

ol (pronounced ole like the English "old" without the d sound)–my olin (ole-IN)–mine

orismë (or-is-MAY)–journey's end

orron (OR-ron)–how

pürdonnen (pure-DON-nen)–anything

rhyd (ruhd)–crossing

saer (sire)–fire

Saer (sire)–one of the major Old Ones

saft (pronounced like the English "aft" with an s on the beginning)–next

schal (rhymes with the English word "all")–fall

scrifail (SKRI-fail)–ruin

se (seh)–I

sel (rhymes with the English "sell")–you

selé (SELL-ay)–we

seli (SELL-ih)–your

Seldenawé (sell-DEN-a-way)–Valley of Thrushes

sely (SELL-uh)–yours

selyn (SELL-uhn)–thanks

sharit (SHAR-it)–love

shynsen (shun-SEN)–a personal practice hall, dojo

stal (pronounced like the English word "stall", but with a shortened L sound)–foal

sym (some)–day

tael (tile)–water

Tael (tile)–one of the major Old Ones

tel (sounds like the English word "tell" but the l sound is shortened)–may

tiom (tih-ohm)–me

tol (sounds like the English word "toll" but the l sound is shortened)–for

tul (tool)–by

tybith (TUH-bith)–restaurant

weal (wheel)–serve

wealtyr (wheel-TUHR)–service

wydd (wuhth)–round, cycle (as in round of the seasons)

yn (uhn)–to

ynes (uh-NES)–time

Ynes (uh-NES)–one of the major Old Ones

yrten (uhr-TEN)–wind

wyn (wuhn)–air

Wyn (wuhn)–one of the major Old Ones

Acknowledgements

Once again, I want to express my gratitude to the first readers of the Chronicles: Stephanie Slocum-Schaffer, Marian Gleba, and Stephen Sherlock. Stephanie and Steve gave me the gift of long conversations about the trilogy and each made an important contribution, especially to this book. Stephanie pointed out several things I wrote that were confusing (for instance, it wasn't clear whether Garth and the figure in black were the same person) and I've tried to make those more clear. The pronunciation guide for character names in all three books was Steve's idea. Once again the team at Damonza turned out an amazing cover. Twice now they've turned out a cover that not only implemented what I asked for, but also tapped into aspects of the books they couldn't have known about (because they haven't read all three yet). It wouldn't take much to convince me that they have a wizard on staff. They are a real joy to work with and I simply cannot say enough good things about them. Finally, as I did in the first book, I want to thank all the people who have worked in the Shenandoah National Park and who have labored over the decades to preserve Virginia's beautiful Blue Ridge Mountains, the place I love best and the inspiration for my Breton Mountains.

About the author

Larry Daily was born in Covington, Kentucky and currently resides in the eastern panhandle of West Virginia. He holds a Ph.D. in Psychology and teaches psychology classes at Shepherd University. *The Chronicles of the Lawbreaker* is the result of a decades long love of fantasy inspired by J. R. R. Tolkien, Ursula K. Le Guin, Patricia McKillip, and Mary Stewart. In his spare time Larry builds HO scale model trains, plays folk music on six- and twelve-string guitars, and devours fantasy novels.

Connect online at http://www.larryzdaily.net/